PLEASING THEM

PLEASING THEM

William Doughty

Nexus

This book is a work of fiction.
In real life, make sure you practise safe sex.

First published in 1996 by
Nexus
332 Ladbroke Grove
London W10 5AH

The right of William Doughty to be identified as the
Author of this Work has been asserted by him in
accordance with the Copyright Designs and Patents Act
1988

Typeset by TW Typesetting, Plymouth, Devon
Printed and bound by
BPC Paperbacks Ltd, Aylesbury, Bucks

ISBN 0 352 33065 1

Chapter One

That summer was a fine one, like none before or since. On a hot and sunny afternoon, with columns of brilliant white clouds towering their bulbous forms into the sky like the clean mountains in dreams, I came to Dreadnought Manor with my beloved husband Robert, unaware that I was about to be plunged into an erotic adventure which I can, without exaggeration, call unique: a time of the utmost excitement, with many a startling development, the memory of which will remain fresh in my mind till death – and, I trust, beyond.

As our one horse chaise rolled along the flat, straight Norfolk road towards my husband's ancestral home, I reflected happily on my marriage of four weeks. In that period, Robert had skilfully initiated me into most of the natural pleasures a man and woman may share. Oh, how I admired his lean, powerful body with its splendidly potent male organ, and how pleasing it was when he lavishly praised my own form, and was so free in his enjoyment of me! I had been a willing, indeed eager pupil, and he the most inspiring of teachers. Together we had drunk deeply the delights of youthful passion.

I had met him at a ball in London only three months before and been captivated by his calm confident manner which gave unusual grace and depth to his every movement or utterance. We had married in almost scandalous haste, and I had even defied my mother, who had wanted me to wait so that she could find out more about him, as she had been concerned by some hint of mystery about his way of life, and whispers to the effect that his financial standing was not secure. Fortunately I had long been able to control my mother.

Financial standing! What did I care for such matters, when my blood sang through my body in his presence? I had married him in haste, before the rumours of his financial problems had been confirmed, in which case I might have been foolish enough to let myself be dissuaded from joining my life to Robert's. It is rare that such rumours hasten, rather than delay, marriage. If accused of possessing a hot-blooded temperament, I would plead guilty without shame.

We had honeymooned in France, touring through the wonders of nature and man alike. Our happy peregrinations had been notable not only for scenic beauties, but for those marvellous, awesome pleasures of the flesh I have already alluded to, as inspiring and wonderful as any cathedral rearing its spires to the heavens or fertile chasm rich in watered greenery.

Now my heart beat with anticipation and some slight nervousness as we approached Robert's Norfolk home, which I was about to see for the first time. We had been met at the village railway station by Robert's chaise and one of his servants, a somewhat grim, muscular man by the name of Franklin. Soon I saw a weatherbeaten wall constructed of round blue flint stones, which, my husband informed me, encompassed the modest grounds of Dreadnought Manor, set in an isolated position among fields and scattered woods miles from any other habitation. We came to the metal gates, and they were swung open by a man with a beaming smile on his sun-bronzed face. I took him to be the gardener by his clothes. He touched his battered hat respectfully as we passed, a hat stained yellow with pollen. I could imagine him bending down to administer to the voluptuous, open-lipped blossoms, receiving from them in turn this gift of brilliant sun-drenched fecundity.

The grounds were well kept and nicely arranged, I saw, as we rolled through them along a gravel drive-way that crunched under our wheels. I glimpsed some impressive oaks, elms and beeches, lawns that were verdant from the morning's showers, good English roses like splashes of blood, and a myriad of blooms as blue as the sea, as yellow as the sun, as purple as themselves. In one corner of the walls was a pond, with a white summerhouse nearby. It was a fine sight, and even if the grounds comprised a mere thirty acres, they made up in intricate loveliness for what they lacked in grandeur. I particularly admired the flowers, at their summery peak of multi-hued glory, contributing a delightful fragrance to the warm air which struck chords at the centre of my being.

The chaise stopped in front of the house. Some large crows cawed and flapped away like broken fragments of night, in a manner I advised myself not to see as ominous.

'Welcome to my ancestral home, such as it is,' said Robert. 'I pray you will be happy here. You will find it an unusual house but I hope you will find its unique qualities to your liking.'

'Unique in what way?' I enquired, though I was not confident of a full reply, owing to the fact that several times on our honeymoon he had made cryptic remarks in a like manner, hinting at some mystery, but avoiding any explanation. My curiosity on this point was piquant.

'Soon you will know all, I promise,' my husband

3

told me with that charming, open-hearted smile of his that I so love. 'I believe the revelation will make your flesh tingle more than somewhat – suffice to say for now that we have thus far enjoyed all the conventional pleasures that a man and woman may share, and, that if you trust me, we may in the seclusion of this remote house, begin to explore what some people would disapprovingly call unconventional, even forbidden, raptures.'

'You know that I am yours,' I murmured, after a little pause of surprise. My heart was beating faster, and my mind raced. I did not know what I was agreeing to, and yet I agreed, I gave my body unconditionally to my mate. What awaited me, in this, my destined abode? My wicked friend Estelle had told me much concerning the less common ways in which human beings (in various combinations of males and females) may taste ecstasy, and I fervently wished to know which of these Robert was alluding to. It was clear to me however, that we could not continue this interesting conversation in the presence of servants, so I did not question him further just then. He handed me down from the chaise and we stepped to the front door, where we were greeted by the butler, introduced to me as Banks, a grave, balding man of middle years who struck me as the very model of what an English butler should be, for he seemed to consist of nothing save respect, competence and discretion. I had met several bishops, but he was more like a bishop than any of them. We entered the house, and I felt, if not rich in terms of money, then rich in mysteries. As life is fundamentally a mystery, then to be rich in mysteries is to be rich indeed.

The house was made of flint in its older parts, of brick for those portions added in the 1820s, and of stone for the facade and north wing which were of more recent origin. There were only about forty rooms, not counting, of course, servants' quarters. My mother had assured me that I could have married a man with a great fortune, thanks to my exceptional beauty, and in this my friends and relatives concurred, but I was happy indeed to have won the amusing and loving Robert Shawnecross.

Robert and I went to our well-furnished and recently decorated bedroom, a very pleasant place indeed. I was greatly astonished by what met my eyes when I opened the door to the adjoining bathroom – here was a sight indeed, of a decadent luxuriance suited to a scene from the *Arabian Nights*. It literally made me gasp aloud. I shall not describe it here, for it would take too long, and besides, I am pleased to tantalise my gentle reader. It will be more fitting and useful to tell you about that peculiar bathroom in a later chapter, when we had a rather interesting time there, as you will see.

'Robert, why do you have such an incredible bathroom?' I exclaimed.

'The improvement of bathrooms is the most important trend in modern civilisation, my dear,' he replied. 'Here one may maintain one's cleanliness, and in addition prove that one's erotic pleasures need not be confined to the bedroom. The pleasures of water and slippery soap await us.'

'So this is one of the unconventional pleasures you mentioned just now. Will you not tell me something of the others?'

'Not just now, for it is amusing to make you increasingly curious, and heated in your anticipation,' Robert laughed.

'You are cruel to me,' I replied, pouting, but in reality I was becoming ever more thrilled by the air of erotic expectation that Robert was creating so masterfully.

After changing our clothes we went back downstairs to the dining room, which was not as grand as some I had seen, but which suited me well enough with its sporting prints on the walls and the shiny cutlery on the big dark oak table.

Soon we were enjoying a pleasant repast, waited on by Banks, the grave butler, and Edith, a cheerful and pretty young housemaid. I was struck by her manner, which seemed unusual for a servant's. There was no doubt but that she was truly delighted to see Robert back from his honeymoon.

'Oh sir, we're all so glad you've come home,' gushed this giddy girl. 'We've missed you so much. It isn't the same without you, sir.'

'Thank you Edith, but we are tired from our travels,' my husband told her quite sternly, 'and would rather not hear your chattering just now.' He glanced at me as though to warn her that she must not let slip his secret in front of me.

'Of course, sir. I am a dreadful chatterbox I know,' said Edith, not at all abashed. She managed to remain silent for the rest of the dinner, though it was obviously a great effort for her, and not one to which she was accustomed.

After our leisurely meal, Robert and I went into the adjacent library. He told Banks to bring all the servants there so that they could be introduced to me, and it was not long before they all assembled. Once again, I shall not at this point indulge in the copious description beloved of so many writers, because those details of appearance and manner will be more useful to the reader in later scenes of my tale, when he or she will find them helpful in visualising some strange scenes of advanced deviation.

Here I shall merely introduce you briefly to Sally, the remarkably large cook, John, the porter and general handyman – and also, somewhat surprisingly, a black man – while of a similarly surprising nature was the fact that we had a stable girl instead of the usual stable boy, and at that she was a highly attractive Indian girl, Darma. The stable man Franklin was the muscular fellow who had driven our chaise from the station, while the man who opened the gates for us was the gardener as I had surmised, whose name, I now learned, was McBean. His Scottishness was not pronounced. Charlotte was a young and petite kitchen girl, Edith and Mary the housemaids. For another surprise, we had a girl assisting the gardener. Her name was Lisa, and her small slender body was dominated by a remarkably large, but high, bosom.

It was a small staff with some singular characteristics. I was not used to having a large staff, for my mother and I had lived modestly after the death of my father, when I was but five, left us virtually penniless, but I had some experience of servants in the homes of my relatives and friends, and I knew that Robert's staff was an odd one, with attractive girls, one of them Indian, working in the stables and gardens. Nor was that all. There was something far from mundane about the way they regarded Robert and I. They betrayed a kind of anticipation and keen interest that amounted to eagerness, as though they were awaiting something from us, something exciting.

It was hard to put my finger on the situation, but of course Robert had already told me I would find this an unusual house, so I was keenly searching for evidence of that quality. I was thus receptive to the servants' manner. Could I be deluded, or was it one I could only describe as lustful?

The staff were dismissed, leaving Robert and I sitting in the comfortable library armchairs, old and dark, which cast their pleasant leather odour into the warm air. The room was flooded by the last light of the sun, a sphere of deepening orange hue that skated along the horizon as though determined not to set, and the countless volumes on their ranked shelves glowed richly in that splendid summer evening light. When we are very old, we shall remember the way the sun set on the happy days of our youth.

'Well my dear,' said I, 'our servants are not quite typical, I know that much now. You have a black man and an Indian. Moreover, the Indian girl works in the stables, and another girl assists the gardener.'

'These are merely superficial deviations from the norm,' Robert insisted, with a dismissive gesture of his hand. 'There are many jobs women could do as well as men, if we did but discard absurd social conventions. There is something rather more unusual about them than such a minor matter, though I hesitate to tell you of it for fear you will be shocked.'

'Perhaps I am not so easily shocked as you imagine,' I told him, thinking, I must confess, of what I had done the year before with Estelle – lovely, red-haired Estelle, a delightfully bad girl of Sapphic leanings. These experiences made me less shockable than some truly innocent girl. I felt shy of my husband's reaction to my adventures with Estelle, and so had told him nothing of her.

'My dear, if I thought you were easily shocked by matters of the flesh I would still have married you, for I love you, but my trepidation would have been troublesome,' said Robert, with the slight smile that was rarely absent from his charming mouth.

'I begin to fear of hearing something along the lines of melodramatic fiction,' I remarked. 'Is your first wife secretly imprisoned in a back attic, or is it a ghost? If I had any say in the matter, I would select the ghost.'

'It is something far more cheerful than any ghost, my dear Jane. The time has come when we must talk frankly. I am, as you know, a passionate man, one who delights in all the ecstasies a woman and man may share. And I tell you frankly that you are an unusually passionate woman. This is not considered a polite thing to say to a lady, but in this conversation now we must be free to move beyond the stifling conventions of our time, of our society. Can you assent to this?'

'Certainly,' I agreed at once. 'I am indeed determined to follow your lead in this as in all other matters, for that is my duty as your wife. No matter what you are about to tell me, it will not affect my love for you, and my desire to do my duty.'

'Nobly spoken, Jane! You are a woman of rare strengths,' Robert exclaimed, taking me in his arms.

What did I fear, so long as I was held in those arms?

'Let me tell you about the servants, Jane. Edith for instance. You may have noticed that at dinner she was pleased, even excited, to see you and I. Did you notice, Jane, that in her manner there was an affection the warmth of which went beyond anything a servant would normally feel towards the master of the house?'

'I saw something of the sort,' I replied softly. My face reddened somewhat as my imagination painted a vivid picture.

'In short,' Robert stated, 'there has been physical intimacy between Edith and I.'

Reader, I was not so upset as many another young lady would have been, though I was surprised, and then gratified, that he was telling me so much.

'Yes, that would explain why she was so delighted to see you,' I said after a pause for reflection. 'You have of course made her happy, as you could make any woman happy.'

Robert proceeded to drop a bombshell of even greater explosive capacity.

'It is not just myself and Edith, Jane. In this house the servants and I know the pleasures of what is popularly known as "Free Love".' He squeezed me in his embrace as though to comfort me. 'Whether this practice continues or not depends entirely on you. If you disapprove, I shall change my ways and henceforth be faithful to but one lady in the world – my beloved wife. If however, you are prepared to indulge in the amusements which the servants can offer, then I shall initiate you into a new class of pleasure, and our life together will be the richer. As I stand before God, I love you, Jane. I want to give you pleasure such as few women have known, I long to delight you with diversity and development in place of the static staleness that affects so many couples. I do not want to be like other men, who visit their mistresses in private and frequent prostitutes. I want to share everything with you, the gorgeous beauty I love more than life itself.'

He went down on his knees before me and clasped my legs in his strong arms.

'You are an exceptional woman, Jane, and you deserve both an exceptional mate and an exceptional mode of living. You will not fly from me now that I have made this revelation? No, you shall stay, and continue to love me as I love you.'

I could not reply for a time, so full of emotion was I. Not only was it startling to be told of the manner of life in this house, but I felt too that my strong, confident husband who usually led me in all ways was sincere when he said he would let me decide our future. This served to increase my amazement.

'Of course I will not leave you,' I said urgently, horrified by the very thought. 'I love you. I shall follow you wherever you lead me. If you would prefer me to join you in these special pleasures, then of course I will.' It was a fateful proclamation on my part, and one which, no doubt, many of my readers will be certain no young lady should make under any circumstances. But I loved him so.

Robert laughed with relief and kissed me. He sat in an armchair and pulled me on to his lap, then told me more about his domestic arrangements.

He had decided, on his father's death three years ago, that he might as well have servants who shared his philosophy of pleasure as ones who did not, so he had deliberately set out to recruit a few men and a larger number of women who were aware of their bodies' capacity for rapture. The females were those whom society absurdly calls 'fallen' women. Some of them had had problems before they came to his house: Lisa for instance had a baby, but not its conventional accompaniment, namely, a husband.

These servants had been carefully selected, not merely for their appearance, but for their attitude, for that is the key attribute necessary for true delight in matters erotic. I was naturally pleased when Robert added that I was unique, for I combined exceptional beauty and the charms of youth with a great capacity for the pleasures of the flesh.

I asked him how it was that the girls of his staff were not more or less continually with child, and he replied that they used recently perfected devices known as Dutch caps, which freed women from the drudgery of having too many children and allowed them instead to concentrate without fear on the responses and delights of their own bodies.

Lastly he emphasised that these servants were

singular men and women indeed, as each of them had highly individual, even peculiar, erotic specialities and preferences. He promised me that each of them was fascinating as an individual, and that, when taken together as a group, the combinations they could form were beyond anything the most fevered imagination could devise.

Robert hinted at some of the servants' proclivities, and then, in response to my eager questioning, gave me such facts as filled me with astonishment, and I must confess, profound erotic arousal. I will not share this information with you just yet, gentle reader, for it is my womanly pleasure to tease you just a little, though you may rest assured that in the end every startling detail will be divulged for your delectation.

We were seized with a mutual desire to be alone together in our bedroom, that we might indulge the amorous feelings which had been engendered by our conversation concerning these servants and their bizarre erotic lusts. So Robert informed Banks of our decision to have an early night, and then he and I adjourned to our spacious and pleasing bedroom.

'My darling,' breathed Robert, embracing me fervently. 'I want you to realise fully that it is you I truly love. What I do with the servants is amusing in the extreme, and I feel some affection for those females, but the activities I share with them are not attended by those passionate feelings that love alone can bring to the erotic act. They are not of my class, but you are my social equal, and my moral superior. And now I invite you to admire yourself in the mirror while I help you undress, so that you will be forced to admit you are gorgeous, the perfect woman. If you see yourself with honest eyes, you will know that only you can bring me to the highest peaks of rapture.'

There was a full-length mirror in one corner of the bedroom, and my masterful husband had me stand in front of it as he gracefully removed my dress and undergarments. This naturally took quite some time, as there were so many tiny buttons and hooks to undo on the dress, and so many layers of garments underneath. With sure hands he removed my frilly underskirts, silken bodice, and white silk stockings. He unlaced my corset, which in the fashion of the time was of strong, heavy construction, and very tightly fastened, so that on its removal I felt as light and free as a gazelle.

Lastly he removed my knickers, and I stood naked before my master and the mirror.

'Oh my God, how beautiful you are,' breathed Robert, in a rapture to think that I was his. He closed his eyes and gently caressed my body as though unable to believe his good fortune.

He went on praising me in an undertone, and it sounded like a prayer. I, too, was in a state of rapture, receptive to all sensual pleasures.

Robert kissed my behind and ran his tongue up and down my spine, his long artistic fingers stroking my belly and breasts. Quivers of pure pleasure danced up and down my every nerve. Oh, and our room faced west, it faced west indeed, so that although the sun had set, the light from a sky awash with living colour flooded the room and caressed my flesh with a vibrant symphony of reds, oranges, and purples. There were salmon-pink high clouds to the east, orange clouds to the west, all in a dome of deepening blue, as blue as Robert's eyes. All this visual wealth cast a living, immediate light into the room, and all over my naked flesh. I looked into the mirror. I saw that I was beautiful. Desirable.

There are precious moments in life when someone

invites us to admire ourselves and we know they are sincere. I admired myself. Reader, I must here admit that I was beautiful, for this would not be an accurate narrative if I failed to put aside the usual constraints of modesty and make that point clear. My body, face and hair were such that any man would have given his soul just to be allowed to kiss my foot.

Because I knew I was desirable, I knew that my husband desired me, so I felt more confident than a less attractive woman would have done in my place, and thus willing to admit the possibility that the servants might well afford Robert some harmless amusement that in no way detracted from his love for me. I knew it had to be me he truly loved, for I had eyes, and I stood in front of a full-length mirror.

I unpinned my hair and tossed my head so that it fell in pleasing disorder, winding down the ripe contours of my body like twisting mountain rivulets made golden by sunrise. Streams of gold ran down my flesh, caressing me intimately. My large but firm round breasts tingled under the silky touch, and my nipples, which are of a somewhat large size, and much given to swollen rigidity, stuck out shamelessly through the curtains of my golden hair.

'You are so beautiful,' Robert groaned with reverence, placing his hands on my tiny waist and kissing my shoulders. 'I am going to penetrate your body, dearest, and give you my gift of semen. But first, admire yourself in the truest way. Love yourself for me. Make love to yourself, this other self of yours in the mirror, as a gift to yourself and to me.'

To show me clearly what he meant, he took my hands in his and placed the right one at the very base of my belly, on the nest of golden hair that springs there, and the other on my left breast. He moved them gently back and forth, then withdrew his own hands. I was so wrapped in pleasure that I could do nothing but continue the movements, pleasuring my body. I had never done this before with him, and for a moment I was shy, for of course it was daring and shameless simply to be seen naked by him, instead of covering myself with a nightdress in an adjoining room – so how much worse was it for me to masturbate in the presence of a man! According to Victorian sensibilities, no words were strong enough for what I was doing. The truth must be that in encouraging me to such shocking acts, Robert had good material to work with, for I must have had a strong streak of wanton wickedness to allow myself to be led into such outrageous vices.

With self-love in my heart, coupled with a love for Robert which dwarfed that self-love, I continued the motions of my hands upon my flesh, to please him by pleasing myself. Waves of delightful sensation passed not merely through my flesh, but to the core of my being, to my soul. I had been endowed by my Creator with a great capacity for pleasure, so was I not following His plan in enjoying that capacity?

I caressed myself with greater abandon, thinking of what Robert's penis would do to me, and of what he had told me about the servants. The movements of my hands become more wanton, and I moved them from one place to another, varying the sensations of erotic pleasure. I smiled at myself and at Robert in the mirror, where I observed this shameless young minx caressing her beautiful body. I had drunk a little wine at dinner, which perhaps contributed to my abandonment. Robert stared at me in fascinated wonder, then began to tear off his clothes. At this shattering of his manly self-possession I felt an altogether womanly triumph.

I played with my hugely engorged nipples, and

gathered my flowing natural juices to spread them over those nipples, making them gleam wetly. I tweaked my nether lips and made them slippery too, and I rubbed the area of what Estelle had told me the proper name of, that is, my clitoris. I arched my long, slender back, flaunting the taut pear-shaped roundness of my buttocks, while tensing the muscles of my thighs, which Robert was once pleased to insist were of a startling and superbly thrilling length and shapeliness. I even parted my legs and leaned forward a little, so that my buttocks were presented to my mate, with the wet reddish-pinkness of my nether lips glistening in invitation to his penis.

Robert seized me and kissed me passionately. I had triumphed.

'You wonderful witch!' he exclaimed. 'You seem so angelic and demure that nobody would think you capable of any erotic activity save of the most passive and lifeless forms. Yet there is in you a joyous demon perhaps even more powerful than my own. We shall find out all your secret lusts my dear. You and I and the servants will all find out what we are truly made of. It will not be boring.'

Suddenly he lifted me in his strong arms and threw me down on the bed, leaving me breathless. Casting off his remaining garments, he pounced on my naked, aroused body, his superbly rigid male organ quivering with desire like the nose of a fierce dog that is about to make a killing. He plunged it into me with one mad, irresistible lunge that made me gasp with pure rapture. Once more we were joined together as we should be!

Robert thrust back and forth, up and down, as though his maleness were an imprisoned animal of deadly ferocity fighting to escape its confinement by main force, determined to destroy its prison or die in the attempt. Our tongues and lips met in savage gnawing, his hands clasped my shoulders tightly to hold me in position against the power of his mighty thrusts, and his belly ground against mine while the shield of his chest held my yearning bosom in sway. I arched my back, rubbing my sensitive nipples against the corrugations of my mate's ribs, pleasuring myself against his magnificent body.

With such a masterful male pleasuring me so very passionately with desperate lunges of his superb penis, it was not surprising that after a fairly short time I was swept beyond the world of reason into the vale of pure ecstasy. A sky full of fireworks erupted behind my tightly closed eyelids, and the music of the angelic chorus sounded in my soul as I died and was reborn.

When I had recovered my senses and lay gasping, Robert turned me over and rode me from behind, holding my breasts tightly, bringing me to further violent spasms of ecstasy.

'And now, my darling, you can replace your vaginal juices with another kind,' he announced, withdrawing from me once I had finished spending.

I saw his meaning, and, as he knelt by my head and presented himself to my face, obediently put out my tongue and licked his penis all over, like a kitten licking a finger that has been dipped in milk. I tasted myself on his male flesh.

His organ throbbed with his heartbeat, so strong was his excitement, and I loved the way it jerked back and forth with the rush of blood through his splendid body. I flickered my tongue at high speed over the rim of his helmet, and sucked the tip while fingering his testicles and thick-veined shaft. I was gratified to hear him moan with rapture. How wicked I was thus to serve his manhood with my mouth –

17

what perversities I could now not merely take part in, but actually enjoy with a vivid satisfaction!

After I had thoroughly licked him, leaving his organ wet with my saliva, Robert lay on me again, sliding his bespittled penis into the slithery warm depths of my being. I embraced it tightly, squeezing my vaginal muscles as he had been training me to do, and once again I was delighted to hear him utter little gasps of delight in acknowledgement of my determined efforts. I was getting stronger.

For a time Robert alternated between either end of me, using first my mouth and then my vagina, and I greeted his penis with my mouth in a new way every time, now grazing his helmet rim with my teeth, now taking him into my cheek, or wrapping my fingers around his shaft and tormenting the little slit in the end of his knob with the tip of my tongue. I was happy in my depravity.

Perhaps a correct young lady would have been horrified to be thus used, but I was far beyond being correct, and was only too pleased that he used my orifices with utter freedom.

Finally he had me squat down on all fours in front of him while he sat on his haunches, body upright and knees apart, and pulled my buttocks down onto his lap to impale me on his organ. He gripped my hips tightly in both hands and moved me up and down and around to suit his penis absolutely, and in this he suited myself also, for I spent powerfully again. A short time later he shot amazingly powerful spurts of life-giving milk into the core of my being, which tingled and throbbed with the force of his repeated hosing until I almost feared I might burst like an overfilled sausage skin. My darling gave a long series of choking gasping cries as though he were being strangled. That animal sound is in my memory again as I write, and I am glad.

Later I tried to sleep, but for a time it was difficult, despite my weariness after our travels. What would tomorrow bring? I thought of the servants, and wondered whether I could be capable of such peculiar erotic adventures as Robert clearly hoped I would attempt. Tingling anticipation thrilled my every nerve as I slid into the oceanic depths of dreams.

Later I tried to sleep, but for a time it was difficult despite my weariness after our travels. What would tomorrow bring? I thought of the servants, and wondered whether I could be capable of such peculiar erotic adventures as Robert dearly hoped I would become. Time and time again I cleared these from my nerve as I slid into the oceanic depths of dreams.

Chapter Two

After a voluptuously late rising and a hearty breakfast, Robert and I made a tour of the house and gardens. There was pride in his voice as he pointed out to me the finer features, and I was glad that he was proud, for I wanted him to be happy, and pride in something is necessary to happiness despite what we are told about pride being a sin.

If not as grand as some, the house and gardens were neat and pleasant, and I looked on them with joy, for it was here that I would make my love with my beloved mate. I shall here briefly note a few points about this house that are salient to my narrative.

Upstairs were two striking rooms designed purely for erotic pleasure, this pair being known as the large and small soft rooms. Robert pointed out that it is just as logical to have rooms purely for pleasures of the flesh as it is to have kitchens for cooking and libraries for reading, and this point is, I am sure, unanswerable to those who admit logic into their hearts. I shall also say here that the house had gas, which was so useful for heating in winter and for cooking and lighting all year round, as well as for the baths and showers which my husband so enjoyed. You may be surprised that we had gas so far out in the country, but Robert's father had bribed an official with the result that a pipe had been laid from North Walsham, which had a gasometer, to a village which did not, and this pipe – which I fear cost the shareholders some loss – ran by our front gate, thus allowing us all the benefits of this modern gas age.

Another interesting point that struck me about the house was that Robert had installed a feature of Russian houses, namely double windows. This consists of two layers of glass with a space between them to cut out draughts and loss of heat during the winter. I was pleased to see this further sign of his industry and acceptance of innovation. He said that it was an idea whose time had come, and that by 1910 every home in Great Britain would have double windowing.

Noon came, and we had a light luncheon. I wanted to ask him about my initiation into new forms of erotic delight, but it did not seem quite ladylike to speak in this manner, so I refrained. My curiosity was so strong however that I could hardly keep it in check, and I was profoundly glad when he brought the matter up.

'My dear,' he said, 'would you be interested in partaking of the kind of pleasures I alluded to yesterday, namely those involving the staff? For this, the first time, you might prefer to watch rather than participate, for you are not used to this form of amusement I know. Besides, observing is itself a fine sport.'

'I am willing to follow your lead, confident that you know what is best for the two of us,' I replied in a manner that was, considering my passionate nature, close to being hypocritical.

Certainly it was too lukewarm and good-girlish for my husband's tastes.

'Come Jane,' he said laughing. 'Admit that you are extremely curious about the capabilities and capacities of the staff. Do not try to make it purely a matter of a wife obeying her husband.'

'You know my heart so well I need hardly ever speak,' I laughed in turn.

How delightful it is to have a mate and friend who understands one so totally. To be thus understood is to no longer stand alone, and that is a splendid thing, for every man and woman is endangered by loneliness.

'Of course I am curious,' I continued. 'This morning, on our tour of the house and grounds, I was dying of curiosity every time we met a servant going about his or her duties. When I talked briefly with some of them, I longed to enquire what manner of erotic rapture they habitually shared with you, and when we admired Lisa's darling baby – which I am glad is not yours, for then I would be jealous – I wanted to ask her if, from the making of it, she had great pleasure. So you see, I possess every bit as much curiosity as you could wish me to.'

'I'm glad to hear you say so,' Robert told me, his kind smile warming my heart like the rays of the sun. 'So now let us go to the small soft room and savour its singular comforts.'

We went upstairs to that singular place, designed and used purely to facilitate lustful pleasures. In the centre of the room were two large mattresses placed side by side, covered in red silk, with brightly coloured cushions scattered about on them, ready to assist in comfortably maintaining the postures of those engaged there in physical union. Along two walls were large mirrors placed there to heighten one's level of visual stimulation, while along the other walls were comfortable chairs and sofas for what I may call the audience. Above these hung drawings and paintings, the nature of which I can only term licentious. They showed such scenes of depraved and peculiar erotic activity that I almost quailed, and at the same time thrilled, to suspect that I might be called on to indulge in similar activities. Little did I know that the reality was to be stranger than the products of these artists' inflamed lusts.

Robert pulled the room's bell cord, and the portly, grave butler, Banks, arrived promptly in response to the summons.

'Banks, have Mary come here at once,' ordered my husband. 'And when I ring the bell again, you are to send Sally and John here.'

'Very good sir,' Banks intoned. He departed as noiselessly and gracefully as though he levitated above the ground rather than sullied his feet by walking upon it.

'Mary is an intriguing girl,' Robert told me. 'She has an unusual erotic propensity which I shall demonstrate to you today in a mild form. She is also a competent housemaid, as indeed she must be if she is to remain here.'

It was but a short interval before Mary knocked on the door and entered the room, making a curtsy. She wore a black and white housemaid's uniform, of rather better material and cut than average. Thus she presented herself for our erotic pleasure. She seemed outwardly calm, but I could see a fierce light in her eyes and a set to her mouth that betrayed passion.

'Do you feel like joining us here and now, Mary?' Robert enquired.

'Of course, sir,' Mary replied in deep tones of Northumberland origins. 'You know I always feel like doing it, sir.'

'And would you tell my wife, your new mistress, what your favourite pleasure is?'

'I'd be glad to tell you ma'am, and I do hope that you will help give me what I need, for I do need it something fierce. All the servants look forward to your getting pleasure from them, if it isn't taking a liberty to say so. As for me, I am a wicked woman, for I love to be tied up in all kinds of ways, and teased, and used as you please, and even punished a little, though not too much for all that I want to be punished too much sometimes, if you see my meaning. I deserve to be punished because I am a wicked girl who wants to be made helpless so that others can use my body. Nothing else gives me the same pleasure. I had bad luck before I came here, Miss. Men were either frightened of what I wanted from them, or else they used me too cruelly and looked down on me. Only in this house have I got just what I need. The master is a great man.'

I was greatly surprised by this recitation, for I had only been told by Estelle that some men and women liked to be tied up as an erotic pleasure, but had never until now been faced with the curiously thrilling prospect of witnessing such *outré* raptures. I felt an excitement I can hardly describe in ladylike terms – I can only say that I became intensely aware of my own body and its capacity for ecstasy.

Mary was entirely sincere in what she said, that was obvious – she truly desired to be bound. It was a thrilling sight indeed to watch her disrobe with an eagerness that made her clumsy, fumbling as she slowly undid the buttons and hooks of her black and white uniform. I felt a keen interest in this unveiling of her flesh, for as you have gathered by my references to my friend Estelle, I was first initiated into the pleasures of flesh by girls, and have kept a liking for my own sex ever since, though men certainly satisfy my needs at a deeper, more basic layer of being.

Mary managed to remove her uniform and set to work on her petticoats. What a fine thing it is to watch women slowly disrobe, hampered by the many levels of clothing society demands that they wear, with all its complex fastenings. To watch a woman win free of her clothes is like watching a butterfly struggling to emerge from its imprisoning chrysalis, and it will be a sad thing if fashion ever permits women to remove their garments quickly and simply, as then their nudity would be too easily achieved, and hence less valued.

So now did Mary gradually emerge, her face reddening with her haste and her peculiar desires. Her dark eyes shone. She was handsome rather than beautiful, but with a tall and shapely form that more than compensated for any deficiencies in her features. Her legs were long, and powerful in appearance, her waist comely in its smallness even without the corset which she now removed. It had been laced extremely tightly, and was of a heavy construction, so that I guessed she enjoyed the feeling of confinement it gave her as she went about her duties. Her bosom was of a pleasing shapeliness, and boasted a remarkable pair of nipples, exceptionally large and turgid. I stared at them, they were so large and proud, and in fact I longed to play with them. Carefully she removed her black silk stockings, and then, without shame, she pulled off her drawers and knickers. A sight of rare interest met my gaze, for no less remarkable than her huge, engorged teats were her private parts, which, when unveiled, also fascinated me, as her nether lips protruded a surprisingly long way, like the distended petals of some lush bloom flowering in a fever of growth amidst the wild jungle growths of the hot and humid tropics.

She let down her long hair, which was light brown in colour and parted in the middle. The large bun dissolved into a mass of falling strands that fell about her body in caressing waves, a sensuous disarray that somehow made her seem more naked even though it partly covered her white skin. The sight of this strong-bodied woman offering herself would have been highly stimulating by itself, but when coupled with what she had told me about her charmingly perverse desires, it was a moment of overwhelming intensity.

She stood there before us in seeming submission, silent, with burning eyes turned to the floor, a mere servant offering her splendid body to be tied and teased, rendered helpless and tormented. She should have seemed weak – but believe me when I say there was something fiercely demanding and powerful about her, some spiritual strength, even a kind of mastery. Perhaps she was strong because she knew precisely what she wanted, and even though what she wanted was to submit, in precise knowledge of one's desires there can be born a formidable power.

It was we who were submitting to her desires, not she who was submitting to ours.

The tension in the room had mounted formidably during her prolonged disrobing. Some strands of hair had fallen across her face, but she made no move to brush them away. She was as still as a statue.

'Is it not interesting to have a servant such as this?' Robert asked me. 'And you know, my darling, you need never be jealous, for you are my chosen partner, my soul mate.'

'I will not be jealous,' I replied, and I spoke truly, for I knew I was the one he loved. I was of his class, and he had chosen to marry me. It could not have been for my fortune, for I had none, so it must have been for love.

'Now we will give this splendid woman what she likes. Are you ready to begin, Mary?'

'Oh sir, you know I'm always more than ready,' the servant replied gravely, in her deep, almost hoarse voice. She gnawed her lip fretfully.

Robert reached out to a black, red and gold Japanese lacquer box that stood on one of the triangular shelves occupying the angle of two corners in the room, and removed from it a scarlet silk cord.

'Put your hands behind your back,' he commanded.

She peeked at him from between the strands of her hair, then obeyed, also turning her back to him, her master. With the swiftness of skill that must have been born of practice, he bound her crossed wrists together. The ends of the cord hung free. He led her to one of the large heavy mirrors, and used these free ends to tie her to the ornately carved frame, which was of darkly varnished wood. That mirror was strongly fastened to the wall, and I was certain she could not free herself by any exertion, however frantic.

'Now Mary will have to watch whatever happens, and she will have no way of slaking her lust,' said Robert, in a serious, factual tone. 'And of course, should we choose to do anything at all to her lovely body, she would have to endure it as best she could. She has no choice.'

My husband now rang the bell that summoned, as he had arranged earlier with Banks, Sally and John. Sally, you may recall, was the immensely fat cook, a woman whose intellectual limitations were only excused by her capacity for erotic pleasures, while John was the handyman, a black man from Jamaica, a fine young fellow not merely handsome and cheerful, but even competent.

They merely glanced at Mary, taking in the fact that she was naked and bound without the least show of surprise. They did however betray an eager anticipation of what might now occur.

'I assume the pair of you will be willing,' said Robert, 'to put on a show for my wife and I.'

'Yes sir' they replied in heartening unison.

'Then undress,' Robert commanded.

They hastened to comply, and once again I had the arousing pleasure of watching others undress for my enjoyment. John was only the second man I had ever seen naked, and the first black man, so the degree of my attention may be imagined. He was pleasingly muscular, with an organ that was fully erect by the time he proudly revealed it to my eyes. It was large, and in its darkness, impressive. I found it not uninteresting. As for Sally, her fatness was awesome. Fat? By herself she was a very landscape.

The strange thing is that her fatness was attractive, for she carried her obesity with happy, lustful confidence, and indeed it was hard to imagine her looking any other way. Had she been thin she would merely have been diminished. There was some hypnotic power in the sheer bulk of her breasts, belly, buttocks and thighs, and she was both a parody of femaleness and its very epitome. In her immensity she was immensely female.

I felt shy and hardly dared to look at either of them, especially John with his powerful maleness, but all the same I naturally had to take a look now and then, if only so as not to aggravate Robert by seeming to be unwilling.

The clothes removed by all three servants were now placed in an adjoining room. Robert ordered John and Sally to have a quick wash, as they had been perspiring at their duties. They soon returned. I sat on the sofa with Robert at my side, and you may be sure that the rate of my heartbeat did not decrease when my husband made the following outrageous suggestion.

'Sally, you will sit on John's face. John, you will lick and suck Sally as though your life depended on giving her full satisfaction.'

This was something new to me indeed, and I must admit I could no longer take my eyes from this unmatched couple. John lay down on the red silk covering of the mattress in the centre of the room, and the huge cook ponderously squatted over his face and slowly lowered herself, her massive hindquarters and generously proportioned private parts engulfing his features utterly, obliterating his head so that it was lost to the world. I hardly understood how the poor fellow would be able to breathe.

His male organ, which Sally was facing, at once pulsed with a new urgency, so it was clear that John found his unorthodox position one that afforded him no little stimulation. I tried to imagine what it was like for him to be, as it were, consumed by those huge buttocks and gaping private parts, and likewise, when Sally squirmed and sighed with delight, I wondered how it felt to sit on the face of a man and have him serve you with his mouth. I knew the joys of cunnilingus, as it is properly called, but never had I dreamt of trying it in such a peculiar manner. I could not help but feel that it was rather exciting.

As though what had already occurred was not shameless enough, Sally now acted in a way that fully revealed the depths of her wantonness: she raised herself a little, reached under herself with both hands, and pulled open the fleshy lips of her femaleness to hold them far apart while she settled down again on John's face, covering it with her wet, slippery vulva as though she hoped to draw his head into her womb. There passed through my own frame a voluptuous shudder.

I thought Sally showed her selfishness by not touching John's staff, but perhaps she was enraptured by her own pleasure, which seemed great in proportion to the size of her body. She rolled her head, made grunting noises like a sow, caressed her own bosom and lower belly, then gave a strangled cry I took to be a result of her spending, arching her huge body and shuddering like a jelly on a plate during a severe earthquake.

All of this Mary watched intently, a sullen look on her face, a hungry gleam in her dark eyes, all the while betraying her lust by the rigidity of her remarkable nipples, the shifting of her legs, and the manner in which she gnawed her lower lip.

Only now did Sally condescend to give John some pleasurable stimulation. She leaned forward and regarded his organ with a dreamy smile as it pulsated and twitched, then she reached out and playfully flicked it with her fingers, grinning, as she did so, an almost imbecilic grin. She went on flicking her fingers at the helmet and testicles in a manner that must surely have given John some discomfort, if not pain, but perhaps he was in a state where he enjoyed such treatment at her hands. His only response was to grasp her immense thighs and lift her a little off his face, so that he might, I realised when I heard his panting breaths, gain access to fresh air. I glimpsed his face, and was surprised to see it shining with wetness.

'Sally lubricates at a great rate,' Robert told me. 'John will be half-drowned in another minute.'

It was certainly curious to know that her parts were slobbering all over the face of a man who was serving them so devotedly, and indeed he was serving the rest of her elephantine body too, for he reached up to her huge breasts and squeezed them rhythmically. Sally gripped his male organ at its base and moved her hand slowly up and down while the other caressed his big balls, which made him thrust his hips upwards, trying to bring himself off, but this effort was soon thwarted by Sally, who let go of his shaft and strengthened her grip on his testicles, making him squirm. The fat young woman grinned as though she had achieved a great triumph.

Some minutes passed with variations on the themes I have outlined above. Sally gave John alternate discomfort and pleasure, but was careful not to make him spend, which would have shortened their amusing game. She used her fingernails on his helmet, making him moan, then kissed it and caressed it with her tongue. She writhed her hips in rapture, grinding her private parts against his face, revelling in the pleasure his mouth gave her intimate parts. Occasionally I glimpsed his tongue worshipping her pink wet flesh with a speed and articulacy born of fervent lust. I shifted a little uncomfortably in my seat, aware of my own increasing arousal. Increasingly, John cried out, but his cries were muffled by the weight of female flesh engulfing his mouth.

Sally remained at or near the peak of rapture, spending three or four times in rapid succession. I heard a lady give a little sigh of envy, and realised it was none other than myself.

John was now overcome with lust, and reached up to take hold of Sally's head, pulling it towards his organ. Far from resisting, she took his shaft in both hands and planted her mouth on the splendid bell of the glans, kissing and sucking it before using her thumbs to prise open the little mouth at the tip, into which she flicked the tip of her tongue. I reflected that I was learning a good many tricks to try with Robert, as he had no doubt hoped I would.

Sally took the knob into her mouth again, sucking on it hard, grazing it with her teeth, rubbing her lips along its rim, lashing her tongue back and forth, and all the while she pumped vigorously at the long thick shaft with both hands. She squeezed and shifted her cunning cook's fingers, strong from pastry-making, until John gave a muffled, impossibly drawn-out scream as he began to erupt into her mouth and over her face as she bobbed her head back and forth, letting her lips slide over his exploding knob. Some she swallowed; some, in seemingly endless spasms, lashed over her face like white leather whips.

The fat young woman, her female bulk all glistening with sweat, drank the male substance not merely shamelessly, but avidly, as though this vital fluid were the most delicious and nourishing of foods. I was fixated by her attitude, and by John's prolonged spasmodic writhings, which showed that his was an unusually extended example of masculine rapture. All through his ecstasy, Sally's fingers clenched strongly, somewhat in the manner of a gorilla strangling a deadly snake, which I warrant added rather than detracted from John's pleasure. When he was finally done, the obese cook grinned at us and licked her lips. She exuded pride.

32

Chapter Three

John emerged from beneath the giantess, and lay panting for a while, exhausted by pleasure. His face and hair were soaked in the fluids generated so generously by Sally's excited parts.

'Thank you for watching us, ma'am,' he said to me, once he had recovered somewhat. 'We are all happy to have you here.'

'Thank you both,' I replied, 'for the fine show.' I was in fact distinctly pleased by the manner in which my life was developing.

Sally said nothing, but merely grinned again. In truth she rarely spoke, and seemed more animal than human. Still, she was an entertaining animal, which is surely preferable to a boring specimen of humanity.

'You may go now,' Robert told them. 'And well done, the pair of you. Sally, I trust the beef will not be overdone tonight. You are, in general, an excellent cook, but at times a little inclined to the incendiary school of cooking.'

'Yes sir,' Sally replied.

They departed. Robert and I were left alone with Mary, who you recall was naked and bound. I felt aroused in the extreme by what we had just witnessed, and Mary was clearly in a similar state, as I could clearly tell from the glistening of her private parts and the turgidity of her remarkably large nipples.

'Let us disrobe, my dear,' Robert suggested.

'In front of Mary? It makes me blush to think of it,' I protested. In truth I was exaggerating my shyness, for I had undressed with Estelle, Julia, and other girls to enjoy Sapphic pleasures, but I was sure Robert knew nothing of this, so I pretended to be nervous now in order that he might have no suspicions. In truth I was desperate for my lust to be relieved.

'Once you have been totally naked in front of the servants a few times you will feel comfortable enough,' Robert stated, smiling at my modesty.

In a matter of minutes we were undressed, for as the reader may imagine, we were more than somewhat aroused by the antics of Sally and John, and in no mood to disrobe with our usual care and grace.

Mary gazed at us, especially at me, with wide eyes, then cried out, 'Oh ma'am, you are so beautiful! You and the master are so fine together, such a splendid couple. I have always dreamed of being tormented by a superb man and wife acting in concert. Now will you be good enough to make me comfortable, that is, to touch me in a certain place?'

'We shall touch you when and where we choose,' Robert said sternly. He took me in his strong arms and kissed me passionately. I felt the hair of his chest caress my nipples. He lay me down on the bed and entered me forthwith, neither of us having any need or desire for further preliminaries. There are times when one only craves one thing, and that was one of those times. How delicious it is to have but one craving, and to be able to satisfy it so immediately! All too often in life we are possessed by a multiplicity of desires, but in erotic lust one finds the release and joy of simplicity.

It was good. Robert's rigid maleness probed the

depths of my body in heroic motions, all fluid in grace, agile as a fish. The fires of ecstasy were lit in my body more rapidly than I had ever known, and so strongly that for a short period I swooned.

I was confident I might die of such delight, and that it would be a good way to enter paradise. Robert could not dally either, but thrust at me again and again with superb strength, bringing me to the eruption of unbearable rapture as his splendid penis beat about in my woman's parts, lashing at their creamy, slippery flesh. I was delightfully aware of Mary's thwarted lusts, and so was my husband, who glanced at her from time to time as he enjoyed my clenching love muscles. Suddenly he acted as though he had been stabbed in the back. Deep grunts issued from his throat, while his vivid eruptions beat against the very centre of my earthly form, mastering my womb with male power. Again and again he gasped, all the while arching his back and writhing his hips as he buried his large organ entirely in me and emptied himself into my receptive and caressing warmth.

Mary watched us avidly, unable to relieve her own aching lust. Robert and I kissed, and smiled at one another. It is always pleasant to have something that others do not, and so he and I were especially pleased to have pounded our bodies together in rapture while Mary could only sigh and wriggle – indeed she wriggled her naked body as though trying to seduce one or both of us.

We lay tenderly for some minutes, whispering those sweet nothings that mean so much more than nothing.

'Oh please sir, ma'am, do something to make me feel better,' she pleaded huskily, 'or at least untie me so I can do something for myself.' She strained fruitlessly against her silken bondage.

'That's about enough of your impudence,' Robert

snapped. 'Another word out of you and it will be the worse for you, my girl. You ought to know your place by now.' Although he sounded genuinely angry, he squeezed my hand reassuringly behind his back, out of Mary's sight, and I took him to mean that he was play-acting so as to give this servant the unusual pleasure she craved. For his part, it was clear he greatly enjoyed the game, so it was, as the best things in life are, a mutually satisfying exchange.

'Come my dear,' he said to me. 'Let us amuse ourselves with the thwarted lust of this girl, who has made the considerable mistake of placing her body at our mercy. She will find only a lack of mercy.'

Robert got up and approached Mary, while I remained lying on the mattress for a while, delightfully lulled into a state of torpor by the powerful, if temporary, satisfaction of my desires. I watched fascinated as he first touched the tops of Mary's thighs – heavens, I was seeing my husband touch another woman! – and then lightly caressed her huge teats, which, improbable as it seemed to me then, actually grew more hugely taut under his fingers. I caught my breath, but found there was nothing of jealousy in me, for he did not love her.

I looked in a mirror, and saw my big blue eyes, long golden hair that hung down in such interesting waves, and splendid body. I opened my thighs, and saw male juices exuding frothily from my pink lips. I displayed myself to Mary, and was gratified to see her eyes widen still further.

Mary, too, opened her legs, wider than I had, for she was desperate for my husband's caresses, and only desired to make herself more accessible to this splendid man. He obliged her by laying the palm of his hand against her nether lips, which you may recall were uncommonly elongated and distended. I gasped, as in her shameless wantonness the debauched girl thrust her parts against his hand, trying to attain the peak of pleasure, only to groan in frustration as he withdrew his hand. He showed me his palm. It was wet.

'Here is another female of such lewdness that she gushes rich secretions to welcome the passage of a penis,' he stated. 'I'm sure it will look attractive if we were to transfer some of these juices to her breasts. Poor Mary, we are going to tease you so!'

My husband's organ was already reviving with astonishing rapidity as he wiped his hand on her right breast, to make it gleam in a manner that was most appealing. He repeated the process of collecting the female fluid, and applied it to her left breast. I imagined how the liquid must evaporate from Mary's taut teats, thus imparting a piquant coolness. The thought made my corresponding parts stand to attention like soldiers, and in addition, to demand attention.

As Robert went on with this splendid game, Mary kept trying to obtain stimulation from his hand, but each time he touched her too briefly for there to be any possibility of her spending. She sweated, and arched herself, pushing out her lower belly at him, trying to thrust her private parts against his flesh. In a curious way, I envied this young woman. I had never been so extremely tantalised, and I was intrigued to know how it would feel. I wondered if I would ever be treated as she was being now, and the thought made me get up and join my husband, to kiss him and hug him so that my body was pressed against his. I fondled his rigid maleness, and he fingered the split flesh between my legs, giving me the direct stimulation he had so cunningly denied our helpless maid.

I played the amusing game of teasing Mary, finding

her parts to be almost bloated with lust, and unnaturally hot. Juice streamed from the entrance to her body in great profusion. It was most interesting to play with such elongated lower lips, and such turgid nipples. The scent of her aroused femaleness wafted through the warm summer air.

'Now her breasts are well-coated and slippery,' Robert mused, regarding his captive with the air of a connoisseur. 'Let us seriously massage one breast each, my dear, and drive her completely insane.'

It seemed we would indeed achieve this dubious ambition, for as we enjoyed squeezing and stroking her fine orbs, paying special attention to the outrageous nipples, Mary writhed and cried out for mercy, by which she meant orgasm, and called on help from God. I grew somewhat concerned. My husband assured me however that it was only her way, and did but prove she was enjoying herself, so I continued to tease and caress her breasts in every way I could think of, kneading them like dough, tweaking and rubbing the lubricated flesh with the greatest sensations of pleasure. All the while, Robert and I fondled one another lewdly, so that I spent.

'We shall do the poor girl an injury,' I said afterwards. 'Let us release her.'

'You have a kind heart,' replied my husband. 'But when you know Mary as well as I do, you will realise that she loves a greatly prolonged session of captivity, with many episodes of teasing, intercourse, humiliation, torment, and binding in fresh positions. It is an art. What we have done with her so far today would normally be merely the entrée.'

'Oh ma'am, I beg you, pay no heed to him,' Mary gasped as though in the last stage of human endurance. 'I shall die if I'm not let go now.'

I gave Robert a beseeching look. He smiled at me

in return, then untied the servant in a moment. Quick as a vixen, she threw herself onto the red silk-covered mattress and clutched her private parts in both hands, from front and back, so tightly that it looked as though she were trying to squeeze out her own juice by main force. She spent almost at once, with the most extravagant display of contorted face, arched back, spasmodically jerking limbs and the like that I had even seen from a woman. Her body rolled off the mattress on to the carpet with a bump, but she did not seem to notice.

After an inordinately long time, the housemaid ceased her self-worship, for that is a more accurate term than the hateful and foolish one so commonly applied by the ignorant, namely, self-abuse.

'When you feel ready, you may go,' Robert told her gently.

'Yes sir. Thank you so much for teasing me sir, and you too ma'am. But give me leave, if it isn't forward of me, to tell you ma'am that the master was right, and though it was very kind of you to have mercy on me, it would've been so much nicer if you had tied me up more and used me cruelly for a much longer period, as it is so lovely when done right. If my words do get on your nerves, why, you can gag me in a minute. I only tell you so that you may get the best out of me, ma'am.' Mary's words were apparently respectful, but from the light in her eyes and a slightly resentful undertone, I knew she thought me a milksop. She was a remarkably demanding woman even though what she was demanding was to be bound, gagged, teased and used.

'But Mary,' I protested. 'You kept begging us to stop teasing you and let you go.'

'Well yes, I would, wouldn't I? I was tied up then, and that's what I have to say or else there's no point.

39

Never mind ma'am, I know you meant well. Next time, take my advice, gag and blindfold me and don't be distracted by my pleading voice nor eyes neither.'

With that, this astonishing young woman took her leave.

'Never mind, she is never satisfied,' Robert laughed, and pulled me down on to the mattress. 'I am delighted you have condescended to use the servants for your amusement. Am I not right in saying that you have enjoyed yourself not a little?'

'I was glad to see you enjoy yourself, of course,' I replied, still attempting to appear correctly modest.

'It seems to me that you take naturally to these unconventional practices, Jane. I had feared you would be shocked, and would flee the house to return to your mother. Could it be that you have taken part in similar activities before?'

'Oh Robert, how could you?' I cried in horror. I tried to rise from the mattress, but he smilingly held me down. 'As if I, a pure girl, knew anything of such depravities. Shame on you for insulting me.'

'Well my dear, I had heard that some girls enjoyed themselves in their youth with others of the fair sex, and it occurred to me that you might have sampled such harmless diversions. I was not, of course, accusing you of being involved with other men before your marriage to me. That would be unthinkable.'

As my husband spoke, his eyes twinkled as though he were enjoying some secret and amusing knowledge.

'I am glad you realise it,' I told him sternly. I had indeed never known the touch of a man before him, but I then went on to tell an untruth, owing to my wish to seem pure and unsullied.

'I must also make plain that I have never indulged in anything unladylike with others of my own sex.

That is something men are all too prone to imagine, but the reality is quite another case, I assure you.'

'You never so much as kissed another girl?' Robert enquired, his busy fingers tickling my rump the while.

'Certainly not,' I replied. Reader, forgive me for that lie. I had been strictly brought up, and felt I had to conceal the delights I had shared with Estelle, Julia, Carlotta and the others. Life makes many of us hypocrites.

It was then that my husband dropped a bombshell.

'I have heard a somewhat different story from a friend of yours,' he told me with the smile of a man rich in erotic knowledge. 'In short, your friend Julia has told me all.'

'Oh, the traitor!' I exclaimed, blushing deeply. 'And you have caught me out in a lie – I am doubly ashamed.'

'Hush, hush my dear,' Robert told me gently, patting me on the back. 'You have nothing to be ashamed of, either in your past activities or in your white lie. And far from betraying you, Julia did you and I a great service, for the knowledge she imparted to me helped me decide to marry you. It is a fact that in our society it is almost impossible for young ladies to partake of erotic pleasures with men, for they would be condemned, so those girls of a sensuous nature do often find solace with one another. Julia was sure you preferred men, from the way you had questioned her about her experiences with them. It has all worked out for the best. I knew that a girl like you, curious about men, and having indulged in orgies of the Sapphic variety, would have a good chance of adjusting to the unusual conditions in this house, if we did but love one another with all our hearts.'

I had started to sob in the shock of having my secret known to my husband, but I was immediately reassured by these words of his, and indeed, I soon felt deep gratitude to Julia for telling Robert about my desires. He and I now snuggled together in a great surge of passion and love.

'And now that you have had experience of both sexes,' said Robert, 'tell me which you prefer.'

'Men of course,' I replied truthfully. 'Men have that powerful organ designed to give delight both to its male owner and its female recipient. I am suited by nature to enjoy it, as well as to revel in the hard muscular strength of men's bodies, and their handsome faces, of which yours is a prime example. Men such as you are strong, Robert my darling, and that strength makes me feel safe and snug in my security. Yet I would not decry the pleasures my own sex have given me. Women have a pleasing softness, charm and delicacy, as well as a formidable capacity for prolonged erotic pleasures.'

'I am glad to hear you sing the praises of women,' said Robert. 'For they are so delightful that it would be a stupid girl who did not find a strong attraction from her own sex. Now tell me in more detail of what you did together, for it pleases me to hear of erotic delights from your sweet lips.'

So I told my husband everything about my group of wicked friends, of whom Estelle was the accepted leader. I talked, and we caressed one another intimately. I told him of how we kissed one another's breasts, and rubbed the lower part of our bellies together for mutual satisfaction. I talked mainly about Estelle herself, with her beautiful face and figure and her long auburn hair.

'Tomorrow we shall take your initiation one step further,' Robert observed lustfully. 'For instance, you might make love with another woman, and then watch me enjoy one of the female servants.'

'I may be very jealous of her if you do,' I warned him. 'I might hate you for putting your penis into her.'

'We shall see,' Robert murmured, then fell to sucking my breast.

Heavens, how fearfully aroused we both were by our licentious plans and conversation! I thought I would die for my desire of his rampant manhood.

'You are more than ready for another new experience,' Robert announced and with that went to a corner of the room where stood a chest of dark old oak. This he opened, and from it took, to my excited amazement, a most curious collection of black leather straps with shiny steel buckles. I was both frightened and enthralled – a potent mixture indeed.

'This is a love harness,' my husband stated. 'You see, this belt buckles around my waist, and these go from it around your shoulders. From the waist hang these long adjustable straps with stirrups at the ends, just as one uses while riding a horse. I shall harness you, with your permission Jane, and thus achieve a deeper penetration and degree of control than has hitherto been the case. You will be my good strong mare, and I shall ride you.'

I confess I did not need any persuading, but eagerly helped Robert strap the thrilling harness to my slender young body, lifting my long golden hair so that it did not get caught up in the straps. I even urged him to do the straps up tighter, for it was a thrilling sensation indeed to be harnessed like an animal. The torso straps crossed from left to right, thus making an 'X' on the front of my body and the back, with a silver ring between my breasts at the point of junction. Although my limbs were free, my body felt most deliciously confined and compressed.

43

I was so aroused as to be eager only to be used by my husband, and lay down on my back. He entered me at once, and I felt a warm surge of delight. Next he put his feet in the stirrups and pushed down against them, with the magical result that he seemed to thrust deeper into me than ever before, while his pubis ground against the area of my clitoris, bringing me so rapidly to the peaks of ecstasy that I was amazed.

My splendid mate rode me magnificently, both front and back, using me as his mare, his pleasure horse that responded faithfully to his every whim. He wallowed in my body, until finally he shot his male fluid into its centre with the force of a gun, at which I was again burned up by rapture.

When he undid the harness I was utterly spent, like a formerly frolicsome mare that has been ridden thirty miles across rough country.

The strong leather straps had left red marks on my white flesh, marks which Robert kissed tenderly. I felt proud of them, for they were like a soldier's minor wounds gained in the service of the queen.

I lay there and felt a vast love for him whom God had given me for all eternity. I knew that on the morrow I would endeavour to please him even if I had to watch him copulate with a servant. We dressed and went down for tea.

That night I prayed God to make me a good wife to this fine man, and to obey him in all things. I prayed for the power to satisfy Robert's great erotic drive, as was both my duty and my pleasure.

Chapter Four

It was at breakfast the next morning that I had a strong intimation of the crisis which was soon to break over us: a dire emergency that led us into a truly bizarre sequence of erotic endeavours, achievements, and suffering.

The reader may recall that my mother had evinced doubts as to the financial standing of my husband, and I may add that even on our delightful honeymoon there had been moments when he seemed preoccupied with some concern, though he would quickly shrug off the mood if I enquired whether he was worried. Now the morning mail was to add to my fears that Robert had a serious problem.

At first I thought the post of unusual excellence, for I had a letter from my beloved bad girl, Estelle, containing news which sent a reminiscent shudder of voluptuous pleasure through my body and soul. I was about to tell Robert what the missive conveyed, but then restrained myself, for the wicked thought came to me that this information was of a most stimulating nature, as there was little doubt that Estelle would join in our interesting activities, and therefore it would be amusing to hold it in reserve, as it were, for the moment when I desired to give my mate an extra stimulus that would grant us both additional erotic delights. Accordingly I resolved to keep this exciting news from Estelle to myself until such time as Robert and I were once more engaged in the happy toil of love's sweet labours. I felt proud of my own cunning.

My happiness fled, however, when I looked up from my letter and across the table laden with porridge, toast, oranges, chicken livers, boiled eggs, tea and kidneys that formed part of our morning repast, for now again I saw on Robert's face that look of deep anxiety which I had occasionally been surprised by on our honeymoon. Now I resolved to study him at leisure unknown to him, so as to confirm my suspicions before he had opportunity to recompose his features in their usual cheerful form.

He had forgotten me for the moment, that was plain enough, and though I do not suffer overmuch from vanity, nevertheless it gave me no little discomfort to witness his utter absorption in the letter he was reading, an absorption strong enough to obliterate any thought of me for the moment. It was clear from the movements of his eyes that he read certain passages over and over again, and from the look of despondency that settled like London fog over his features, it was all too plain that the comfort he searched for so desperately was not to be found in the letter – which had, I noticed, a foreign stamp on its envelope – and that in this communication all was bleak and barren.

It made my heart ache to see the man I loved in such a state as this, and every iota of my being yearned for him to confide in me and give me the opportunity for me to show that I would stand by him whatever trouble he might be in. I felt that his caresses had strengthened me, that I was now a woman on whom he could rely to the end. In fact, such were my romantic notions, I almost hoped that he was in trouble, so that I might prove my faithfulness to him come what may. I trust the reader will forgive my foolishness.

'Is it bad news, dearest?' I enquired at last.

So totally had he forgotten my existence that, at my quiet words, he gave a start of surprise.

'What? Oh, it is nothing,' he muttered after staring at me for a moment as though seeking to recall who the deuce I might be.

'Will you not share your life with me?' I enquired timidly. 'If your letter contains bad news, I –'

'My dear, this is a business matter. Business is the man's domain as the home is the woman's. We must get this necessary division of responsibilities quite clear at this, the start, of our married life.'

'Of course I shall obey you in all matters,' I agreed meekly. Naturally I was disappointed in his not confiding in me, but at the same time I was pleased by his display of masculine strength of character, for I would not have married a milksop.

'Thank you, my darling,' Robert said with strong tenderness. He reached across the table to squeeze my hand. 'Let us now look at the newspapers, and then we might have a walk. I shall write some letters, and then, after a light luncheon, we might take a bath – together.'

I was deeply thrilled by this idea of mixed bathing, a daring notion indeed which made me blush for the images that thronged my mind. My anticipation was the greater for the knowledge that the bathroom was one of sybaritic luxury and elegance such as would have befitted a sultan, where a couple could enjoy all manner of erotic sportiveness. We might even be joined by a servant! I could hardly wait, and yet the waiting was highly worthwhile too, for I knew it would make the eventual pleasure all the stronger.

We passed the morning hours as my husband had suggested, and on our walk we talked briefly with some of the servants as they went about their work.

In the garden, McBean and Lisa were weeding, while Lisa's baby, Arnold, lay asleep in the shade. In the stables Darma, the Indian girl, had just brought back Robert's gelding, Blaze, from his exercise and was brushing him down. She loved the horses, that was plain to see. The stable man, Franklin, that muscular, quiet man who was indeed stable, had taken a cart into town in order to buy fodder, and John had gone with him. Robert told me that it was Franklin who made the erotic leather items such as the harness I had tried the night before, for he was skilled in making and mending harnesses for horses, and to make them for men and women was something he found even more stimulating.

Everyone in the house enjoyed dreaming up new designs for him to make, and apparently some of those Mary had suggested were cunningly restrictive. It was curious to think of the strong, silent stable man spending many hours making such items with loving care. Still, I daresay it is a good thing to have a hobby.

It was another beautiful day, and, protected by my parasol and broad white hat against the unfortunate browning properties of the sun, I greatly enjoyed our stroll. I did not attempt to question Robert about his worrying letter, for I respected his decision not to tell me about it – and besides, I had a premonition that the truth would out, and that when it did, it would not be pleasant.

When Robert went to his study to write his letters, I visited Sally and her little helper, Charlotte, in the kitchen, where they were busy making strawberry jam – the strawberries were exceptional that year. I instructed them to prepare a light salad for luncheon, and later I consumed this with Robert. After we had concluded, I sat and wondered if he had forgotten what he had said that morning about our sharing a bath. I hoped he would bring the subject up, for I did not want to suggest such a thing myself and so seem utterly abandoned.

'Let us go to our bedroom,' Robert proposed suddenly, and I was delighted to hear it, for it was clear he was thinking of pleasures of the flesh. When we reached that room, he had another suggestion. 'Do you have any objection to Banks joining us, Jane? I have in mind his seeing you in a state of nudity, and of his doing something that will touch you without his actually touching you.' He smiled. 'You will find out soon enough what I mean, so ask no questions.'

'I have no objection, since it is your wish,' I replied, again somewhat hypocritically, for I was naturally curious about Banks, the imperturbable butler. I had been brought up not to show signs of enthusiasm, as it was thought common.

Robert pulled on the bell rope, and Banks arrived promptly as ever, his face a mask of respectful anticipation.

'Banks, we wish you to take out your penis and amuse yourself while my wife undresses. Refrain from spending as yet. Jane, it would give Banks and I pleasure if you were to divest yourself of your apparel in a slow and sensuous manner.'

How can I describe my feelings as I prepared to undress in front of a man who was not my husband? I was certainly embarrassed, and uncertain as to what might occur next, yet at the same time it was so delightfully wicked that it felt exciting. This was forbidden, and yet I was going to do it!

I stood up and began to unfasten the many straps, hooks and buttons of my dress. Banks undid himself and took out his male organ without embarrassment, then moved his hand back and forth on it so that it became erect. I blushed to see it, but he maintained his usual grave and respectful manner as though nothing untoward was occurring.

After some time I took my dress off and began on other garments, moving with deliberate slowness so as to tease both men, though this, my first performance in this line, was as nothing compared to the skills I later acquired. It was good enough however to thoroughly arouse both Banks and my husband. Robert undressed very quickly, revealing his organ in magnificent tumescence. As for myself, I felt intensely female and vulnerable in a thrilling way, and was keenly aware of every part of my body as I revealed it to the men's hot gazes.

After some time I bared my breasts, and had the satisfaction of seeing Banks' eyes widen. With slow care I unrolled my silk stockings and gradually removed my other garments until I was naked. I could see that Banks was showing self-restraint, for every now and then he paused in his manipulation of his organ so as not to spend.

'Jane,' said my husband, 'I propose that Banks adorn your nudity with his manly fluid, an act that will give both he and I pleasure. I hope you can enjoy it too. If not, just say so, and he can spend in another manner.'

This was quite a proposal. I now understood Robert's words earlier, when he said that Banks would touch me without actually touching me. I felt a little shy, and almost declined the proposal, but then I reflected that Robert was worried about the letter he had received that morning, so it was my duty to help distract him. Besides, I wanted to proceed bravely with this process of initiation, and not be thought of as a killjoy.

I signalled my compliance with a slight movement

of my head. At once I felt exquisitely wicked, and a thrill of pleasure coursed through my soul.

'Lie on the bed near the edge, my dear,' Robert advised me. 'Banks, you may spend over my wife's belly and breasts.'

'Yes sir,' the butler replied, still without showing signs of surprise, though he did seem quite pleased.

I lay naked on the bed as directed, feeling deliciously aroused and vulnerable, and at the same time both shy and brazen. Banks stood next to the bed so that his manhood was standing above my belly – surely my husband must intervene, thought I, he cannot be serious about this wickedness. But no. Robert watched intently as Banks increased the frequency of his hand motions until he spent copiously, with the stuff pouring rather than shooting out of him owing to his age. Banks, I realised later, liked to save himself for such special occasions, and so the unusually thick cream came out again and again to pour over my breasts and belly as if it would never stop. Finally it did, by which time I was aghast at the mess all over my body.

Banks gave a deep sigh, regarded for a moment what he had wrought, and gave me a little bow that might have looked sarcastic from anyone but him.

'You may leave us now, Banks,' my husband stated. 'Oh, and Banks, do keep the housemaids up to the mark. I could almost discern dust on some books in the library yesterday, and dust is something one should never be able to almost discern.'

'Very good, sir. I shall talk to Edith and Mary immediately.'

As the door closed behind the butler, I looked at his creamy substance, which oozed slowly downwards over the curves of my body. Robert took my hands in his and placed them on my breasts, then moved them slowly back and forth. I blushed afresh, for he was forever surprising me afresh with his powerful imagination. I wanted to please him, so I continued the motions of my hands even after he withdrew his own. In another minute I was enjoying the slippery feel of the stuff, and my own sense of wickedness. A caress is more of a caress when it is lubricated, and here we had a fine lubricant indeed, both in slipperiness and odour.

'It is now a fact that you are besmirched with filth,' Robert observed cheerfully. His penis was superbly erect, mighty in its lustful arrogance. 'As you are filthy, you must be cleansed.'

Abruptly he swept me up in his strong arms, and effortlessly carried me into the adjoining bathroom. Here we were both surprised to see Edith, that giddy young housemaid.

'What are you doing here?' Robert enquired. 'You should not be cleaning the bathroom at this time.'

'Oh sir, I thought I should do it special – I heard you say you would have a bath together – and please don't send me away now I'm here, for I can help.'

'So that's it,' said my husband. 'You wanted to join us in order to slake your lust and curiosity.' He set me down gently on my feet. 'That smacks of getting above your station, Edith.'

'Oh I wouldn't do that sir. I know my place,' the maid insisted in her strong cockney accent. I shall not be discourteous enough to the reader to attempt its reproduction here. 'I only thought as how I could help.'

Despite my embarrassment at her seeing me in my smeared state, I felt sorry for the girl, who doubtless had a strong desire to be pleasured by my husband. In the setting of that unique household I could not feel jealous at such an idea, and besides, to be jealous of her would have been to regard her too highly. Therefore I intervened on her behalf.

'You could let her join us, Robert,' I murmured coaxingly.

'Ah, you find her amusing, do you?'

'Yes, I do,' I admitted, blushing.

'You may stay Edith, thanks to my wife's kindness. No, do not remove your uniform just yet. And remember, if it had been up to me I would have sent you away after a harsh scolding.'

'Yes sir, you're very strong,' the maid said complacently. 'Thank you ma'am for letting me stay. I'll run a bath, shall I? I put in a lot of cold water already, as it's such a hot day, and the gas do make the water so hot.'

She turned on the hot water. I shall now describe the bathroom, for it is certainly worth describing for the way in which it was designed to facilitate erotic delights.

The bath which Edith had begun to fill was an exceptional affair made of green marble. The top of it projected above the level of the floor, while the bottom was sunk lower than that surface. The bather mounted three steps to get into it at one end, and at the other end and on both sides were mounted brightly polished brass rails, the purpose of which was to give support for whatever interesting erotic activities the bathers were enjoying. The bath was more than long enough for a tall man like Robert to lie down in, and so deep that if I stood in it when it was completely full, the water nearly reached my bosom.

The whole floor of the bathroom was tiled, and sloped gently towards unobtrusive drains. One corner of the room was lined with black tiles, and here was a fine example of modern inventiveness, namely the several roses of an all-round shower. In another corner was a black inflatable mattress made of vulcanised rubber, that new wonder material.

The walls of the room were blue, like tropical seas, and decorated with paintings of gorgeous mermaids most skilfully executed. Another striking feature of the room was the long, very shallow white enamel bath sunk into the floor and projecting into a little turret with windows all round, which extended nearly to the floor, with the result that one could sit or lie in that bath and have a view of the gardens and the flat Norfolk countryside all around one. This bathroom was not uninteresting.

Edith threw generous handfuls of bath crystals into the waters of the deep bath and began whisking them to encourage the formation of foam. Hot water jetted into the bath from the highly efficient heating apparatus.

My husband led me to the black-tiled corner and turned on a cold spray, which hissed against my skin and made me gasp, though it was not unpleasant, the day being so warm. He then had me lie face down in the shallow bath, and I looked through the window at the fine view of the splendid old trees, lawns, and brilliant flowers in the garden, as well as the fields of golden corn ripening outside our walls. I thought how odd it would be to lie there in the winter, naked in hot water while having a clear view all around me of frost, icicles, and snow-covered woods and fields, all white and chill.

Robert slowly and sensuously soaped my back, thighs, and buttocks, arousing me by the skilled touch of his loving hands, which knew so perfectly how to handle my willing flesh. After squeezing my nether cheeks and tickling the flesh between them he moved on top of me, and I was surprised when he did not enter my female channel, but rather slid between my soapy thighs. He lay on my back and reached under me to toy with my breasts. I was sandwiched between the coolness of the enamel bath and the warmth of his skin, with the view of the countryside laid out before my eyes, and in this happy state we stayed for some time, while he gently moved his organ between my thighs, indirectly stimulating my private parts. Then Robert led me back to the shower to rinse off, and he held me in his arms and kissed me while the cold spray came from several different directions, making me deliciously aware of every inch of my skin.

After we were thoroughly cooled, we made for the big marble bath. It was one of those magical moments that effortlessy crosses the barrier of the years in my memory as a lightning flash crosses from sky to earth. The sun streamed in, making the tiled floor gleam like ice, and the beauty of everything was deeply affecting. Robert, so tall and handsome, could not take his eyes off my naked body, decorated with my wet golden hair.

The water in the bath was now quite deep. Robert jumped in boyishly with a great splash, then lifted me into the bath and laid me down in its gentle warmth, transforming me into a mermaid like those painted on the walls, a naiad in the foaming, forbidden waters of lust. Robert gazed at me hungrily, his penis actually pulsing with his heartbeat.

It was delicious how the foam tickled my skin, and whenever a movement of mine trapped some of it beneath me, it rose to the surface, caressing me all the while as though it had a life and desires of its own.

'Here is a servant for our every need,' said Robert. He took Edith by the hand and pulled her gently but irresistibly towards the water.

'Oh sir,' squealed the maid. 'My uniform will get wet.'

'Yes, it will look amusing,' my husband replied, smiling.

The girl slid helplessly over the rounded marble lip of the bath, and gave forth a great cry that was cut off as she splashed into the bath. She rose up spluttering, her black and white uniform all drenched, clinging to her tightly to outline every curve of her young body like a second skin. She protested, but in reality the girl was clearly delighted to join us.

'Do your duty,' Robert told her. 'Clean your mistress thoroughly with your hands and tongue.'

'I'll be glad to do it, ma'am,' the servant breathed, and in her eyes I saw that she found me attractive.

She rubbed and caressed me with the copious foam, gently pleasing every inch of my body with her work-hardened hands while sucking and licking my breasts and private parts. I was greatly pleased.

'Please sir, may I be allowed to take my uniform off now?' she pleaded prettily. 'It won't do it any good, being worn in a bath.'

'I know you are in fact only thinking of your own pleasures,' Robert told her. 'You think your voluptuous sensation will be enhanced by nudity, do you not?'

'I'm sure I couldn't think of anything as clever as that, sir.'

'All right, take it off. But I am thinking of the pleasure your naked body may give my wife and I, not of your pleasure.'

It was amusing to see the maid struggling out of her wet uniform in the deep water – Robert would not give her permission to leave the bath – especially as Robert and I teased her by pushing her over now and then when she was entangled in a garment she was fighting to remove. We also splashed and groped her unmercifully, so the frustrated, highly aroused girl took a long time to gradually win free of her confining clothing. Her dark brown hair soon fell in disarray over her body.

Edith was a very pretty girl, and it was delightful to see her white wet skin gradually emerge from her garments to gleam in the sunlight.

Robert now sat on the edge of the bath to give us more room, and to watch us like a god, ready to swoop down on two aroused females whenever he chose. Edith and I kissed passionately and pressed our bodies together, too overcome with desire to be restrained. It was delightful how the blue crystals Edith had added to the water made our skin feel slippery, so that we could writhe and wriggle against one another as we stood there, satisfying our own needs and each other's in the way that makes the erotic act both selfish and altruistic, a delicious conflict of ever-shifting motives.

In a way we were competing too, for that male organ which stood so rigid and tempting, like a prize one of us would win. We displayed our attractions and our arousal to Robert more than we did to one another, and even as I held the slender, slithery servant in my arms and pressed my breasts against her smaller ones, I was thrillingly tormented by the thought of Robert taking her in my presence. She fingered my cunnie and I returned the favour, trying to imagine how she would feel to his penis.

We tried several positions, showing off our knowledge of the many forms of Sapphic indulgence. We stood and rubbed one another's private parts with our slippery thighs, and then I turned around, bent down and stuck out my behind so that she could play with my nether lips, running her fingers up and down them very rapidly before crouching down to stick her tongue inside. I reached up to fondle Robert's testicles.

'This is splendid,' he breathed. 'You are marvellous with another woman.'

Assured of his warm approval I grew still more lascivious. Edith and I lay down in the water and floated there on our sides, face to face, pressing our bosoms and pubic mounds together, wriggling back and forth so that we both attained the heights of rapture. We gasped and thrashed about in the water, pressing ourselves together, using all our strength.

Robert entered the bath, and Edith and I at once turned our attention to him. We were all eagerness, kissing him and caressing his splendid body. He turned me around so that I had my back to him.

'Hold onto the railing,' he stated.

I did so, finding how useful it was for the kinds of copulation that involve the full exertion of muscular power. I looked over my shoulder and saw Edith prove herself a useful servant indeed, for she took my husband's organ and slipped it inside me. I gasped with pleasure as he thrust home, driving manfully into the centre of my being and occupying me with his strength, stretching and filling me. His hands mastered my breasts, my back, my broad hips that he held as though they were handles for the convenience of men coupling with their mates. Our bodies moved in tender motion. I arched my back and wriggled my behind, squeezing him now and then while he thrust in and out with splendid power.

After countless spear thrusts at my body and soul by my man, I reached the sun-kissed summits of ecstasy, and the extent of my rapture was such that I felt I was being taken apart by angels and put back together again in a better way, to reside henceforth on a higher plane. I slid down into the warm foaming waters as though surrendering myself to the depths, and Edith loyally supported me. As my body clasped at Robert he gave deep sighs of delight, and collapsed on to my back, holding my breasts while his manly fluid hosed vibrantly against my innermost flesh. What perfection of pleasure!

For some minutes we could only sit sighing in the bath, while Edith caressed us gently. It took some time to recover our wits after such a shattering release of all tensions, but then it struck me that it would be a good idea to share with Robert the news I had received that morning, for it would encourage the welcome revival of his manhood. Was I not a cunning wife?

'Dearest, I have had a letter from my old friend Estelle, the Sapphic beauty,' I told him. 'She will come to visit us soon, that is, if you are willing.'

'I am more than willing, I am eager,' Robert replied. 'I have heard much of her, though our paths have never crossed, and it will be pleasant to meet her at last. The woman who initiated my dear wife into the pleasures of the flesh! You shall write to her by the evening post inviting her to come as soon as she can. Inform her of the fact that she can enjoy herself here with you and the female staff, and that no man shall bother her.'

'Perhaps she will let you watch if I ask her nicely,' I said, at the same time reaching out to grasp his maleness. 'It will be a sight worth seeing.'

As I had hoped, my news of Estelle greatly interested Robert, and as I moved my hand up and down, his organ revived rapidly. Soon it had regained all its steely pride. Moved by a generous impulse, I took Edith's hand and placed it higher up on the shaft, so that Robert could have the pleasure of two females holding him in that place most loved by men. I felt a deep sense of joy, and inwardly gave thanks to God that He made me capable of enjoying such delights.

'Oh look sir, your cock is huge again,' said Edith in artless admiration, her eyes wide as half-crowns.

'I'm not sure that is proper for a servant to make comments on the intimate anatomy of her master,' Robert observed. 'However, as your comment was not of an adverse nature I shall let it pass.'

We now dedicated ourselves seriously to the building up of our amorous inclinations to the point where we could once more savour love's highest expression. Edith and I moved our tightly clasped hands up and down Robert's manhood and stroked his superb body, while he caressed and probed us both to good effect.

'Sir, I wonder who you mean to fuck?' said Edith. 'It would be so good if it were me, because I do need it so much. Oh ma'am, do say he can do it to me.'

'Robert, I have no objection if you cared to enjoy the girl,' I said. The reader may think me a bad woman for speaking thus, but in the situation and state of excitement we had reached, it was only natural. I was highly aroused, and deeply curious besides to see what a man and a maid might look like together, especially as that man was my husband. I blushed slightly, but it did me good to speak so sincerely. So many people go their whole lives without ever saying what is truly on their minds, so that, in effect, they have never lived at all.

Robert was deeply moved.

'You are an excellent woman, Jane,' he avowed, taking me in his arms and kissing me.

What a mixture of feelings I had as Edith and Robert caressed and kissed one another prior to coupling! Many strong emotions mingled in my soul, making the scene a gripping one for me. At least I knew at that moment I was truly alive, not merely going through the dull motions of existing.

Robert lay back in the water and the servant straddled his body. I was suddenly filled with a sweet love for my husband, and wanted him to enjoy the girl as he might enjoy a glass of brandy or walk in the countryside, so I took hold of his penis and held it at the required angle.

'Thank you indeed, ma'am,' said Edith.

She impaled herself upon it. As I watched it slide home into her cunnie, I felt the most exquisite thrill of arousal shiver through my every nerve, and then I knew what we were doing must be right, or it would not feel so good.

Edith reached out to hold the railings on either side of the bath, and with their support was able to copulate with the greatest vigour, exerting the full strength of her arms, torso, and legs. As Robert was floating, she was able to use her long, powerful legs to good effect, moving his body as she chose. It was fascinating to watch her lithe young body, gleaming wet in the sunshine, arch and writhe with taut muscles. Their gasps told me the tale of their delight, and I shared it, caressing them both and pressing my body against portions of Edith's as well as Robert's.

The servant stood on the bottom of the bath, flexing her leg muscles, moving her body and his up and down as he floated in the warm foaming waters. I reflected that servants, by their labours, must attain some physical strength, and resolved to exercise more in future. Robert caressed us both indiscriminately, sometimes clutching at my buttocks and pressing his face into my cunnie while thrusting up into the housemaid.

Robert now had me stand over his face, and he licked me fervently while Edith leaned forward and kissed me. They both played with my breasts. I found it exquisite to be with a man and woman at the same time, and grew dizzy with pleasure as Robert's lips and tongue served my tumescent parts with love. I spent, and my rapture was heightened by the clever way Edith squeezed my breasts in a rhythm to match that of my rapturous gasps. Then Robert, too, spent, and his cries of triumph shivered through the sensitive flesh between my legs, vibrating it delightfully. I thought of his cock erupting in the servant girl, and was ripped apart by a savage orgasm which seemed to last a million years. Dimly I heard Edith's rapturous panting as Robert's final thrusts threw her over the brink into the oblivion of ecstasy.

After tea, I wrote to Estelle, asking her to come as soon as she was able. Happily I anticipated fresh pleasures – what would I do next, and with whom? I wondered how Robert would enjoy the other female servants, and was eager to find out. What a prospect now opened before us!

Little did I know at that moment, but in fact this way of life, so novel and exciting, was under dire threat. A period of great anxiety, severe trials, and bizarre erotic strivings was about to begin, so that what I had done with Banks and Edith, and thought so delightfully wicked, would seem as child's play compared to the trials we all had to undergo.

Chapter Five

The next day I dedicated to work, for life cannot be
all pleasure or that would become one's work, and
very boring work it would soon become too. There
was much to investigate both in the house and in the
garden, and I busied myself profitably by finding out
everything from the amount of jam being made to the
frequency of washing the servants' bed linen. In a
house of any size at all there are a thousand matters
to consider, and when one has duly considered them,
why then, one finds another thousand matters that
were hiding behind them out of sight. I was pleased
to find that most of the house and its routines were
in reasonable order, though I was able to make some
improvements that made everything still better. It became clear to me that Robert made sure the servants
fulfilled their household duties with the same thor-
oughness with which they ensured their own erotic
pleasures.

Indeed, the house had a happy atmosphere. Everybody was pleased to be living in a place where even
their most unusual appetites could be satisfied without censure, and indeed it must have been partly
this happiness that led them to work hard at mundane tasks such as cooking, cleaning, ironing etc.,
which leads me to the conclusion that if anyone wants
good servants, they must allow them to be happy.
I am aware that this is a radical proposal which will

condemn me as a freethinker in the eyes of many, but I can only report faithfully what I have experienced, which is that the more one enjoys oneself, the better one can work.

In the evening, Robert had news for me.

'I must leave early tomorrow on business,' he said. 'I may be gone two or three days.'

'Must you go, dearest, so soon after we have arrived here? I shall miss you dreadfully.'

'Indeed I must go, but do not worry yourself, for it will be delightful to hurry home and hold you in my arms again. This brief absence shall but heighten our mutual attachment.'

So I helped him pack, though with a heavy heart, for I feared his trip was connected with the letter that had so worried him, and I had a sense of foreboding that no good would come of his travels. Indeed, after he had departed, I felt depressed. I tried to busy myself with plans for the garden, and willed the hours to pass, but time hung heavy on my hands. I did not even have the heart to pursue erotic pleasures with the female staff.

Robert returned after a three days' absence, and I felt certain, as soon as I saw his face, that dark clouds were gathering around our life together. I asked him nothing about his concerns, which I presumed were financial, for, you recall, he had forbidden me to do so, and I was perhaps rather too obedient. A man may give strict orders to his wife and be disappointed when she obeys.

On the same day came a letter from Estelle accepting our invitation, and informing us that she would arrive at the village railway station at ten past three on the following Tuesday afternoon.

The Sunday and Monday passed with Robert spending almost every minute in his study. He wrote letters, reread old ones, and tied papers into bundles, among other activities. He would not let me or anyone else give him any assistance.

Then it was Tuesday. There were thunder showers around noon, but they had passed by the time Estelle's train arrived, so the world was all washed clean and fresh in sunshine as my dear friend got off the train. John was with me, and he piled Estelle's luggage into the chaise, experiencing a little difficulty in fact, for she was a fashionable young lady who took a large quantity of clothing wherever she went, even if she spent a major part of her visits naked.

Reader, I wish that I had the literary powers of Dickens or Austen that I might write a description of Estelle which would do her justice. I have not those powers, so I can only do my poor best. Picture for yourself, then, a young lady with a perfect figure and a calm, aristocratic face. Imagine her movements to be pure grace in motion, and be impressed by her air of absolute confidence and self-possession. Now you know something of this young lady. I can only add that her long, rich, wavy auburn hair was the envy of every female who saw it, as were her perfect white teeth, so frequently revealed in a smile which was usually mocking.

'Oh Estelle, how lovely to see you again!' I cried. 'What fun we shall have together, I'm sure.'

'I'm not so sure that fun exists in Norfolk, which is famed rather for its agricultural pursuits than for orgies. I may be the one to introduce the concept of pleasure to the miserable puritans who choose to live here – though "live" may be too strong a word for what people do in Norfolk,' Estelle stated in her crisp, clear pronunciation. We kissed, and she gave me a penetrating look from her bright hazel eyes, seeming to see into my soul. 'How beautiful you are now, Jane. It is depressingly obvious that the male sex suits you.'

John drove us the few miles home, and I told Estelle about the unconventional pleasures that we indulged in at Dreadnought Manor. I had not told her in my letter, as I thought it too delicate a matter to trust to the post.

'And you were such a quiet girl,' was Estelle's response. 'Now you have not only undergone a transformation to that dubious virtue, a love of the opposite sex, but you have married a man who is even more clearly a lunatic than most men are.'

'Oh Estelle, how can you say such a cruel thing? You are the one who introduced me to erotic pleasures with you and your friends, so how can you say Robert is a lunatic when he is only doing the same thing – well, with men as well as ladies.'

'The same thing, only totally different,' stated Estelle.

'Why, before I met you, I was totally innocent.'

'Good God, as bad as that? What a boring life you must have led until you had the good fortune to meet me. I saved you from the horrors of a life of unrelieved virtue. What you do not understand, child, is that while a sharing of pleasures between ladies is beautiful, it is not the same thing when a man ruts with the servants and encourages his naive young girl of a wife to do likewise.'

'Oh, you are simply prejudiced against men,' I protested. 'When you meet Robert you will feel differently.'

'Besotted, besotted,' Estelle laughed, shaking her head. 'If he told you to hop on one leg into a burning building while balancing a jug of cream on your head, you'd do it like a shot, I know, and assume he had a perfectly good reason for asking you to do it.'

'I'm sure he would,' I replied heatedly, leaving logic some way behind. We both laughed at my foolishness.

'I hope he appreciates having such a slavish admirer of his fair male person,' said Estelle. 'I hear he isn't even rich. If you're going to be so perverse as to marry a man, you might at least have married a rich specimen.'

'Really Estelle, as if worldly wealth was of any consequence where love is concerned.'

'When it matters, you'll find out just how much it does matter,' Estelle stated, declaiming as though we were acting in a play on the stage. 'My heart bleeds to hear such pitiful innocence.'

We came to Dreadnought Manor, and my husband came out of the house to give Estelle a warm greeting. In his superb bearing and manner he was every inch the gentleman, and I felt proud to be his mate.

'Welcome to my house, Miss Havisham. I hope you will enjoy your stay here very much.'

'Not half as much as I hope I will' she replied.

Fortunately I had warned Robert of my friend's particular form of speaking in friendly insults, so he was not taken aback, and indeed enjoyed her badinage. I took her to the pleasant room we had selected and prepared for her. I had personally arranged the flowers in the vases. John, Banks and Franklin carried up her bags and trunk.

'And have you sampled that fine specimen of Jamaican manhood?' she enquired of me, referring to John. Thankfully she waited until the men had left the room.

'Of course not Estelle!' I exclaimed. On reflection, I added – as I was an honest girl – 'Not yet at any rate. I have merely watched him being sat on by the cook.'

Estelle turned to me and regarded me as though I was an interesting scientific specimen.

' "I have merely watched him being sat on by the cook",' she said, in a sickly sweet voice which I imagine was intended to be an imitation of mine. She gave a great sigh. 'Only such an innocent girl as you can be so truly depraved, Jane. I envy you.'

'I am not so innocent,' I protested. 'I have come a long way.'

'Yes, and all of it downhill.'

I left my friend to refresh herself and change her dress. She came down for tea, and I was delighted to see that she and Robert got on very well indeed. They were both very clever, and conversed on any number of topics with ease and enjoyment. After tea I showed Estelle the new dress I had bought in Paris on my honeymoon, and the time until dinner passed quickly. Estelle retired soon after this meal, for she was tired after her journey from Rutland, where she had temporarily based herself in an unsuccessful attempt to seduce a nun.

'An interesting young lady,' Robert said to me that night, and I praised him for showing such good sense.

In the morning, Estelle was equally approving.

'I like your husband,' she told me privately. 'It's clear he loves you madly, and that alone proves his fine character.'

She and I walked in the gardens after breakfast, for it was another sunny day, although the wind was a little strong for our parasols. I told my friend more about the female servants, which were of course the only ones she was interested in. I pointed out Lisa doing some weeding amongst the roses. She was a quiet and sweet girl, and excellent in her work. Her illegitimate and charming baby Arnold was asleep in a cot under an elm.

'An attractive girl, and an interesting figure,' Estelle mused, regarding the servant. 'Your husband certainly chose his staff with all care.'

We talked with Lisa, who wore a man's work shirt and trousers for convenience in her work. What a shocking thing it was to see a girl dressed like a man! Her male costume did not distract from her female charms however, most remarkable of which were her very large, milk-turgid breasts.

'We would like you to join us this afternoon,' Estelle told her after chatting about the baby. 'Is there someone who can take care of Arnold for you?'

'Oh yes, Darma, the stable girl, can do it, miss. She loves little Arnold.'

'I daresay you will feed him before joining us,' mused Estelle. 'Tell me, does he drink all the milk you produce?'

'No he doesn't, miss. He is not thirsty enough to drink all the milk I make,' Lisa said without embarrassment. 'You can see, I am a big girl in that way.'

'Yes, I can see,' Estelle agreed. 'And what do you do with the extra milk, that which Master Arnold does not require?'

'Charlotte begged me to let her drink it every day,' Lisa replied. 'So she has it, Miss.'

'Charlotte is a greedy girl. Such greed may be amusing, so we shall have her with us this afternoon too,' stated Estelle. 'Please do not give Charlotte any of your milk today, unless I ask you too. Join us in the dining room at two o'clock.'

We let Lisa return to her duties and walked on. When we were beyond her hearing I asked Estelle what she intended to do with Lisa's milk.

'I don't know yet, but surely a woman in milk must offer scope for some unusual pleasures,' my wicked friend replied.

We repaired to the library, where we passed the time pleasantly by looking at books and photographs of an erotic nature. After further discussion of the servants, Estelle was also eager to try Mary, the masochistic housemaid, so we told Banks to deliver the news that she and Charlotte were required in the dining room at two.

'Three servants and two ladies,' mused Estelle. 'Plus, perhaps, some toys. If one is going to be disgusting, one might just as well be completely disgusting.'

Robert had lunch delivered in his study, so busy was he, leaving Estelle and I to share our midday repast. Punctually at two, Lisa, Charlotte and Mary arrived, and Estelle regarded them with a keen interest that was reciprocated. We all went upstairs and undressed in a spare bedroom. The reader has already been acquainted with the interesting features of Mary's naked form, namely her unusual nipples and sexual parts, but I must describe what Lisa and Charlotte had to offer for our pleasure.

Charlotte was a short, very slight girl who might, when clothed, have been mistaken for a boy, as her light brown hair was so short. Her hips were narrow, her breasts indiscernible, but in her gentle, shy face were large grey eyes that seemed to drink in everything with a great intensity of interest. She had suffered much as a child, I found out later, and in this house was tasting happiness for the first time. She was still adjusting to the novelty of not being shouted at and beaten.

As for Lisa, she too was of slight build save for one significant detail: her breasts were exceptionally large, and, owing to her slightness and the fact that she was lactating, they were indeed impressive. Estelle gently moved Lisa's long black hair from those breasts and looked at them with frank interest. She was clearly pleased with all three servants, and indeed I may make here the general observation that naked women are often of greater interest than naked men, unless one is in love with the man, as they exhibit a far greater variety of physique than does the male sex.

I was thrilled indeed to be with Estelle once more, that expert in depravity, for it was she who had taught me to enjoy my own body, and all of us have a special place in our hearts for that first partner in sin, that dear originator of our sweetest delights.

The five of us went naked to the luxurious bathroom I have described before, where we enjoyed a shower in order to erase the odours of their morning's work from the servants' skins, making them fresh and palatable. We towelled ourselves dry, then went to the small soft room, where it pleased us to fasten a thin piece of red silk over the window, dimming and colouring the light in the room, so that we felt like visitors to some *Arabian Nights* setting where anything might happen. We bolted the door and fastened over it a sheet of white silk, so that we seemed to be in a room without exits, a soft, warm, comfortable place outside of mundane reality, a self-enclosed pleasure dome in which we could indulge our every sensual whim.

We had brought with us a bottle of white German wine and five glasses, and this we happily shared. We all started sharing gentle caresses and sweet kisses in that leisurely way girls generally have when they are together without men. How delightful it was to feel the warmth and softness of one another's skin! I looked into bright sparkling eyes, and kissed rosy lips. I found Lisa's breasts surprisingly firm considering their great size. They were pleasing.

Charlotte had a ruling vice: she loved to give

pleasure by sucking while at the same time frigging herself. I do not mean this was the only act that gave her pleasure, but it was certainly something she reverted to by choice, as she did now, for she tried us all in turn, going down on the mattress and mouthing our private parts as if the natural lubrication we produced there were her favourite food. How delightfully she used her mouth! All the while her hand was busy between her legs, pausing every now and then as she teased her own body. That kind of self-teasing is, I believe, the mark of a true sensualist, indicating a propensity for prolonged pleasure rather than a brief ecstasy.

Estelle looked in the old wooden trunk in the corner and took out a strap-on dildo. It was made of polished black leather sewn around some padding and a hard core, so it felt like an erect male organ. At its base were straps so it could be worn by a woman. We girls giggled to see it.

'Surely you will not use it, Estelle?' said I. 'You used to tell me girls did not need such things when they enjoyed themselves together.'

'I said that in the past because I dreamed of keeping you for myself,' laughed my friend. 'I did not want you to think of men as instruments of pleasure. Now that you are a fallen woman – yes, you are fallen indeed, no matter how you protest, for you have married – we might as well play with these toys.'

'You can use it on me, Miss,' Mary said eagerly. 'And you can be very rough.'

We gathered around the lovely Estelle to help strap on the large phallus. It had a knob at its base which slipped into its wearer's female passage, thus affording her pleasure while also serving to attach the dildo more firmly to her body. Bright metal rings were firmly attached to the base of the shaft, and, fitted to these, strong black leather straps with shiny buckles. How exciting it was to do up these straps and fit the replica male organ to Estelle!

These straps formed a harness, for some went around the tops of her thighs, while others firmly encircled her narrow waist. There was a broad collar around her throat, from which straps descended at front and back, crossing between her breasts and in the small of her back. Estelle had us fasten the straps tightly, finding the sensation of being embraced by leather an interesting one. When we had done, the dildo was as firmly attached as a real man's pride and joy. It looked amazingly provocative, even shocking, for Estelle was so very female, with her lovely long and wavy auburn hair and sweet face, round firm breasts of perfect size and shape, narrow waist and finely flaring hips. She was so very womanly, and yet she boasted a large, black, male organ – the contradiction was marvellous, strange, even sinister.

We all felt in awe of this strong-willed young lady who regarded us with a slight, enigmatic smile. The fact that she was of the highest social class only added to the incongruity and sense of shared wickedness, and you may be sure it played a part in what I had often noticed in my friend, her being convinced of her own absolute superiority.

She kissed and toyed with each of us in turn, and we responded eagerly. Charlotte even went down on her hands and knees to lick, then suck it, looking up into Estelle's eyes with dumb pleading. My friend sighed with pleasure as though the servant had been worshipping her real penis.

'You shall have it,' she murmured, and laid the slightly built kitchen girl on her back.

The rest of us gathered round, fascinated, and gave each other intimate caresses. Estelle fingered

Charlotte and found her wet, then moved into position over her little body and jabbed her weighty dildo at the servant's narrow entrance. I thought she could not go in, but soon she had gained a lodging, and then she pushed home the swollen head and long shaft while Charlotte gasped, rolled her head, and said she could not take it, she was only a small girl.

'It can be done,' insisted Estelle, holding Charlotte's shoulders and ramming the leathery phallus in to the hilt with a mighty thrust. Both girls gave a loud cry.

Their eyes were aflame with passion, and they kissed as hungrily as though they were cannibals who longed to gnaw one another's flesh. Estelle made hard pumping motions, and her little victim moaned rapturously, throwing her head from side to side and beating her fists against the mattress. In a short time she gulped and coughed as she attained the peaks of that ecstatic region which is the most we have to hope for in this world. She stayed there for such a long period that we all envied this petite kitchen girl, but finally she went limp and lay panting for breath as though she had come close to drowning in the warm golden seas of rapture.

'That was quite amusing,' said Estelle. She withdrew the dildo, and smiled at Lisa. 'That work has made me thirsty. May I drink your milk?'

The young mother blushed slightly, but lay down on the mattress and presented her breasts to my friend without protest – indeed, they looked so full of milk that I daresay she was glad of the opportunity to express it. We all held our breaths as Estelle lowered her lips to Lisa's right nipple. Instead of sucking at once, she put out her tongue a long way and licked that swollen teat, flicking at it with her long tongue, tantalising the girl whose milk surged until she could bear the teasing no longer.

'Please suck me Miss,' she cried out with extreme emotion. 'I can't bear it – all my milk needs to come out so much.'

Estelle abruptly sucked hard, and Lisa gasped with a pleasure that I envied, for it was one I had not yet known.

My friend drank deep, then raised her head and pressed her lips to mine. As we kissed she let Lisa's milk pass from her mouth into mine, and I shuddered at the curious sensation. Some of it trickled down our bodies.

'Now lay down, Jane, and you go on all fours over her, Lisa,' Estelle commanded. So strong was her personality that we both obeyed her, even though I assumed she planned something perverse. How right I was! For the bad girl squeezed Lisa's left breast hard with both hands, squirting a jet of milk down over my private parts.

'Oh Estelle, this is wicked!' I exclaimed in surprise.

'Yes, I hope so, or else I'd be wasting my time,' my friend replied, grinning. How proud she was of her deviant act!

I blush to write of it, but Estelle continued to milk Lisa over me as though I were the bucket under a cow, and she rubbed the milk into my skin too, as well as squirting some into my face and hair. I cannot think why I put up with it, except that my friend had such a strong personality. Suddenly she pounced on me, licking milk from my body and then sticking the dildo she wore into my cunnie, acting the part of a man with the greatest vigour. We writhed together violently, venting our lust until a violet and yellow explosion of ecstasy tore my soul to shreds and scattered me to the viewless winds that blow from heaven.

We lay resting for a few minutes, then Estelle discussed with Mary how the servant could be punished

– her ideas were so cruel and wicked that the habitually gloomy Mary showed signs that she had some slight capacity for cheerfulness.

'So then,' said Estelle, 'once we have you bound and gagged, with your genitals open and exposed, you would be grateful if we were to develop some exquisite forms of torment for your –'

At this moment there was a knock on the door.

'I'm sorry,' said the butler, Banks, 'to disturb you ladies.'

'Go away Banks!' shouted Mary.

'Please do open the door. It is the master. He has a revolver and we fear he is contemplating using it on himself.'

Chapter Six

You cannot imagine how terrible it is to hear such words. I was so shocked that I nearly swooned, and it was fortunate indeed that Estelle was there, or I might have completely lost my head.

She unhooked the sheet with which we had covered the door, wrapped it around herself, and let Banks in. He showed no surprise at our nudity.

'Tell us,' Estelle demanded, 'exactly what has happened.'

'McBean, the head gardener, climbed a tree at the side of the house in order to trim off some branches which had been rattling against the windows. From there he inadvertently had a clear view into the master's study, where the master was sitting with his back to the window. McBean saw him take his revolver from a drawer and check that it was loaded, then place it on the table top. He then began to write something.'

'A suicide note!' I exclaimed. 'Oh, I must go to him.'

'Don't be silly,' Estelle insisted, holding me back. 'If you go banging on the study door crying and screaming, it might panic him into the fatal act. Banks, go and tell your master to come here, as Jane has had an accident. She slipped and banged her head – just like you to be so clumsy, Jane. That will bring him running.'

'An excellent stratagem, Miss,' said Banks, and departed.

'There there Jane, remain calm,' Estelle stated, patting me quite hard on the back. 'Do not give way. It will be a long suicide note I am sure, as Robert is a lover of the dictionary, so we'll have plenty of time to stop him.'

'Oh Estelle, this is not a moment for your dubious witticisms. How can you be so heartless?'

'I've had plenty of practice,' she replied in an inappropriately cheerful manner. I do believe she enjoyed any kind of excitement, even the possible suicide of her friend's husband. 'You may go,' she told Charlotte, Lisa and Mary. 'Thank you for the fun we had, and I hope we can do a great deal more very soon.'

Soon after the servants had left us, Robert burst into the room, his face showing the keenest anxiety for me.

'Jane, Jane, are you all right?' he cried, taking me in his arms. 'Does your head hurt very much? I shall send for the doctor.'

I began to cry. Estelle adjusted the sheet she was wearing until it seemed the latest in elegant wear – she has that gift – and then explained to my husband.

'She did not hurt herself. That statement was just a trick to get you out of your study.'

'A trick!' Robert exclaimed. 'Have you taken leave of your senses?'

'Oh my darling,' I sobbed. 'We are sure you have problems, and now you must relieve the burden of those problems by sharing them with us. You were handling a revolver just now – you were on the verge of taking drastic action – Robert, if you kill yourself I must do the same, so you would be murdering me.'

'I checked the revolver because I heard there had been burglaries lately in the neighbourhood.'

'Come, come,' Estelle observed coolly, making a slight adjustment in her sheet to heighten the impression of high fashion chic she was so brilliantly conveying. 'Be a man and tell us the truth. This is not the time for concealment.'

Robert's face had been white when he came in, but now he seemed to turn paler still.

'I – I would not have killed myself,' he said brokenly. 'That is, it was just a passing thought, in the depths of despair. I thought it better to leave you free to remarry. But I shall not do it now that you have forbidden me, Jane.' He sat heavily in an armchair and was overcome for a few moments by the power of his emotions. I held him in my arms.

'Oh Robert, you should have confided in us. That is why God told men and women to marry, so that we could all have at least one person to confide in,' I insisted passionately. 'I have suspected something was wrong in your affairs. You had that letter, then you went on that urgent business trip, then you were so busy in your study. I should have insisted you confide in me – it is all my fault, I have been weak.'

'Jane, Jane,' Robert gasped. He embraced me devotedly. 'Do not blame yourself. I have been a fool.'

'The servants knew you had troubles,' I mused. 'That is why they rushed to tell me when you were handling that gun. I should have asked them the details of your problems. But now we can all stand by you, and I can show how much I truly love you. What is the problem? Is it only money?'

'Only money!' Robert exclaimed bitterly. 'There is nothing "only" when it comes to money. I shall tell you the sorry story, and then you may condemn me for my folly. Pray do not depart, Estelle. As Jane's friend it is fitting that you hear me, so you can comfort her in full knowledge of what has occurred. I

79

encouraged Jane to invite you in the knowledge that she would require a companion she can trust, a lady who will support her in the difficult times ahead.'

'I had no intention of leaving, it's all too interesting for that,' Estelle replied with deplorable lack of gravity. She sat cross-legged on the mattress and leaned forward as though she were at the theatre, her liquid eyes gleaming.

'Tell us all,' said I, 'and perhaps we shall think of a solution.'

'There is no solution,' Robert sighed. 'I am ruined. In a short time we shall have to leave this house. We shall be penniless.'

'Ruined? Is that all?' I replied. 'What does that matter if only we still have each other?'

'After a few months of poverty you will despise me, and I shall despise myself even more,' my husband said bitterly. 'Now I must tell you my story from the beginning: I was raised, you know, to be a country gentlemen, that is, never to work for my living but only to live on the interest of my capital. A fine way to live, except that my father wasted most of that capital before his timely death by making bad investments, by gambling, and by lavish generosity to whores. When he died therefore, I only inherited a small amount, not enough to support me by its interest alone. Since then I have been living on my capital, and that capital has been diminishing to nothing.'

Robert paused and wrung his hands.

'What could a gentleman in my position do except marry a rich girl and get a healthy dowry along with her? Yet this was difficult for me, as I was determined to love the lady I married, and such wealthy young ladies as I met, I did not love. Then, one year ago, my old friend Roger Appleforth told me of his plan to go to Portuguese Africa to prospect for diamonds, and I resolved to stake everything on one gamble. I obtained loans from three men, with this house and its grounds as security. I lent the money to Roger, knowing him to be honest and reliable. Now one year has passed, and I am unable to repay the loan, as Roger has not found any diamonds. My three creditors are claiming the house, and soon they will have the legal right to turn us out. As they will.'

My husband held his head in his hands.

'So now you see what a wretched villain I truly am, for I married you, Jane, when I knew my financial position to be perilous in the extreme. I loved you so much I had to marry you, even though you had no dowry and I feared I would soon have no house or money. I have been a cad. True, I hoped that Roger would come through with the African diamonds, though in my heart I feared he would be unable to – he is a splendid fellow, you understand, but after all, prospecting is a risky business, or else everybody would do it. Oh, what a villain I have been! I loved you so much, Jane, that I married you under false pretences, letting you assume I was comfortably well-off when in fact our honeymoon, modest though it was, consumed almost the last of my financial resources. I have been false and dishonest. I felt sure you would not marry me after my ruin was complete, so I pressed you into a hasty marriage, hoping indeed that even if I lost my home you would stay with me, for I judged you to be loyal and faithful, as so many women are. It was despicable of me to make you mine in that cowardly, underhand way, how clearly I see that now! I knew it all along indeed, but I wanted you so much. And now you must despise me, and want only to return to your mother.'

'Never!' I cried, holding him tightly in my arms. 'I won't go, Robert, I'll never leave you. Did I not vow in church that I would love you in poverty as well as in wealth? Would you have me break my vows to God? Rather you should forbid me to leave you. Now that you need me, I love you more than ever.'

We were both overcome with emotion.

'I have been a cur,' Robert sobbed.

'The only bad thing you did was not to trust me to marry you even after you had been ruined,' I told him. 'To be poor is nothing to me. My mother and I were always poor after my father was ruined.'

'Poverty is a disgrace, and it may kill our love besides,' Robert said gloomily. 'Now you are young and strong, but as the years of grinding poverty roll like millstones you will come to resent the fact that I married you without a penny to my name. You will suffer, and come to despise me. You should despise me. I am a penniless gentleman bereft of vocation or trade, and there is nothing more useless than that on the face of the Earth.'

'Women can endure anything as long as they feel they are loved,' I insisted.

'Heavens, this is a romance!' Estelle exclaimed with irritating brightness. 'How charming it all is, like so much that is impractical. I expect the curtain to drop now, and then we shall find you, in the next scene of the play, living in a country cottage with a baby in a cot. What shall you do Jane? Become a washer-woman? I will always trust you with my unmentionables.'

'It is good of you to try and cheer Jane up with your light-hearted badinage,' Robert sighed.

'Oh dear, I'm not that good.' Estelle laughed. 'I am merely amusing myself. Now then, let me try and think of something practical to save my old friend from becoming gloomy, for I hate my partners in crimes against nature to be anything but absurdly cheerful. How can we get money? I would give you some myself, but I cannot find the large sum we require, for my damnable parents keep me on a tight allowance. Cannot you borrow from somebody, Robert?'

'Alas, I have already borrowed from my friends, and none of them will lend me any more.'

'That is a pity,' Estelle observed. 'Many of the best people in society are ruined, but keep going year after year on loans which they repay with other loans. It seems to me an excellent way of making one's way in this world.'

'There is nothing to be done,' my husband stated in a despairing tone that filled me with fresh concern for his wellbeing. 'I shall go to the library.'

'I shall dress,' said I, 'and join you there.'

He departed. Estelle and I helped one another dress. My mind was overwhelmed with the news of our ruin – how dreadful it all was! Where could Robert and I live if we lost Dreadnought Manor, and on what? Would our poor servants be able to find good positions with new employers, or must they too go down the slippery slope of poverty and despair?

How dreadful it was too, to think that my initiation into the sharing of erotic delights with our servants must soon cease. I have written a full account of the pleasures I shared with the staff not merely for your pleasure, but to make the point that these pleasures were remarkably fine, and that it would be a wrench to give them up – a wrench not only for me, but for Robert. To go from such a delightful home to I knew not where – this was a bleak future. I saw before me an ugly wasteland I feared to enter.

'Estelle,' I exclaimed, 'what will we do?' I turned instinctively to her, as she was such a clever girl.

'Surely you shall think of something that will save us?'

'Perhaps I can,' she drawled. 'If I can think of a plan that will help you, and afford me some amusement, we shall all benefit.'

We finished dressing and joined Robert downstairs in the library. Here Estelle delivered herself of an astonishing proposal, with the smug air of a young lady who is in love with her own cleverness.

'You say your creditors are three men,' she stated. 'Very well then, let us seduce them so that they cancel our debts.'

Robert stared at her a moment, then laughed bitterly.

'I thought for a moment you had a serious proposal to make,' I protested. 'Really, this is too bad of you, Estelle.'

'My friends, I am merely using my common sense,' Estelle insisted. 'It is indeed an irony that this quality, called common, is in fact so uncommon that when it is presented to you, you find it unrecognisable. Think for a moment. Here we are, allied with a group of servants who will surely help, as they can enjoy erotic freedom here. We must persuade those three men to accept the hospitality of this house in return for cancelling your debts to them – they can cancel the debts in stages, over a period of years, if they like. What man could resist such interesting girls as you have here? It is true that rich men can enjoy themselves in brothels, but prostitutes are depressed, tragic, and depressing to meet, whereas the female servants here are acting out their true desires, and so are happy. A man who enjoys himself with such girls will become happy too.'

'But these men love money, as all men do,' replied my husband. 'They want their money back, and if the only way to get it is to take possession of my house, throw me out, and sell it, that is what they will do. They have other ways of enjoying erotic pleasures, after all.'

'It's easy to make objections,' Estelle grumbled. 'If you can think of a better plan yourself, I would be delighted – and surprised. My plan at least offers hope. If it fails you will be no worse off. Now tell me a little about these three creditors we must seduce. All you have to do is give them anything they want.'

'David Haddisfarme is a strong, worldly man,' said Robert, with a weary air of humouring her as well as he could. 'He is certainly a sportsman and a lover of women, so if your plan could succeed with any of the three, it might be him. You might be able to capture his imagination, but I'd put the chances at forty to one against myself, for he loves money. As for the other two, they are simply impossible. Stanley Blanking is a pure young fellow, the very model of what a modern young man is supposed to be; that is, boring and puritanical. He is very likely a virgin, and might well report you to the magistrate and the church authorities if you tried to seduce him. He hates all hints of eroticism and sensuality – it is madness even to dream of corrupting him, he is a cold baths man. As for the third creditor, Sir Horace Withington-Blathers is elderly, bitter, and money-grubbing to the last degree. I hear he is a cruel sadist where matters of the flesh are concerned, who takes his pleasures cheaply by whipping girls who are literally hungry. Why should he forgive me a large debt in return for tying up Mary, for instance, when he can give a girl a sovereign to be whipped bloody? Now do you begin to see how utterly hopeless your proposal is?'

Estelle slowly shook her head. A faint smile curved her full lips, and there was a determined glint in her eyes.

'What I see is a wonderful challenge,' she stated.

'And it is only the challenges that make life worth living. And I also see a man – if I can even call him that – who is surrendering before the fight has properly begun. It is fortunate that you are not with our gallant forces in Afghanistan or the Sudan, for then your fellow officers would have to do your share of fighting as well as their own.'

'Good God!' my husband cried out, starting from his chair. 'If you were a man I would give you a damn good thrashing.'

'And if Jane were my wife I would try anything to save her from poverty,' Estelle retorted, standing her ground with flashing eyes like a lioness.

'My dear,' I interpolated, afraid that the scene would develop along unfortunate lines. 'Let us go along with Estelle's scheme. I know her well, and can assure you that she is a cunning, ruthless, scheming girl whose splendid stratagems have accustomed her to winning, by fair means or foul – usually foul. She is a thoroughly bad girl, therefore she is right.'

'Thank you Jane,' murmured Estelle, smiling. 'Your compliments are music to my ears.'

'In short,' I insisted, 'any plan suggested by my dear friend is sure to be wicked enough to succeed.'

'It would be undignified to try and use my servants to seduce my creditors,' Robert insisted. 'It would be in bad taste.'

'If you will excuse me, I have some business,' said Estelle, and with that she left the room.

My husband and I discussed where we could go and what we could do once we were thrown out of our home. None of the options was at all attractive.

We were interrupted in singular fashion by Estelle, who looked very pleased with herself as she led into the library every last one of the servants, who lined up in front of us.

'What is the meaning of this?' Robert demanded. 'I did not summon you here. Return to your duties at once.'

'If you forgive me, sir,' said Banks, 'we must disobey you just this once. We are here to tell you that all of us are not only willing, but eager, to play our parts in Miss Estelle's plan for saving this house – it is our home too, sir.'

'Since you are all going to lose your places here anyway, I cannot very well threaten you with dismissal,' sighed Robert.

'Mary, would you care to speak first?' asked Banks.

'Well sir,' said the maid, speaking very quietly at first, then in firmer tones. 'I can only say that I have been happy here, and satisfied in every way. Before I came here I had many problems. Some men thought I was mad because I wanted to be helpless and teased, while others hurt me too much. But when I came here you gave me exactly what I needed, and had the other servants treat me in the right way too. You didn't despise me or abuse me. If I have to leave here I'm sure to get into trouble again with cruel men, dangerous men. So we must try what Miss Estelle says, sir.'

'That absurd plan cannot succeed,' Robert sighed, shaking his head.

One by one, the servants spoke, some shyly, but most with the boldness of desperate women or men. Edith, the giddy housemaid, said that she so liked men that she would be sure to get killed by a jealous wife, or by one of her own lovers, for she could not be faithful, it was so dull. The stable man Franklin nervously admitted that he lusted after girls so much that it had led to serious fights with jealous men as well as other problems, such as the fact that now he loved making harnesses and trying them out on girls, which he would be unlikely to be able to get away

87

with outside this special house. This was the only place he had been able to be happy.

John, the black handyman, and Sally, the fat cook, told us that they were in love and wanted to stay together, but it would be very difficult for them to find jobs as servants in the same house, especially as people generally disapproved of a black man loving a white woman. As for Darma, the Indian stable girl, she said that she not only loved the erotic freedom of this house, but delighted in working with horses. She would not be able to do this in any other house, as there was an absurd prejudice against women working with horses. I could see my husband was wavering, but it was Lisa who struck the decisive blow.

'Here I live happily with my baby,' she said quietly, holding that child. 'And I like working in the garden. Nobody would give me a job because I'm an unmarried woman with a baby, so then what would happen to Arnold? I'd have to pay some woman five shillings a week to take him secretly while I went far away to find work, and then he might well die, for those women let the babies die while they drink themselves senseless. So please sir, won't you at least try Miss Estelle's plan, because even if it don't work, me and Arnold couldn't be worse off, could we?' She began to cry.

'I have been wrong,' Robert exclaimed. I clasped his hand, moved by this admission. 'I was thinking of my place in society when I should have been thinking only of you all. We shall try the scheme of seducing my creditors, though I warn you it cannot succeed. I shall write to David Haddisfarme right now to invite him here immediately, as he is the best one to start with. He lives nearby too. But I beg you, do not get your hopes up. Even if we did succeed with him, which is very unlikely, there are two others more difficult to please than he – and even if we somehow did persuade all three to cancel their debt, what then? I would still have no money to pay your wages.'

'We can worry about that when the time comes, sir,' said Edith, and all the other servants agreed fervently.

I now saw clearly how worried they were about losing the house where they had been happy, and which most of them saw as a refuge from an outside world where they had been derided and accused, and in which they felt themselves to be misfits and outsiders. I say they were worried, but I had better say they were frightened. I resolved with all my heart to help them seduce those three men, as I felt such a strong sense of responsibility.

'I promise you I will do my utmost,' Robert told the staff. 'As will you, I know. And now perhaps we had all better return to our duties.'

They thanked him and dispersed. My husband at once wrote a letter to Mr Haddisfarme, urging him to visit us as soon as possible on a matter of importance, which he would find to his advantage. John took the letter personally, riding my husband's mare, and brought back the reply that he would visit us the day after tomorrow.

That night, just before going to sleep, I had an unpleasant thought, namely that the idea to try and seduce the three creditors was Estelle's, and she might merely be using the situation for her own enjoyment. In the morning I put this point when she and I were alone.

'Yes, of course I suggested it for my own amusement,' she replied placidly. 'You know me, Jane. I live for pleasure. This little scheme of mine should be fun.'

'Fun?' I protested. 'Estelle, we are talking about my home.'

'And of course I shall do my best to help you keep it,' she replied. 'If I have fun at the same time, two good ends have been served instead of one. Besides, it is more likely Mr Haddisfarme will be tempted by our offer if he sees a happy face, namely mine. The danger is you will all be so worried and serious you will put him off.'

I had to admit Estelle talked a good deal of sense, even though the way she talked it was so irritating.

In the morning Estelle suggested to the servants that they refrain from erotic activity until Mr Haddisfarme arrived, so that they would all be fresh and eager. She also talked with each one individually that day, finding out the details of their erotic preferences, skills and talents. Finally Robert, Estelle and I discussed and planned how to make the approach to our creditor, but I shall not report what we said and decided, for it will be better by far to show you those memorable and exciting events, the recollection of which thrills me to the core.

Chapter Seven

You can imagine how all of us, with the exception of
Estelle, were caught up in a rising tide of conjecture,
anticipation and nervousness on the morning Mr
Haddisfarme was due to arrive from his estate on the
other side of North Walsham. With what keen curiosity and downright fear did the servants observe his
arrival surreptitiously from various vantage points,
trying to gauge the manner in which he would take
his sexual delights with the servants offering themselves for his limitless pleasure.

He came on horseback, as he loved to ride. David
Haddisfarme was a hale and hearty man, in his mid-
thirties, smiling and not unhandsome, slightly over-
weight with dark brown hair which was starting to
recede at the front. Overall he gave the impression of
being a man of business, energetic and cheerful. His
first words on meeting me were these:

'Why Robert, you are the most fortunate man in
England to have a wife such as this. I am delighted
to make your acquaintance, Mrs Shawnecrosse.'

We went indoors and were soon on first name
terms, so I shall refer to him as David from here on
in this account. I felt that the female servants would
not be adverse to give themselves to him, for he was
attractive in his way. I wondered whether it might
not turn out to be my duty to give myself to him
also – I had not discussed this with Robert owing

to my shyness in bringing up a matter of such extreme delicacy and potential offensiveness.

You can be sure that we gave David a splendid lunch, for which my husband brought out what was practically the last bottle of his best madeira, and that we were determined to amuse him with our wit and compliments. Even Estelle was polite and charming instead of rude and offensive. After we had given the sherry trifle dessert a reasonable opportunity to be digested, Robert proposed that we go into the library, where he would reveal the matter he had invited David to discuss.

'Fine,' said David. 'I shall be glad to hear whatever you have to propose.'

'It is as much a matter of seeing as of hearing,' Estelle told him. 'And I must leave you for a few moments to attend to various matters.'

We gave her, as it were, a head start, then went to the library, where the three of us sat in armchairs that had been moved from their customary position in the centre of the room to stand near the shelves on one side of that large room. David made himself comfortable with a cigar and a glass of fine brandy. I was far from comfortable – in fact I cannot describe the mental agony I experienced in knowing that if David refused the attractions of the servants, we would be ruined and homeless. It is beyond my poor abilities to find words for such terrible fears, so the reader will have to imagine what I felt, perhaps drawing on his or her own experiences of extreme anxiety.

'What are you going to show me, eh?' asked David.

'It is a surprise, so we cannot tell you in advance,' replied my husband with a laugh in which I could detect his anxiety. 'It will be here soon enough.'

Just as he said these words, Estelle entered the room with Edith. That giddy young housemaid had her long yellow hair stylishly arranged for once, and was dressed in singular fashion: she wore a strong, tightly fastened red leather corset which left her breasts bare, and from this corset were suspended red silk stockings. She wore a pair of red leather shoes with such absurdly high heels that she could hardly walk, and, in order to balance, had to adopt a pose in which her bare behind was stuck right out.

Edith blushed and smiled. She surely found the experience of exhibiting her body like this to be a pleasurable one. I was surprised to notice that not only were her nipples erect, but they were shiny wet. It struck me that somebody might even have sucked them to make them stiff – I looked at Estelle and knew she had done it. What a bad girl!

David overcame his first surprise sufficiently to regain the power of speech. He turned to my husband.

'Surely you are not going to propose –'

'I beg you to do me and my wife one favour,' Robert hastily interrupted. 'No matter what you think, simply enjoy the little show we have prepared for you, in which all the servants will take part. I am sure you will find it amusing. Afterwards we can talk.'

'Yes, please do watch it before you talk with my husband,' I pleaded, touching David's arm.

'Very well,' he agreed. 'When such a lady as yourself makes a request of a gentleman, only a brute would deny it. I shall watch what does indeed promise to be an amusing show.'

Estelle now gave a description of Edith which was intended to arouse. My friend was enjoying herself immensely – she was the centre of attention in a situation of profound excitement and absolute wantonness. How her hazel eyes shone, and how bright were her teeth flashing in her smiles.

'This woman adores men, and loves to fuck,' she

93

stated matter-of-factly. 'You can see she has a splendid body, and a cheerful, open manner. She loves to try unorthodox pleasures if she thinks they might afford either herself or her partner some enjoyment.' Estelle knelt down on the floor and stroked Edith's thighs. 'Her legs are splendid, strong and long, powerful but silky-smooth,' my wicked friend mused, gently stroking them with a kind of wonderment in her face. 'Her behind is nicely round and impertinent.' She kissed Edith's buttocks in turn, taking her time about it, then stood up and dismissed the flustered, aroused girl by thanking her.

Edith left the library and Sally entered it. The enormously fat cook's otherwise naked body was decorated by a black suspender belt, black silk stockings, long black leather gloves and a black domino mask. She also wore calf-length black leather boots with high heels on which she walked with surprising grace. They made her look even taller, and so even more physically imposing. A little olive oil had been spread over her huge breasts and buttocks, making them gleam. She was impressive and attractively bizarre.

'This is a woman indeed!' Estelle exclaimed. 'Noted more for her size and sensual appetite than her intelligence, Sally has the hunger of a giantess when it comes to men. Just look at her – what a lot there is to get hold of! A big fat girl like this can take any amount of the most vigorous fucking and still want more, for she is so well-padded against violent motions. You can lay on her with all your weight and swim on her as you swim on the waves of the sea. You can safely let all your feelings loose upon her, using all your muscular strength, and she will simply moan in ecstasy. She is a big, healthy, happy animal.'

Estelle held up one of Sally's mammoth breasts

with both her hands, showing its weighty substance to the audience of three as though she were an auctioneer displaying the finer points of the cattle she was selling. Sally grinned.

'This is good female flesh, you see,' Estelle continued with the enthusiasm of a woman who loves her own sex. 'We have more flesh on our bodies than men, and our breasts and buttocks have quantities of fat to make them look rounded and attractive to men, so a fat woman is more of a woman than a thin one. Turn around, Sally. You see, she has the buttocks of a queen, which any man ought to be willing to give his right arm to serve, either by riding her from behind or by having her sit on his face. In her essential selfishness she is capable of being cruel and domineering if the man urges her to behave so, yet at the same time she would enjoy a light spanking.'

Estelle sent Sally away, and the next servant to put herself on show was Charlotte, the young kitchen girl with her tiny body. She was shy enough to blush. Her otherwise naked body, so small and thin, was adorned with necklaces, rings, bangles, and a black leather belt decorated with silver. With her short hair and undeveloped little body she might have passed for a boy, especially as she stood with her hand covering her private parts.

Charlotte was a touching sight, like a slave of antiquity going on the auction block, her fate entirely in the hands of her buyers.

'Here is a striking contrast to the giddy wanton, Edith, and the full-fleshed Sally,' Estelle announced. 'There are advantages to her slightness which are not to be despised. Her young little body is unusually flexible, and like a circus gymnast she can take up an interesting variety of positions with ease. Her skin is unusually sensitive, because, owing to its smaller surface area, it has more nerve endings per square inch than a fat girl's. I know by my own experience that these little girls are extraordinarily sensitive to the lightest caress. Charlotte loves to suck, and is extremely proficient in this important field of eroticism. Thank you, Charlotte.'

As the kitchen maid left the library, I glanced at David, on whom rested our frail hopes. He seemed as interested as any man would have to be in such a display of females, but after all, Robert had told me he had seen such shows before. I could only hope he had not seen such a varied group of women described by such a wicked girl as Estelle.

The next servant to stand before us was Darma, the Hindu stable girl. She looked ravishing, with her glossy, straight black hair hanging in smooth waves below her hips. It was like a tent she inhabited gracefully. Her dark-skinned form was lightly covered in transparent green silk scarves that had been tied around her breasts and hips. A gold ring glittered in her pierced navel.

I noticed that Estelle regarded her with special attention and admiration. She spoke with a seriousness unusual for her, as though beauty was the only quality she could take seriously.

'Here is a young Indian woman with black, yet bright, eyes into which one can happily gaze for hours,' stated Estelle, fingering a strand of Darma's black hair.

The servant looked at Estelle gravely. Her oval face with its high cheekbones radiated gravity, composure, and in her eyes, outlined with kohl, gleamed a powerful intelligence.

'It is delightful,' my friend continued, 'to feel the caress of her gorgeous long black hair against one's skin – it is a delight one wishes could be endless. It is so long and soft. She likes to gather it in both hands and caress the sensitive parts of her fortunate partner. I would like to make ropes of it, soft yet strong ropes, and use them to bind me to her. Had I but the voice of a poet, I would – but I am only myself.'

My friend took a deep breath and then spoke coarsely, as though trying to trample down the finer feelings in her heart which, I surmised, alarmed her by their sincerity and power – for surely she was falling in love, and did not want to fall.

'If I were a man,' Estelle announced, 'I would wrap her hair around my cock and spend upon its blackness so that my cream showed to good effect – as indeed it would upon her skin. And I must mention too that she was trained to squeeze her internal muscles strongly, so that any man lucky enough to penetrate her with his penis will find her a fine ride.'

There was an inscrutable flash of emotion in Darma's eyes as Estelle spoke with this deliberate coarseness, and then the Indian girl departed, and Lisa took her place. She was wearing long black silk gloves and a matching basque that had open cups under her large breasts, raising and supporting them charmingly while leaving them bare. The assistant gardener's breasts looked swollen with milk.

'What could be more divinely female than a lactating woman?' Estelle demanded with a return to her usual high spirits. 'Lisa is of a gentle, loving nature, and she greatly enjoys sharing her milk with those who give her erotic pleasure. It is a fine thing to drink milk from a young girl. It is the deepest intimacy and trust, that intimacy and trust for which we all crave even while we pretend we are looking for wealth or pleasure. A man can drink her milk and give her his own, from his penis. Such a fair exchange, and one that gives mutual satisfaction, cannot be despised.'

Estelle, as though overcome by her own words, gave Lisa a tender kiss while caressing those remarkable milky globes, which seemed to grow even bigger and firmer under this stimulation. Certainly it was a sight of unusual interest to see such magnificent, milk-turgid mammaries, with swollen teats that seemed to be straining to deliver their full load of creamy love into any eagerly sucking mouth.

After Lisa left the library, Estelle went to the entrance being used by the servants and did something that caused David to start with surprise: she led Mary in on a rope, as though she were a horse at auction, a pleasure-mare that any man must lust to ride, and ride hard, as her master. The tall young woman was naked save for a black silk blindfold. The rope tying her hands at her back passed between her legs.

Estelle was holding it high, and keeping tension as she pulled Mary along, so that it was firmly placed between her sex lips, which you will recall, were uniquely elongated. I thought of the stimulation Mary must be receiving from that coarse rope held tautly against her most sensitive flesh while she displayed her helpless, vulnerable nudity, and a thrill of excitement shivered through my body and soul.

Mary herself was aroused, as was evident from the state of her nipples, which stuck out in extreme engorgement. This statuesque woman in a state of arousal and captivity was by no means the kind of sight one meets with every day, and I hoped fervently that David could not resist this intriguing collection of females who offered themselves to him so generously. I wondered what David would have them do if he accepted their offer – he looked a strong and knowledgeable man, one capable of leading them a merry dance.

'Here we have that rarity, a masochist who knows

exactly what she wants and is determined to get it,' Estelle stated. 'She is satisfied with what she is, she is happy. She enjoys confinement in all its infinite varieties, and loves to be placed in positions where she must obey the outrageous commands of men. She has a superb body which cries out for special treatment. Her bum is spankable, her impertinent nipples seem to cry out for control, her large labia stimulate the wildest fantasies.'

Estelle then did another disgusting thing, namely, she let the rope go loose and placed her hand on Mary's parts. She brought it away shiny with wetness, and displayed it to her audience.

'You can see,' she stated, 'that this is a highly excitable young woman who loves restraint and strictness. She has greatly enjoyed being tied up and brought naked before you.' She led Mary off stage as it were, then returned again holding a rope. This time it was attached to leather collars worn by three men in a state of absolute nudity: Franklin the taciturn stable man, John the black handyman, and Banks the grave butler. They had their hands immobilised at their backs by leather straps, and their penises had been stimulated to a state of full erection.

'These men, the male staff – in more senses than one – come to you helpless as a symbol of their acceptance of your will,' Estelle stated.

She now held her riding crop, and to my amazement she touched this to each penis in turn, gently tickling it to keep it in a state of throbbing erection. Estelle, the dedicated lover of women, arousing men in this wicked way, without the least idea, I am sure, of satisfying their lusts. What depths of wickedness was she plunging into so recklessly?

'Their cocks will enter any mouth or cunt, and spend where you order,' Estelle said with apparent coolness, though in fact I am sure she relished every word. 'This concludes my show in which I have displayed to you the staff. Remember, they are not merely willing to satisfy your every desire, they are actually eager.' Wickedly, she again touched John's cock with her riding crop, then thanked the three male servants, who departed, though John looked like he would have liked to throw himself upon Estelle, despite being bound.

'There remain a few other points I should mention,' my bad friend continued. 'This house has some excellent rooms designed specifically for sensual and erotic pleasures, namely a luxurious bathroom, and two bedrooms with mattresses laid on the floor for group enterprises. We also possess numerous amusing aids to pleasure, such as harnesses, gags, strap-on dildos and everything else of that ilk, many of them beautifully made by our very own stable man, Franklin. There are also books of extreme licentiousness should we require inspiration – though in fact I imagine that between us we shall not run short of ideas. All in all, I very much hope that you will agree with what Robert will now say to you.'

Estelle sat in an armchair beside ours. Robert then spoke, assuming a cheerful, casual manner I know he was far from genuinely feeling.

'I daresay you've already guessed what I'm going to say, David, so I'll make it short. As you have just seen, I have an unusual group of servants here who would be delighted to serve you with their bodies. They are eager to go on living here with my wife and I, safe from the problems they had in the outside world. Yes, in a sense they are in retreat here, like monks and nuns, but they are not retreating from the licentiousness of the world, but rather from its puritanism. I am making a simple proposal – you come here whenever you like, and each time reduce my debt to you. We shall be comrades together in a great erotic adventure.'

David did not reply for some time. He swirled his brandy in his glass and held it up to the light-filled window, then sipped at it, evidently deep in thought. As we waited for his response I yearned for him to say yes, for it was dreadful to think of Robert losing his ancestral home and being cast penniless into the cruel world. I prayed inwardly.

'Have you put this proposal to my fellow creditors?' David enquired.

'Not yet,' replied my husband. 'You are the first we have approached.'

'They will never accept. One is a virginal milksop, the other a money-grubbing man who buys his cruel pleasures cheaply.'

'You can enjoy the staff now with no obligation,' said Robert. 'Only if the other creditors agree to the same proposal will you begin to reduce my debt.'

'They will never accept,' David stated. 'Though in the unlikely event that they did I could afford to write off the debt, as I made a great profit on some steel shares the other day, and am about to sell forty acres near Norwich for housing. You are lucky, you have caught me in a good mood.'

Reader, I thanked the Creator for His unexpected intervention on our behalf.

'I must ask a question or two first,' stated David. 'Estelle, I was deeply impressed by your free use of language and strong understanding of erotic pleasures you showed while introducing the staff to me. I would like to know whether you will yourself –'

'I am complimented by your interest in me,' my friend replied. 'I must tell you my pleasures are exclusively Sapphic – I only enjoy women, and have never let a man so much as kiss me. However, I would be glad to make love with other women for your visual entertainment, and can promise an interesting show of female lusts. In addition I am toying with the idea of teasing a well-tied man in the company of other women.'

'Oh Estelle!' I exclaimed, amazed at her shameless wickedness. (Later I wondered if she were not trying to submerge her tender feelings for Darma beneath a sea of extreme corruption.)

'Your reply pleases me greatly,' David said warmly. 'You would not be offended by any suggestions I might make as to what you could do with a girl, suggestions of an obscene nature?'

'That would be a new form of pleasure for me, and therefore one I would find greatly diverting,' my friend assured him with a smile of supreme wickedness.

'My next question may cause offence to you, Robert my boy, but it is one that simply must be asked,' David stated. 'This concerns you, Jane,' he added, looking hungrily at me. 'I will tell you frankly that you are one of the most charming and desirable young ladies I have ever had the good fortune to meet. I must be explicit so that there is no misunderstanding – I am only willing to accept this offer if you are willing to give yourself to me.'

'My God!' Robert exclaimed, jumping to his feet. 'You insult me beyond my powers of endurance! I cannot prostitute my own wife to pay back my debts. Surely you can see that your request is ungentlemanly in the extreme.'

'Then I cannot accept,' David said with equal high temper. 'I suggest you prepare to leave your home.'

At these awful words I nearly swooned. It had all come to nothing then, and I was the reason for this disaster.

Chapter Eight

I saw to my alarm that Robert had clenched his fists, and gave every other indication that he was about to throw himself upon his creditor and give him a sound thrashing. I clasped my husband's arm to prevent him taking such drastic action.

'Calm yourself, dearest,' I told him. 'Our guest is merely being honest. Under the circumstances, his words are natural.'

'You are correct as ever, Jane,' Robert agreed reluctantly. He sat down again and took a deep breath. 'Now then David,' he went on with a brittle calm. 'Perhaps you would like to reconsider. Think what can be done with the servants. They offer remarkable satisfactions, I assure you.'

'The servants are a fine bunch,' David agreed. 'But your wife is exceptionally lovely, possesses a great charm and grace, and besides, is of my class, so it will be especially delicious if she surrenders herself to me. I must have her, or I am not interested in your offer.'

We seemed to have reached the end of our hopes, but now my clever friend Estelle had something to say.

'Robert, you have not even asked Jane what she thinks of this, and surely you should, as she is the one most intimately involved. It may be that she has another way of looking at this situation. She may not simply see it as a matter of paying your debts for instance.'

I understood that Estelle was giving me hints as to the attitude I should adopt in order to save the situation, and I strove to understand her meaning. She looked at me, saw my puzzlement, and spoke more explicitly.

'I have known Jane for longer than you, Robert, so I can say that beneath her gentle, somewhat aimless, bland, even vapid exterior, there beats the heart of one of the great libertines of history. It may be, in short, that she is greatly attracted to David.'

'What you say is true,' stated Robert. 'I should have asked your opinion, Jane, for in this house we do not follow the outmoded custom of the men speaking for their wives. Nor do I insist on women being property of husbands, and remaining faithful to their husbands even while their husbands enjoy other women. You must speak for yourself, Jane.'

What a dreadful dilemma for me! I could see that David was implacable in his demand that he possess me, while Robert was equally determined to maintain his honour, and not prostitute me to cancel a debt. The two men and Estelle all stared at me, waiting for me to speak. I saw what Estelle had been hinting at, and knew it gave some hope of success – but the risks were appalling. I risked offending my husband so much that his love for me might die. Was ever a woman placed in such a position? Yet it was my duty to accept the danger, as it was the only way to help my husband and save our home.

'My dear,' I said, trying to speak lightly. 'Estelle was surely right when she said there was more to this matter than simply paying off your debts. Look at how Estelle is enjoying herself – she is far from thinking only of the money involved, and so am I. In short, I would be more than willing to try what David has to offer, as I was willing to try the servants when you suggested it to me. I tell you frankly – though this may shock you – that this is purely for my own pleasure and has nothing to do with your debts.'

'Heavens Robert, Jane is surely the most exciting wife a man ever had,' Estelle said brightly. Her eyes sparkled. 'Every man, and some women, must envy you.'

Robert looked hard at me and chose to believe that I was only thinking of my own pleasure, and not of the debts.

'If money is not your motive, I cannot be accused of prostituting my own wife for my financial advantage,' he said at last. 'You are thinking of your own pleasures, and that is what I wish my wife to do. I agree that you have the right to give yourself to David if that is your desire.'

Reader, we had saved face. Estelle's clever intervention had saved the day. In truth, I was not ashamed or afraid to give myself to David so long as my husband approved, for Mr Haddisfarme was a handsome, well-built man of pleasingly determined character and a cheerful disposition.

'I am delighted by your decision, Jane,' David said warmly. 'Now we must look sharp, for I'll have to leave tomorrow morning. I have a business meeting in Paris concerning the plans to launch a company to build a channel tunnel.' He rubbed his hands together. 'Let me make one thing clear, though. The servants must obey my every order absolutely. They must follow my instructions to the letter even though it will be very difficult for them to do so. If they fail, you will have to pay me what you owe me or else leave this house. You had better get your staff to obey my every whim.'

'On the contrary,' Robert replied with spirit. 'They will obey you if they choose to. I shall not even attempt to persuade them to do anything against their inclinations.'

'Robert, you are one of a kind.' David laughed, putting a hand on my husband's shoulder.

Perhaps he thought his attitude foolish, but for my part I was proud of him for refusing to coerce his servants.

'I have a lot to think about,' said David. He smiled at us, obviously enjoying the anticipation of rare erotic delights. 'I believe I'll take a stroll around the garden while I plan my campaign.'

'We'll be waiting,' Estelle told him, 'with keen interest.'

David left us, and we were left to our own thoughts. Robert was plainly worried, Estelle excited, while I felt greatly agitated, wondering how David would use me. No man had possessed me save my husband, but now there was to be a second, and in curious circumstances.

'I fear he means to do us down,' Robert said at last, pouring himself another glass of wine.

'We must give him such a good time that he won't be able to resist coming back for repeat performances,' Estelle insisted cheerfully.

I thought this was easy for her to say, as David would not even touch her. Little Miss Sappho could simply enjoy herself while the rest of us strove to please Robert's creditor.

We asked the servants to wait in the large soft room, and instructed the women to remove any stockings which they had worn during the show. We passed half an hour in the greatest suspense.

When David returned I knew at once he had thought of something that would afford him considerable pleasure, for he had a rather self-satisfied smile.

'An idea has occurred to me,' he said. 'It would

amuse me to enjoy all the lovely ladies while you, Robert, and the men on your staff, look on without intervening in any way until I ask you to. It will be a valuable test of self-restraint, and as we are always being told that self-restraint is the basis of a good character, you may regard this as a character building exercise for your men.'

'I congratulate you,' Robert said in a resigned manner. 'You have certainly thought up something that will be difficult for us and enjoyable for you.'

'You would do the same in my place,' David laughed. 'Oh, it will be a fine piece of sport. I wonder if you would prefer to undress here or upstairs, Jane? And you, Estelle. Of course I want to watch in either case. You shall undress too Robert, in case you unfortunately lose your patience and throw yourself upon a girl, or even your wife.'

We all four disrobed in the bedroom I shared with Robert. I was sure that Estelle took the keenest pleasure in perversely stripping herself naked before men, and she smiled at them as though teasing them while slowly removing item after item of clothing. It was a deeply erotic undressing for all of us. I was myself aroused, and the men both boasted huge erections which literally pulsed with their heartbeats, a phenomenon indicating the greatest excitement in males. Estelle eyed these curiously. Her nipples were erect, the minx. How dare she, who only loved women, undress with two men! It showed how much she trusted Robert – or perhaps she enjoyed thinking of the risks she ran. She was a Sapphic beauty indeed, skilled in lust and sensuality, yet never having let a penis touch her lovely young body. What a devil she was to be naked with two lustful fellows whose cocks were almost bursting with lust for her delectable cunt!

David's eyes shone with wonder as he regarded the slowly disclosed flesh of Estelle and myself.

'What incredible beauties!' he exclaimed. 'What lovely, lovely girls you are! God, I have never seen upper class ladies behave with such wantonness.'

We joined the servants in what was known as the large soft room. This had three large mattresses laid out on the floor, covered in silk sheets of bright red, yellow and purple, with numerous cushions of various sizes scattered about ready to lend their support to lustful bodies in interesting attitudes. On the walls were hung erotic charcoal sketches by Robert and Mary – Mary's were somewhat extreme in nature – and generously proportioned mirrors which served to give additional views of events on the mattresses. There were wardrobes in two of the corners containing all manner of clothing, harnesses and toys for erotic pleasures, while against the walls were set three sofas. Sunlight streamed in the big windows, casting bright rectangles across the room like the fingers of a hand reaching out for love.

As we entered, the servants regarded us with the keenest interest and anticipation. All showed evidence of sexual arousal. Robert briefly explained to them what David had told him about his possibly being willing to reduce the debt in stages, and how the male servants must now sit and watch until told otherwise.

'If one of you jumps on a girl without my permission, I will be greatly offended, and will withdraw my offer,' David stated.

I thought it likely that one of them would not be able to restrain himself, and guessed that David intended this to happen, so that after enjoying us all, David would be able to say he had not been obeyed, and would not cancel the debt. I saw that the men looked grave, so they were doubtless thinking the same as I, namely that our situation was desperate.

'This is simply capital!' David exclaimed. He showed no shyness at being naked in front of so many people, but rather displayed his fine body and large erect penis with pride. 'What wonderful times you must have here! No wonder you are keen to save this house and stay together. Oh, by the way, let me make it plain that none of you gentlemen may play with himself unless I give you permission, though the ladies are free to do so if they please.'

'Oh good,' Estelle exclaimed.

Personally I felt embarrassed and anxious, especially when David looked at me in my nakedness. I was utterly vulnerable and exposed, and knew we were all in danger, not merely of losing our house, but of allowing ourselves to be cruelly used and humiliated in order to save it. At the same time however I experienced a keen tingling in my private parts and bosom, and it struck me that when a feeling of danger attended erotic incidents, the excitement of the participants is heightened beyond that which they would experience in conditions of perfect security.

'Come ladies, come my pretties,' David cried, in the manner of a farmer summoning his livestock. 'Let us lie comfortably on these mattresses and enjoy ourselves while these gentlemen watch and die of envy.'

Robert and the male servants, that is, Franklin, John, Banks, and McBean, sat themselves glumly on sofas while David surrounded himself with eight naked young ladies. What a delightful position David found himself in! It was not simply that he had so many women to choose from, but that they were such a comely group, with varied physiques and equally varied erotic inclinations as well as highly developed skills. My husband had taught them not to be ashamed of their desires, and they had learned their lesson well.

Imagine David surrounded by naked, willing females of every physical type. He could enjoy the sight and touch of composed lovely Darma, petite and shy Charlotte, Lisa with her milk-swollen breasts, masochistic and statuesque Mary, fat Sally with her grin, and slender tall Edith, that giddy girl. Then there was the beautiful lesbian, Estelle, who alone would not let herself be touched by any man. Lastly there was myself, and I shall merely observe that I was not unattractive.

Wherever the eye glanced it met with some example of female loveliness: Darma's lovely black hair falling about her big dark breasts, Mary's taut nipples thrusting out, Sally's huge buttocks, Edith's fine long legs, and so much else besides. How lovely women are! What pleasing variations one may see in a group of ladies, how soft and curvaceous, so warm and huggable – and how eager we are to be penetrated by that hard male shaft men are so justly proud of!

David stood like a god with naked women kneeling or sitting about him, fondling his body. His cock jutted magnificently, ready to shoot spunk into or over us. We waited to know his pleasure.

'Now then ladies,' David announced cheerfully. 'I shall lie here and you shall surround me, doing your utmost to arouse me by touching and kissing me, by rubbing your parts upon me, by touching each other, or by playing with yourselves.'

David lay down on a red silk sheet covering the mattress in the centre of the room, and we ladies clustered around his powerful body as though eager to pay homage to his engorged penis. There was already an air of lustful tension about the men watching. I understood that, for David, having them watch was an integral part of his entertainment. It pleased him to contrast himself, who could do as he liked, with those frustrated men who could do nothing without his leave. It was a mild form of sadism, and one that showed cunning. Indeed, most of us are the same in everyday life, enjoying our pleasures all the more if we can feel that others do not have such good fortune. David was giving the torment of Tantalus.

I saw too another curious facet of this situation: anything we ladies did to please David would arouse the watching men also, and increase the risk that they might lose their self-control, which might in turn cause David to later cancel any debt reduction. Yet, of course, we had to try to please David, as he was our creditor. Was ever a lady in such an erotic predicament?

Seven of us were now touching and stroking, kissing and rubbing, every part of David, while Estelle caressed us with all her skill so that we became highly aroused. She began with me, and as her deft fingers found my most sensitive spots and her lips grazed my skin like a zephyr, my nipples hardened and my private parts moistened. Estelle moved on from one woman to the next. She gave Darma, I noticed, rather briefer attention than the others, as though to deny that she had any special feelings towards the dark-skinned young beauty. David meanwhile touched our breasts and cunnies, and especially played with Mary's elongated sex lips, squeezing and pulling at them while her juices poured out and made his hand gleam. He pulled back the loose flesh and gave a whistle of surprise at the size of her erect clitoris. How she shivered when he gently caressed, with slippery fingers, that burning, throbbing jewel!

Our caresses of David's fine body grew ever more fervent. He sighed and moved restlessly. Charlotte put her long tongue right out and licked him like a cat, up and down his thighs, while Lisa suckled on his nipples. Darma and Mary took strands of their long straight hair between their fingers and tickled his genitals and belly with them, stroking him as though they were artists holding black and brown brushes. Edith gently squeezed his testicles while Sally frigged her with two fingers.

All the watching men were now discomforted by their powerful erections, and they stirred restlessly on the sofas as though trying to find a more comfortable way to sit. All might be lost if they threw themselves upon our aroused female nudity.

David pulled Lisa to him and suckled her milk to their mutual satisfaction. Some of it ran down his neck and chest, and Charlotte eagerly lapped it up. Lisa was grateful for this attention, as she had an excess of the motherly fluid, and besides, she did so enjoy being drained thus through her sensitive, swollen teats.

Darma stroked David's penis with her hair, then performed a curious act with the long fingernail of the little finger of her right hand, using this like a special tool to actually probe inside the slit in David's helmet, holding it open so that it looked like a baby bird's open beak. David squirmed and gasped, evidently experiencing that kind of exquisite discomfort on the borderline of pain which seems stimulating when we are aroused.

I could not leave all the work to the servants, so I took strands of my golden hair and coiled them around David's shaft, as if it were binding myself to his penis. Mary took the ends of those strands and held them taut, compressing his male organ, and she moved her hands slowly up and down, so that the outer flesh of his penis was set in motion as a captive of my hair. He groaned. Mary paused now and then, taking great care to extend his delight by not making him spurt too soon – she above all understood the importance and value of delaying rapture and so heightening its intensity. Darma again opened the little mouth of David's cock, but this time she inserted the end of a strand of her hair, thrusting it into his tender flesh again and again. Her face was impassive. Estelle, I noticed, watched her with rare absorption.

Suddenly shaking her head as though to clear it of something, Estelle crossed to one of the cupboards and took out two dildos. They were about the size of an average male organ in a state of pride, and were made of black rubber, that wonder material which is now coming into use for so many items of manufacture, though probably the inventor of vulcanisation did not envisage its being used to form imitation penises that can be thrust into women's cunnies.

Estelle had Charlotte go on all fours with her private parts presented to David's face, and then she inserted the dildo so that he had a splendid view of it sticking out of the petite kitchen girl. He played with it happily, sliding it in and out of her, while Estelle used the other one on us, poking us all into a state of advanced lust without granting us the release of orgasm.

At Mary's suggestion we all used our teeth on David, nibbling every exposed part of him as though we were cannibals eating a helpless prisoner alive. We then all blew together on the patches of saliva our mouths had deposited on his skin, to give him a sensation of stinging coolness. Next we all bit him once each – Mary bit him quite hard, so that he exclaimed. I daresay she did this on the principle of doing to others as we would have them do to us, which is a principle of erotic excitement as well as of Christianity.

Charlotte leaned forward and put out her tongue, touching just the very tip of it to the helmet of David's male organ, and moving that tip around with the careful precision of a surgeon wielding a scalpel. She was a devotee of paying oral homage, as you may recall, and was astonishing in her bold expertise. She lay on her side with her thighs together, holding the dildo inside her vagina.

It was instructive to witness how Charlotte gradually increased the pressure and frequency of her ministrations, while the pressure of her fingers holding David's shaft likewise developed. Darma, Mary and I caressed David with our long hair while the girl served his penis, and David began to gasp as though he had just fucked seven girls and had an orgasm in each and every cunt.

What skill Charlotte deployed! She suckled briefly on the very tip, then flicked her strong tongue around the rim. She grazed his knob all over with her teeth, then nibbled on the shaft. She took his balls into her mouth while tickling the knob with her fingernails, then she took the knob into her mouth, laying it in the softness of her cheeks. She worried inside the little slit with the tip of her tongue, then pulled back and spat repeatedly at the big glistening glans, making David shiver as her globules of saliva struck his most sensitive flesh. She was a veritable witch of cock-sucking, making it an arcane art. Her long flexible tongue darted out like a snake's, but had the force of a bull's. Its muscles were remarkably strong owing to her frequent, passionate, use of them, and when she repeatedly struck her tongue at high speed against that shiny helmet, she was subjecting David to a veritable whipping. At the height of eroticism there is often found torment.

She played a thousand cunning tricks. She rolled

her head rapidly from side to side, letting her teeth graze that knob which so resembled a fruit that it almost seemed she must bite into it and savour its living juices. I cannot enumerate her ways, it would take a book in itself. Charlotte was normally so quiet and insignificant a little thing that one could practically bump into her and still not be aware that she was present, but now, in her apotheosis, she was revealing her absolute female power. I was moved.

The girl's rapturous enjoyment of her task emanated from her slight body, arousing us all to new heights by some contagion of mental energy which spread its tentacles through the warm air of late summer. How much longer could the man stand it? Surely this clever girl would, in another minute, make him erupt. Instead the man spoke with the self-possession of the devil.

'Charlotte, your mouth is paradise, but stop for a moment because I do not wish to spend just yet.'

Charlotte moved away with reluctance. She looked dazed, like one coming out of a mesmeric influence, and seemed surprised at being the centre of attention.

The men were restless, I noticed, especially John, who, as the youngest, possessed the keenest lust. I hoped David would take pity on them, but then recalled that he was a man of the world as they say, by which people mean a man is wicked, as though the world itself were not wicked rather than good. This is a curious contagion of God's great creation, which must be good, with man's wickedness.

Forgive me this digression, reader – I merely meant to say that it seemed unlikely we could hope for pity from David, who had our naked bodies at his mercy. I feared his mercy would be evidenced by its absence.

'Lie down Charlotte,' he now stated. 'I will fuck you.'

115

He did not mount her in any orthodox way however, but instead squatted between her legs, lay one hand on her scant pubic hair, and with the other pumped the rubber dildo in and out of her tight little cunnie. He jabbed her at angles, and twisted it round and round at high speed, playing as many tricks with it as she had with her mouth, until she spent with the utterance of whimpers, as though she were a bad child who had just been whipped. David lay down beside her and stared at her face in rapture as though eager to drink her ecstasy. I afterwards found that he was always fascinated by the apparently agonised contortions of ladies' faces in orgasm, finding in them the reality of their natures which in general they hid. He was hungry for the truth behind our dissimulation; he yearned to see our secret animal selves.

'Now my cock has calmed down somewhat, I will fuck you with it,' he stated, and with that mounted the small body of the kitchen girl, thrusting his arrogant penis into her with a grunt of satisfaction. He rode her hard, as though paying her back for so teasing his organ with her mouth – men often seem, even with those they love, to take revenge with their cocks.

'Ah, you are a cock-pleaser as well as a cock-teaser,' he gasped. 'Yes, what a lovely little slut you are! I've half a mind to spank you. My God, how tight and juicy you are!'

He held her slender shoulders and used her with all his strength, devouring her face with his mouth. There was something ancient and primitive about the scene: a small, young, submissive female being so completely taken by a man of powerful build, who bucked his hips against her as though he were engaged in some kind of desperate fight to the death.

Finally she gave a shrill scream, not of agony but of its counterpart that so often wears the same ex-

116

pression, namely rapture. David stayed in her until she was done, enjoying her contractions, as he showed by grunts of pleasure, and then he abruptly pulled his organ out of the kitchen girl with a wet plop.

It gleamed with her juices, and seemed larger than ever, a veritable monster of male strength and pride.

'You, Sally isn't it,' David said with the confidence of one who knows his most outrageous sexual demands will be met, 'go on all fours over the Indian girl and rub your cunt on her face.'

This was coarse language indeed to use with ladies, but I have to write it here or else the reader would not grasp the whole flavour of the scene.

Sally, of course, was nothing loathe to perform any erotic act – she somewhat resembles a pig in her lack of delicacy, I have often thought – and at once mounted Darma and began pressing her private parts to the dark-skinned woman's features, fairly enveloping them in her fleshy femaleness from which so much juice streamed that poor Darma's face was as wet as if she were washing her face. David meanwhile played with Darma's parts, then stood for a while with his shaft in his hand and his knob in Sally's mouth while Charlotte licked his behind and Mary stroked his thighs and belly with her knowing fingers. David was a strutting cock now, displaying himself and his ability to use we ladies' orifices as he chose, moving from one to the other on a whim.

Next he took Sally from behind, first lightly slapping her massive buttocks, which truly were wondrous objects in their female majesty. He slid his penis into her cavernous vulva then proceeded to smash into her huge fleshy mass with repeated blows of his weighty maleness. She grinned and grunted. He had Darma put her tongue out to lick his balls as they danced over her face, and instructed Edith to straddle Sally's strong back facing him, and masturbate. They continued in this fashion for some time, with David giving every sign of delight, while Sally wriggled her bulk with eyes closed, enjoying, as was her fashion, a continuous string of orgasms, like pearls on a string. David paused now and then to conserve his semen.

'Now then,' he announced, 'I do believe I shall spend. Let us construct a new tableau, my pretty mares.'

He withdrew his penis from the fat cook, who rolled off Darma and lay panting on the next mattress.

'Let us set up something truly outlandish, even disgusting,' David laughed. 'I will spend in such a way that it will be memorable as well as damned enjoyable. But which lucky lady should I honour with my spunk?' He eyed Darma, her sweet dark face wet, as was her hair, with Sally's copious vaginal flow. 'Now then, let me try your cunt, my girl.' With that he lay on her and jabbed his penis into her, sampling her as a lady might finger a piece of cloth she was thinking of purchasing. 'Ah, this is a fine cunt!' he exclaimed. 'Heavens, she squeezes me as though she were coming! She has full control of her muscles – she is an expert in vice.'

Delighted by Darma's powerful cunnie, David quickly gave instructions to the rest of us. Some of these were very shocking indeed, and deplorable in that we were being treated like animals that existed solely for his enjoyment. Estelle was asked to ride Sally on the next mattress, and to rub her breasts and pubic mound hard against that fat cook's. Mary was told that if she truly liked to suffer, she could kneel near David and dig her fingernails into her own breasts as hard as she could stand it. Edith and Charlotte had to caress and lick David all over, and as for myself, I blush to admit that I was politely asked to stand and masturbate with a dildo, and this I quickly agreed to do, not just to please him, but also because I was by now in serious need to relieve my lust with ecstasy.

Most shocking of all was Lisa's part. The girl was instructed to kneel over Darma's face and squeeze her own breasts so that her milk spurted over the dark beauty's face and breasts! This was indeed most unorthodox and deplorable in the extreme.

David reared up on his outstretched arms and fucked the Indian girl while Lisa manipulated her huge, milk-laden breasts. Several of us gasped as her milk squirted out like the leaping semen of a man in orgasm, spraying over Darma, and indeed David. He laughed, and wriggled with delight, enjoying to the utmost Darma's strong and slippery flesh, that innermost female part of her which was now stretched and filled by an occupying power.

The men watching now looked as though they might go mad with frustration as they witnessed this outrageous scene of depravity. We ladies all played our parts as instructed, and David looked around at us all, drinking in every detail of the bizarre tableau he had created from the depths of his wicked mind. Minutes passed like eternities. Mary groaned as her fingernails dug into her breasts, her eyes flashing with a lust that was not altogether sane. Estelle gave a little cry of orgasm. Edith and Charlotte licked David's behind. I reached the heights of rapture and sank groaning into a pile of silk cushions. David opened his mouth to receive Lisa's milk, then licked Darma's face, letting the milk dribble out of his mouth. She parted her lips to receive it. David gave a weird cry.

Was he having a heart attack, or was he spending?

Or could it be both at once? I was genuinely uncertain, so appalling were his orgasmic cries – I could almost say screams – that he uttered as he blasted spunk into Darma's slippery, clutching, succulent cunt.

He held her tight and cried out again and again. It was stunning. It seemed he would never end – certainly he went on far longer than men normally do. His face was racked by what looked like the sufferings of a soul in Hell. At last he made agonised croaking sounds, then finally collapsed on the Indian beauty like a corpse.

This startling display of orgasmic force was the last straw for Franklin. With a peculiar cry he leapt up and threw himself on Sally, who received him willingly enough, you may be sure. Robert, McBean, John and Banks all moved to try and pull him off, but they might as well have been the unworthy knights striving to pull Excalibur from its stone.

'Leave him be,' David gasped.

Robert and his men ceased in their fruitless efforts, and Franklin gave a choked gasp as he emptied himself into the cook, laying all his weight on her yielding belly. David sat up and shook his head.

'I told you that you must obey my instructions completely,' he stated in a cool manner. 'It is a pity you cannot try to please me, as I am your creditor. I fear you must lose your house.'

'For heaven's sake!' my husband exclaimed. 'The man was goaded beyond endurance. It is astonishing that Banks, John and McBean have managed to restrain themselves thus far.'

'If you will not follow my instructions there is no point in going on with this,' David sighed, as though more in sorrow than in anger. 'My pleasure is diminished if you simply do what you like rather than saving yourselves for the interesting scenes I had planned. In this situation you should all be thinking of my pleasure rather than your own.'

My heart went out to the unfortunate servants, who listened to David with every sign of anxiety. What a disaster it would be for most of them to be thrown out into a world for which they were but ill-fitted.

'Oh sir,' Lisa exclaimed. 'I am sure we shall all obey you. Do give us another chance, I beg you.' She was tearful.

Her fellow servants joined in her pleas, making a chorus. Indeed, David gave every appearance of toying with us as a cat toys with a mouse before slaying it mercilessly. He raised his hand, and they fell silent.

'I don't see why I should give you one more chance,' he sighed, shaking his head. 'Those who have failed should be punished for their failure, that's my philosophy.'

'Well, I hope you might change your mind just this once,' said Estelle, giving him her most charming smile. 'Because I'm having such a good time.'

'Indeed,' David replied, 'it is delightful to witness your pleasure. Yes, perhaps I should make an exception in this case, and give you a second chance. But mind! It shall be the last. From now on, absolute obedience.'

The staff all promised to obey, and Franklin muttered that he was sorry. I thought our chances of success were very slight, however. David would use us as lewdly as he pleased, and then invent some pretext for refusing to cancel Robert's debt. He now turned to regard our masochistic housemaid, whose breast bore the marks of her own fingernails.

'Mary, I see by the cruel way you treated your own breasts at my request that you do truly love to be ill-treated, and that this is not just an invention to arouse my interest.'

'Yes sir,' Mary replied gravely. 'I love to be tied and teased, or humiliated, or even punished a little.' She took pleasure in saying these words, which were themselves humiliating.

'You are a handsome woman,' David mused. 'It would certainly be interesting to subject you to some humiliation.'

'Thank you sir,' Mary said, even managing the ghost of a smile.

'I think your master and these three fellows should ejaculate over you,' David announced with good cheer. 'And you shall rub it in to your skin, do you hear? And after that everybody in the room shall spit on you as much as they can. What do you think of that, eh? Is it too degrading for you.'

'Oh no sir, I think it's very fine,' Mary said with an animation unusual for her. 'You're very cruel in a clever way sir. I'm glad to have made your acquaintance.'

'You're an interesting young lady,' said David laughing, after looking taken aback for a moment by the way she received her humiliation. 'Now then, you three men, gather round the girl. Kneel here girl, and the men shall stand around you. Handle and suck their cocks, talk lewdly, beg them for their spunk, then show delight as they shoot it all over your body.'

This was a wicked scene indeed, and even as it began, David's penis grew back to its former formidable size and rigidity, so aroused was he by his own conception.

'Come men, spunk over the girl,' he demanded. 'Let us see her wet and creamy all over her naked body.'

After all they had witnessed, my husband and his

three men were not in any state to avoid a rapid spending even if they had tried. Within a minute or so John's dark organ vomited a large quantity of semen over Mary's breasts and belly as he knelt in front of her. The force of his spending was such that his semen made an audible hissing sound against her flesh, a sound that was thrilling in the extreme. Then Banks was drained of his creamy yield as Mary's tongue served him. She let his spunk fall over her long brown hair, her shoulders and her left breast. McBean was the third. Mary held his cock tightly in her right hand, pumping it as it spat jet after jet of male cream all over her face. My husband saved himself until last: Mary lay down on her back and he knelt between her legs. She fondled his lovely organ in both hands until it jetted forth great amounts of spunk all over her belly, breasts, and thighs, with some going on her face. The amount was startling, and with the force of ejaculation made a splendid show. I felt proud.

Mary was now drenched in the spendings of four men, and she followed David's instructions by rubbing the stuff into her skin, building up a thick, rich white cream all over her breasts, belly and upper thighs, as well as her cunnie, which she rubbed vigorously.

'Now spit all over her!' David exclaimed.

This was disgusting. We all gathered around Mary and carefully deluged her with our saliva several times each, so that there was soon a great amount of our spittle on her statuesque young body. She gathered it up and used it as a lubricant for masturbation.

It is a very curious feeling to spit on a young woman, but I did not feel too bad about it because I was sure from her rapt expression that she was far from hating us for what we did to humiliate her. There was indeed an expression of strength and pride on her features. She was proud of enduring what others could not.

David did not spit on her at all, as though he were above such acts, and left them to us, his puppets. I saw clearly how right Robert was when he told me there was a danger of our being tempted to take part in advanced deviations which we might otherwise never have tried, and so going too far.

Mary reached orgasm soundlessly, curling up into a ball like a woman hugging a secret. After she had done, David had her hold his shaft in both hands and suckle on the knob like a baby suckling a breast. She looked up at him, her brown eyes shining.

'Make love to her now,' he told Mary, and withdrew his maleness from her facial orifice.

Mary obediently got on top of Edith, the woman he had casually indicated, and moved back and forth on her body. There were obscene squelchy sounds. David had Lisa lay flat on her stomach and enjoyed her vagina while watching Mary and Edith, just trying the young mother's cunnie as he put it, but after a few minutes he took his maleness from her body and regarded us with a thoughtful air.

'This first course, the entrée, has been amusing enough,' he announced. 'But in the second we shall see what some of you ladies are truly made of. Now, who shall I choose? It shall be a stern test for you, and if you are to have any chance of saving your home you must serve me perfectly in every way, no matter how hard it will be for you.'

Reader, as is the way of women, I both hoped and feared that he would choose me.

Chapter Nine

'You mentioned a luxurious bathroom,' said David. 'I'm intrigued.'

'Yes, it is an excellent setting for the pleasures of the flesh,' Estelle assured him fervently.

David went to look at that room, with Banks to show him the way. The butler was every bit as grave when he was naked as he was in his normal attire, which says a lot for his character. They soon returned.

'I shall try that fine bathroom,' David announced. 'Now let us form a select group. Will you not be one of those heroines of the watery depths, Estelle? And I should also like to invite Darma, for I suspect there is a tender bond between you two, and tender bonds always make erotic acts far more erotic.'

Curiously enough, Estelle blushed at these words. Extraordinary lady! I had never seen her blush when somebody suggested some advanced erotic deviation, but now she reddened, and for once no badinage or sarcasm came ready to her lips.

'We must have Mary,' David continued, revelling in the luxury of choosing us for what I feared would turn out to be an exercise in extreme wickedness. 'And lastly, I hope you will be good enough to join us, Jane. No need for more. This will be an intimate group – everything will just be between the five of us.'

My heart beat faster at this proposal. I took from

his self-satisfied smile and erect penis that he had in mind some unusual erotic acts for us, and he would be the only man present. A shudder of anticipation and trepidation passed through my flesh.

'As for the rest of you, you shall go downstairs and stay in the library,' David stated. 'There you shall stay and rest – save your spunk for later, you fellows – and await my further instructions.'

'Don't do anything with him unless you truly want to, Jane,' Robert told me firmly. 'The house is not worth so much as that, as God is my witness.'

'I promise I shall only do what amuses me,' I assured him, seeing his deep concern.

David and we four ladies he had selected went to the bathroom while Robert and the other servants went down to the library. The bath was already filling.

David was filled with enthusiasm by the sybaritic splendour of that magnificent setting for aquatic disports.

'Good God! This is a marvel. What a time we shall have here!' He looked around the room with us, making crude comments on how he could enjoy our naked bodies in the bath, on the rubber mattress, standing against the wall of the shower bath, and so on. He fondled and kissed us, and we caressed his penis. It was very strange for me to touch the cock of a man who was not my husband, and David took a keen pleasure in my hesitation, shyness, and sense that what I was doing was very wicked.

'It will amuse me to see you ladies dressed up for my pleasure,' he announced.

How strange it felt for me to be directed by this heavy-cocked man without even having Robert present to give me his advice and protection. David was growing in arrogance as we went on gratifying his every whim, and I wondered if we were encouraging the worst aspects of his character by our repeated acquiescence. I feared we were, by constantly giving in to him, creating a monster.

We went to Estelle's room, for as I told you, she had brought a great deal of luggage with her, and this included part of her collection of erotic underthings, in which she enjoyed dressing her pretty bedmates. David amused himself by rifling through these Parisian creations and holding them up against our compliant skins. He aimed to further inflame his own lust, for of course semi-nudity can be more exciting to men than simple nakedness, which can seem pure rather than wicked.

Estelle donned scarlet silk stockings, a red leather suspender belt with six straps, red leather calf-length boots with high heels, and a broad white hat. Darma was dressed by David in long white leather gloves and a broad white leather belt tight around her waist. Her feet were the same size as mine, so I fetched her a pair of white leather calf-length boots with high heels. For myself there was a strong black leather corset strengthened by whalebone, with leather drawstrings which David himself pulled tight, constricting my waist almost to nothing. My bosom and cunnie were left bare, and I blushed to see how my breasts were raised up with erect nipples owing to the constriction of the corset, so that they looked as though they were straining to touch a man.

'These might come in useful,' suggested Estelle, taking out two dildos from her trunk. One of them was of normal size, but the other was enormous, a phallic monstrosity the sight of which made me wince.

We returned to the large soft room and looked in the cupboards. David marvelled at the craftsmanship and ingenuity of the leather harnesses for men and women made by Franklin the stable man, some of them very restrictive. David handled them with reverence. After a time he selected two of these harnesses. One might also call them strap suits, for they consisted of interconnected adjustable black leather straps that embraced the whole body in a strong grip. I shivered to look on them and think of the things a cruel man could do to a lady held captive by such a suit. Would it be Mary and I?

'How lovely your breasts look,' David said to me. 'Please help me put this suit on Mary, Jane.'

Mary liked this sort of thing, so it was no cruelty to fit the suit on her. In fact, her eyes gleamed darkly with an equally dark pleasure. We fastened the straps, which were of strong, glistening black leather: four on each leg, three on each arm, one around the throat, one above the breasts and one below, with one broad one around the waist, all connected by a central strap at front and back that divided into two to pass over her shoulders. David and I did up all the shiny buckles tightly so that Mary's statuesque body was held in the grasp of strong black leather. Her every movement made a creaking sound. She could still move her limbs, though a little stiffly, but attached to certain points of the strap suit were smaller straps, so that, for example, the wrist straps could be attached to the back straps, or to the ankle straps – in fact the permutations were nigh endless. I was fascinated by the suit and by Mary's love of confinement – there was in me a strong curiosity towards this aspect of eroticism. Attached to the neck strap was an elaborate set of straps to hold a large red rubber ball in the wearer's mouth as a gag, but David did not fit this yet.

David now took from the cupboard a cat-o-nine

tails, a large and wicked device with thongs of knotted leather. The handle was wrapped in the same black material. I could hardly bear to look at the nasty thing, it seemed so dangerous. I was frightened. I thought I should fetch Robert.

'Oh thank you sir,' Mary said to David, and there appeared on her face that rare thing from her, namely a smile.

I decided after all not to bother Robert just yet.

We returned to the bathroom, where we poured blue crystals into the bath and agitated the deepening waters in order to produce the foam which offered a variety of erotic pleasures. Then David locked the door. He shot a heavy bolt, and it made a sound that seemed deeply ominous, almost final. We were sealed in with this strong man, and those who might help the foolish females who had placed themselves at his mercy – or lack of it – were on the other side of a stout door. The other strap suit was laid on the floor, together with the cat. I thought they must be for me. I inwardly began to pray. I prayed for strength to endure the ordeal if that was what I must do to save my beloved husband from destitution and shame. I must do my duty.

Without a word, David took Darma and Mary by their hands and led them to the black-tiled shower-bath in the corner, with its several shower heads at various heights, the angles of which could be adjusted. Here the whiteness of Mary's fine strong body, cut into sections by the numerous black straps with their shiny metal fittings, stood out in sharp contrast to the tiles, while the long white leather gloves and broad white leather belt worn by Darma made a similarly arresting contrast, though her dark skin and long black hair looked, amidst those black tiles, wraith-like.

David turned the water on for a minute or two, so that the three of them were soaked as they embraced and kissed. He turned it off and set about the pleasant task of soaping these two shapely young women – Mary tall and lean, Darma shorter and more rounded. The lather looked very white on the Indian beauty's dark skin, while from David's happy exclamations I know he greatly enjoyed the curious sensation of soaping Mary, the ardent masochist, while she wore the strap suit that could confine her in a moment. His hands slipped wantonly over her exposed flesh all partitioned by tightly squeezing straps.

David now went to urinate, and pointed out that if he kept his bladder empty he could delay his orgasm and add to its power.

On his return he used the loose straps in Mary's suit that I mentioned before, fastening Mary's wrists to the strap that ran down her back. She opened her mouth wide for the gag even before he reached for it, like an ardent catholic opening her mouth to receive the host. David strapped it into place, and her mouth was filled with the big red rubber ball. We were all silent, as though attending a religious ceremony. He caressed her body, so helpless and so lovely, then had Darma go on all fours, and entered her cunnie from behind while Mary watched and squirmed with lust, her nipples fiercely erect. He leaned forward and held Darma's slippery breasts in his strong hands, pushing against her while she pushed back at him by placing her hands against the black-tiled wall. A woman on all fours is offering herself unconditionally – she is an oddly exciting sight, so delightfully animal.

David left her after a while and toyed with Mary, soaping her private parts, pulling on her elongated sex lips and toying with her breasts while Darma caressed him with her dark, knowing hands. She wore rings, and used them to give his helmet delicate touches lubricated with soap. He kissed Mary passionately, groping her behind while Darma suckled on his cock, then abruptly crossed with them to the corner of the room where lay the black inflatable rubber mattress, where he had Darma lie down, laid on her and jabbed into her vagina with his gleaming penis, giving her a rapid series of ruthless cock-stabbings, the soap making smacking-squelchy noises between their bellies, until she went rigid with orgasmic rapture. He withdrew from her, and to our surprise, removed the gag from Mary's mouth and freed her hands.

'I refuse to torment you,' he told her, 'even though that is what you want. You are going to have to torment me. But first I will fuck you, to make you even more angry.'

Mary looked very disappointed at being freed. She even pouted. David laid her down on her stomach and entered her from behind, holding the straps of her suit to gain purchase, while she held on to the shiny brass railing that was placed low down in that corner so that men and women could enjoy soapy couplings without sliding helplessly on the smooth black rubber. They bounced up and down on the inflatable mattress as his shiny cock jerked in and out of her vagina, and I was glad when Estelle began to stroke my pubic mound, for the sight of so much erotic activity had made me faint with desire. I had a swift orgasm at the same time as Mary cried out as though in despair, driven helplessly into ecstasy by the formidable power of David's long thick cock driven into her as though by a steam-powered piledriver.

'That's two ladies fucked into spending and I've barely started,' he boasted with a merry laugh, as he withdrew from her tight vagina. He showered with Darma and Mary to rinse off the soap.

'Now then my beauties, you shall torment me, and that way my pleasure shall be prolonged. Mary understands the delights of that, don't you Mary?'

'Indeed I do sir, and I only wish you would do it to me,' that unaccountable woman replied, gloomy once more now that she was not being restrained and used.

'Now help me into this suit,' said David, picking up the second body harness, or strap suit, from the floor. I was greatly surprised by this development, and not a little relieved to find that I was not the one to be rendered helpless. At the same time however – how wondrous are the thoughts of mankind! – I experienced a curious sensation of disappointment, though this was so overwhelmed by curiosity as to what wickedness David would next enjoy.

We strapped the suit around David's body. He frequently asked us to do the straps up tighter, and we would strain to advance the buckle one more hole. Estelle and Mary both proved, compared to Darma and I, ruthless.

'Now I'll lie down, and you can fasten my legs together and my arms to my sides.'

We did up several of the little straps, so that his legs were bound together at ankles, just above the knees, and upper thighs, while his arms were closely connected to the straps around his body by means of the straps at his wrists and just above the elbow. He was now utterly helpless, trussed like a turkey being taken to market. I found it a very curious sensation indeed to render a man helpless. His penis looked gigantic. It was all astonishing.

'Now you must tease and torment me,' he told us. 'Make me desire you, do not let me spend – you can

132

even hurt and frighten me a little. Use the cat. I want you to use the cat on my helpless body, Jane.'

'Oh, I could not!' I exclaimed.

'You must,' he stated. 'Mary will give you advice, she understands the pleasure of restraint. You are to abuse me as your helpless slave for exactly ninety minutes.'

'Fetch my watch from my room, please Darma,' Estelle said. There was a dangerous gleam in her eyes, and I feared she would get over-excited by this wicked novelty, and go too far.

'You must abuse me verbally as though I was a worthless worm, and you are to hurt me, but not so much that I cannot enjoy myself once I am released,' David told us. 'I am not a true masochist like Mary, but I enjoy restraint on occasion, as a change of pace. Abuse me and enjoy yourselves.'

'Let me ask my husband for advice,' I begged.

'No. Either you want to keep your house or you do not. If you want to keep it, obey my command to abuse my helpless body,' David laughed.

'Then I must be cruel to you,' said I. 'It is my duty. I once read a novel in which a woman used men cruelly, so I can use her style of dialogue if you like.' (Who says that reading licentious literature is never of practical benefit?)

'Excellent! Pray do so.'

Darma returned with Estelle's watch. We noted the time, and were ready.

'This will be fun,' stated Estelle with a smile that showed her teeth in a manner somewhat evocative of cannibalism.

'Listen to my final instructions carefully,' David told us. 'Once we begin I shall play the part of a man captured by four cruel women for their own pleasure, a man desperately afraid. I shall beg you to release me, I may insult and abuse you. You shall not release me until the time is up, and you must punish me whenever I insult you.'

We all agreed that we understood. David now flexed his muscles and tried the strength of his captivating harness. It was so strongly made of the finest quality leather that it was clear he could never break free of it, and he was pleased.

'Start with me here on the floor, then move me into the bath, after testing the temperature of the water,' David told us. 'Try not to bang my head on the edge of the bath as I go in. Are we all ready? Assume your parts, ladies, as cruel, vengeful wantons. I shall now assume my role of a terrified prisoner.'

David's whole manner changed as he entered the spirit of the game: he writhed and twisted, struggling to escape from the strong grip of the straps that encased and immobilised his body, while his face evinced every sign of mystification and fear.

'Let me go, I demand it,' he cried. 'Why are you treating me thus? You drugged my wine last night, and this morning I awoke to find myself a bound captive. What is your purpose in treating me in this manner?'

His acting was fine, though for my part I found it a little difficult at first to get into my part. Estelle and Mary were far more experienced in erotic make-believe however (Estelle leads a make-believe life if you ask me, having lost contact with reality) and they were instantly everything David could have desired.

'You have no rights now, certainly not the right to ask questions,' Estelle snapped. 'We have you here for our pleasure, and it is our special pleasure now to torment you. You are doomed.'

'Let's irritate his cock with these, miss,' Mary suggested, detaching two of the small straps that hung loose from her harness owing to the fact that they were not being used to restrict her movement. Mary, as a masochist herself, well understood what to do to David at this juncture.

'An excellent idea,' Estelle agreed. 'Is it not a good idea, Jane? We can restrain and hurt his disgusting male organ.'

'Yes, of course,' said I, managing to enter into the spirit of the game. 'It is only what he deserves, and there shall be far worse to come. Fasten the straps, Mary.'

The servant first tried the straps for fit, then fastened one around the base of his manhood, and the other halfway up the shaft. He protested strongly.

'You cannot do this to me! Women are gentle, loving creatures, not capable of such inhuman cruelty. This must be a nightmare.' He writhed about like a worm, so that Darma and I had to hold him steady while Mary fastened the straps with ruthless tightness.

I found it curiously pleasant to treat a man so. He had been strong and commanding, a ruthless male, as he stabbed his cock into one servant after another, using their orifices as he chose, but now he was utterly helpless, and I could not deny that there was something about the dramatic change I found intriguing.

I heard a crow cawing just outside the window and glanced at it involuntarily, to see the flat Norfolk countryside stretching away in the sunshine. Here we were in England in the latter part of the nineteenth century, at the height of civilization – yet we were engaged in an act that would surely have been regarded as extreme even in the most decadent days of ancient history. It was hard not to be just a little proud of oneself.

'You used your organ against women, stabbing them without mercy,' said I, as I became inspired by some muse of erotic drama. 'Now we will have revenge.'

'How dare he have an erection in our presence?' Estelle cried with such passionate anger that she startled me. 'It is an insult. Stop it at once, do you hear me, you male worm, stop it at once or we shall have to punish you very severely. Make your disgusting penis go limp.'

'I cannot,' David replied excitedly, squirming helpless on the tiled floor.

'You and Darma could use your heels on him, miss,' Mary suggested to Estelle. 'That would make him suffer something fine.'

'Indeed,' agreed Estelle. 'Just think, you piece of male scum – Darma and I are lovers. We don't need men. We don't need your filthy penis.' She kissed and caressed her lover with real passion.

Mary fetched two stools, upon which Estelle and Darma sat side by side. A fine sight they looked, with Estelle in red leather boots, a matching suspender belt, red silk stockings and a broad white hat, while the Indian girl wore, in splendid contrast to her dark skin, long white leather gloves, a broad, tight, matching belt, and my white boots. Both ladies now began to tease and torment David with their high heels, while Mary and I held him steady, placing his body at their disposal so that he could suffer exquisitely.

They were tentative at first, but soon grew more cruel. They kissed and touched one another's lovely bodies, and encouraged one another to dig their heels into their prisoner more savagely. Soon the pressure they exerted was sufficient to leave vivid red marks on David's thighs. After a time they threatened his genitals, then caressed them with their heels. I was remarkably affected by the sight of the large penis and big balls so helpless, so much at risk from those expensive leather boots worn by beautiful, confident women who avidly caressed each other's firm breasts.

'You bitches! You whores!' David cried, his eyes bulging.

'Such language merits the severest punishment,' Estelle told him, and pressed her heel into the base of his penis until he apologised. Her hazel eyes gleamed alarmingly. I knew this was the first time she had ever done anything serious with a man, and it was clear she found the experience thrilling. I feared she would go too far – in general, going too far seemed to be her role in life.

'Suck my heel,' ordered Estelle. 'Clean it with your mouth.'

'I cannot,' David protested. 'It is a disgusting idea.'

Mary quickly punished him by manipulating his genitals in a way he did not like, for he yelped. I think the way she used her fingernails had something to do with it. He agreed to suck the heels, and so served all four, while their wearers masturbated, opening their private parts and showing them off to their helpless prisoner. He also had to lick the shiny leather uppers while Mary tickled the shiny helmet of his penis, which bulged and strained in its leather captivity. David stared enthralled at the shameless masturbators.

'You whores!' he gasped. 'You disgusting sluts!'

Mary pushed a piece of soap at his mouth, and he spluttered and spat most amusingly. She was of course eager to punish and humiliate him in the hope that later he would return the favour.

I decided the others were being more wicked than I, and this naturally made me ashamed. I resolved to play my part, and to be better than my colleagues, which is to say, worse.

'Do you like looking at women's secret flesh?' I demanded of David. 'Then perhaps you would like a better view.'

With that I knelt over his head and held my nether lips apart, so that he could stare at my innermost pink wet flesh without being able to touch it. Shivers of pleasure coursed through my body, urging fresh juices to ooze from my parts. I lowered myself almost to his face, then stood up abruptly.

The high-heeled tormentors amused themselves for a time, pressing their footwear into his helpless flesh. Mary flicked her forefinger against his glans.

'Darma,' I suggested, 'you could sit on his face.'

'And I shall soap her lovely bum,' said Estelle, 'so that she might all the better humiliate him.'

'You cannot! It is – urgghh!' cried David. He became indistinct at the point owing to the way Mary worked a bar of soap in and out of his mouth whenever he opened it to try and speak.

Estelle worked up a soapy lather on the splendidly developed brown hemispheres which constituted Darma's backside. The long-haired Indian beauty then lowered herself gracefully into position, and David's cries of protest became pleasingly muffled.

The servant rubbed her rear back and forth, round and round, thoroughly squelching David's face. She raised her powerful bum now and then to let him burble some exclamations of a protesting and insulting nature, then lowered her weight again to cut him off in a series of soapy bubbles that burst around her private parts. She had an air of gravity and seriousness, but there was the merest hint of a smile on her lips and in her lovely dark eyes, in which lights sparkled like stars in the night sky. Estelle caressed her breasts, while Mary and I, becoming considerably aroused, kissed and touched one another's bodies with growing fervour.

David cut so ridiculous a figure that I began to have a genuine contempt for him. In addition I had a natural grudge against him as our creditor, so it was not surprising that I began to think of ways in which I could humiliate him utterly. Hitherto I had regarded male organs with something close to awe, seeing them as the steely invaders of the secret recesses of women's bodies, but here was one which, for the moment at least, was merely an object of ridicule, a plaything for we four girls, a sorry kind of sausage for our tea.

'Make him lick you,' I told Darma. 'Rinse his face so that he may feast his eyes on your body, but do not rinse yourself. Make him lick the soap from your most sensitive parts.'

'You excel yourself, Jane,' said Estelle. 'You are far less boring than I have hitherto assumed.'

'Oh ma'am, I do so much hope that you will treat me as cruelly as this some day soon,' Mary told me fervently. 'That would be so fine. Indeed, you do have a natural talent for being cruel.'

Darma splashed some water from the tap over David's face so that he could open his eyes.

'Lick soap off her,' Estelle ordered him. 'Lick it off her cunt.'

'No, no, I will not,' he blustered in reply. 'You are witches from hell.'

I picked up the cat-o-nine tails and raised it as though to strike.

'Either you lick her or I whip you,' I stated.

Darma squatted over his face. With a grimace of disgust, David put out his tongue and began, with every show of reluctance and disgust, to lick up and down Darma's private parts. As well as he was able, he spat out the lather. Mary took a long-handled back brush from a corner shelf. It had stiff bristles, and when she touched these to the helmet of our prisoner's penis, he yelped like a coward. I felt irritated by his fear, whether it was real or feigned, so I took the brush from Mary and rubbed it vigorously up and down David's thighs. I then pressed it to his helmet again, harder than the servant had done, making him yell out and beg for mercy in a way that was certainly sincere.

'That will teach you not to cry out until you're truly hurt,' I informed him. 'And keep licking Darma, or I'll rub you a lot more.'

'Why is your cock still hard?' demanded Estelle. 'You are insulting us with your penis, which clearly desires to violate our bodies. We order you to make your cock go soft, slave. You must do it now or answer to the whip.'

I wondered if I dare do such a thing, and then reflected that I must, as it was my duty – and besides, I sensed that Estelle thought I would not dare do it, and I wanted to prove otherwise to her. She was proud of her wickedness, but now I would, for once, leave her in the shade.

'Turn him over on to his front,' I commanded, for all the world like some Amazon queen.

'Don't you dare touch me with that whip,' David shouted. 'It isn't what I truly want. I was only joking before, Jane. Please don't use it on me, I beg of you.'

'Oh shut up,' I snapped. I was in a curious mood, excited by his helplessness, irritated by his begging for mercy. David could not even maintain the courage of his perversions.

Perhaps he was sincere in not wanting to be hurt, yet I no longer thought merely of giving him whatever he wanted and so saving the house. No, part of me was beyond such concerns. Darma and Mary turned our whimpering prisoner over on the white-tiled floor, exposing his defenceless buttocks to my wicked impulses. I picked up the cat-o-nine and it felt decidedly useful. Heavy and dangerous, it was no plaything but a serious object indeed, the possession of which gave me a delightful, tingling sense of power.

And yet I hesitated.

'Forget the house, Jane darling,' whispered Estelle. Her eyes gleamed, and her hands were persuasive. 'Do it because I want you to. I want to watch you whip a man, a helpless man.'

Reader, I hit him on the bum. The first blow was nothing at all, it barely touched him, for I was not only nervous and over-excited, but also unaccustomed to the weight and swing of the cat. David cried out, but it can hardly have been from pain. I paused to swing the cat through the air a few times and so learn how to use it to best effect against the flesh of this man.

'Darma, Estelle, Mary, you are to sit in front of David so he can see your private parts,' I commanded in my lust. 'You are to play with each other so he can see everything.'

When the ladies were in position, caressing one another's private parts and mocking David, I struck my second blow to his buttocks. It was better than the first, but there was still not much in it, for in my fear of doing serious harm I did not put enough swing into it – and this time David did not even deign to cry out! This was most vexing. I saw that I would have to swing the cat in a wide arc to let it gain impetus, or else Estelle would make fun of me as a coward. I decided to hit hard. There was a moist, tingling sensation at the base of my belly, and I rubbed the handle of the cat between my nether lips, greatly enjoying the sensation of the braided leather.

I struck my third blow to his defenceless behind. It landed more heavily than I had expected, and there was no mistaking the genuineness of David's yelp, which he followed with a stream of vile abuse.

'Oh shut up,' I exclaimed. 'You asked me to use the whip, and now you will just have to suffer. And you will certainly have to answer for using such vile language.'

I landed my fourth, fifth and sixth blows on his back instead of his rear, for I am a great believer in the refreshing effects of variety. I paused and stared down at the pink lines I had raised on his white skin.

'Excellent, Jane!' Estelle cried fervently. She was frigging herself practically under David's nose. 'And to think that I have sometimes thought of you as boring. All this time you have been hiding your light under a bushel. You are in fact an accomplished sadist – my congratulations.' Her hand moved faster. 'Hit him again!' she yelled, and enjoyed a splendid orgasm.

David moaned, but did not speak, and I felt he was lost in dark sensuality. I had Mary come over to me and caress my breasts, then kiss my behind. Her hugely erect nipples grazed my legs.

I struck two more severe blows on my victim's buttocks. The sound was sharp, stinging. His flesh reddened. Mary rubbed the flesh around my clitoris. I was breathing hard, rather from excitement than exertion. I knew I was nearing the summit of my pleasure, and it seemed necessary David's pain should also achieve a summit of agony. I knew this would make my own rapture all the sweeter.

I struck my ninth and tenth blows on his back, and followed them quickly with three more on his bum.

'You bitch! You whore from hell!' he screamed.

'You are a very foolish fellow indeed to insult me thus,' I said coolly, and laid five very hard blows all over his reddened buttocks.

'Jane, stop,' he cried. 'I have had enough. You can stop now.'

'Oh, do shut up,' I murmured, absorbed in my own pleasure as Mary manipulated me with fascinating skill. 'Turn him over,' I ordered Darma. She obeyed with a fresh alacrity, as though I had gained a new level of authority.

Estelle looked into my eyes, seemed startled at what she saw there, and immediately mounted her dark Indian favourite. Both women quickly attained the vales of paradise.

I looked down at David's defenceless penis. His eyes widened and he cried out for help.

'Gag him,' I told Mary.

In a flash she had unbuckled the gag attached to her own strap suit, and had it in his mouth as he tried to summon aid with a shout that was muffled into a murmur by the ball of hard red rubber which a strong leather strap held in place. The cat was heavy in my hand. I looked down at his cock, no longer free to probe into the depths of females, but only a piece of silliness.

Mary brought me to the brink, her hands on and around my private parts and her tongue between the cheeks of my behind. I was struck by ecstasy as by a shard of black ice falling from the heavens. I struck out with the whip. I sank to the floor and rolled over clutching at myself. I glimpsed the halls of paradise.

'I doubt if he will ever forgive the debt now, so it hardly matters what we do to him,' Estelle pointed out. Her hazel eyes gleamed like those of some dangerous animal. 'We can enjoy ourselves by taking revenge on him for turning you out of your house, Jane, as he surely will now that you have struck him such a decisive blow.'

This seemed to me an interesting way of looking at our situation, and it impressed David too, for he shook his head, endeavoured to speak through the gag, and even attempted to wriggle towards the door. He looked contemptible. To cap it all, his penis had gone limp.

'Let us see if he has learned his lesson, or if he will dare to have another erection,' I stated. 'Mary, you go on all fours so that your private parts are above his face, and then we shall see if he has yet mastered his unfortunate propensity to offend us with the sight of his erection.'

The statuesque servant, in her tightly-fitting strap suit, took up her position at once, and Estelle seized one of the dildos we had brought into the bathroom with us, and thrust it forcefully into Mary's well-lubricated female channel. She then worked it in and out vigorously so that David's staring eyes took in every detail of the black leather thing distending and tugging the full sex-lips of the statuesque masochist.

I removed the straps we had earlier fitted around David's penis. Quickly it grew in size to its former gigantic proportions.

'Stop your penis from being hard at once,' I said threateningly. 'Or it will be the worse for you.'

Mary rolled her head and grunted, thrusting back at Estelle so as to receive the full reward of the dildo. Her orgasm was so strong it made her cough. When the servant had done, Estelle pulled out the phallus. It made a wet plop.

'You have not heeded our warnings,' I told David. 'Now you will pay.'

'He will pay as no man has ever paid,' Estelle insisted. 'Let us all strip naked, and so be free.'

The four of us removed our items of erotic attire. Our nudity seemed curiously serious after the frivolity of our dressing-up.

'Now we will be gorgeous mermaids,' Estelle, looking at the big bath. 'Cruel, immoral creatures whose one delight is to lure sailors into the deep waters where we are at home, but from which men can never return.'

Chapter Ten

Before we sent David into the watery depths, Estelle suggested to Mary that she wipe her private parts over his face. She held her long, distended flaps open and anointed the captive with her lubricating fluids which had eased the passage of the dildo. When she rose, a long streamer of feminine flow hung briefly from her vagina to his cheek.

We then set to half-lift, half-drag him the short distance to the bath, which the reader may recall, had green marble steps at one end and a brightly polished brass railing around the other three sides.

'Let's launch him like a boat,' said Estelle, and we girls all laughed at such an amusing idea.

David shook his head and made muffled sounds of protest, but we paid no attention. He would not spoil our fun. Darma entered the bath first, both to check the water temperature and to be in position to prevent David banging his head on the far end after we, as it were, committed his body to the depths. We launched him face-up, so that his male organ should not catch on the lip of the bath – it would not be counted a successful launch in any reputable shipyard if part of a new vessel should be torn off.

'I name this ship HMS Preposterous,' announced Estelle.

We raised his legs and pushed him into the bath, slapping his thighs in place of the traditional bottle of champagne broken against the bow. He shot down into the foam and water, to be caught by Darma. The rest of us piled gleefully into the warm water, made slippery with bath crystals, and soon had him back on his feet, only slightly the worse for wear – though from the look on his face you would have thought we had done something quite bad.

We young ladies had a happy time in that bath. It was delicious to embrace, kiss, and caress one another under the eyes of a man whose organ pulsed with lust, our nasty creditor who now could not so much as touch our lovely young nudity. How he would have loved to plunge his steely manhood into our warm, slippery bodies! We teased him outrageously. We squeezed our breasts and held them up to his face, we laid down in the water and held open each other's private parts, we pressed our bodies against his, we caressed every part of him except his huge penis – in short we indulged in every manner of lewdness. How fine it was! One delightful game involved Mary and Darma bending over to display their ample rears, holding open their parts while David strove to stab them with his cock – an effort naturally hampered by Estelle and myself, causing him to become frantic with frustration.

'There is a fine cunt! Surely you can spear it – go for it, lunge for it, you may make it this time!' Such was the manner of the verbal encouragement we gave our captive, even as our hands held him back or else guided him into missing his lush pinky-red target. His cock pulsed so hugely I wondered if it might burst.

We urged him to break his bonds, saying they were nothing, and that a real man would snap them and fuck us all. We splashed cold water on his penis and face. His desperate lust was most amusing. It did not detract from his desire to spill his seed when one of us girls enjoyed the raptures of orgasm, which occurred not infrequently. Mary and Darma switched to enjoying one another, and it was a fine sight to see their contrasting dark and light flesh united in every manner of pleasure, two shapely females all wet and gleaming. Estelle and I pulled David's feet from under him, and he thrashed around helplessly, floating in the water while the two young ladies coupled rapturously.

After they had both spent, we played another wicked game. Mary and I supported David in the water, while Estelle and Darma put their high-heeled calf-length boots back on, my friend's red and the servant's white. They sat on the edge of the bath and pushed their spikes into his skin. If Mary and I held him up, the heels sunk in deeper, but if we let the pressure from the boots push him down, he was in danger of being submerged. We played it both ways. It was greatly amusing to see four heels teasing his genitals while our own private parts luxuriated in the freely given caresses of our hands. Estelle used a dildo on herself, slipping it in and out of her cunnie. David's eyes bulged like a frog's. So passed a happy hour. Well, happy for the female contingent of our little bathing party, at any rate.

'Now we must take him out of the bath and blindfold him,' stated Estelle. 'I have had a good idea.'

Following her lead, we placed him back on the tiles and blindfolded him with one of the red stockings worn earlier by my lesbian friend. We entreated her to tell us her idea.

'I am going to whip him again,' she replied, then gave us a wink which was of course invisible to David. 'It is plain he intends turning you out of your house, Jane. He will never forgive the debt no matter how hard we strive to provide him with erotic pleasures. Therefore we must punish him now, while he is helpless. It is our only opportunity. I love you Jane, and I shall therefore whip this fellow so that he will be unable to enjoy carnal delights for some months, if indeed he will ever be able to enjoy them again.'

You can imagine the effect this had on David – he writhed and moaned and made every effort to escape his tight leather captivity. He was genuinely frightened. Estelle had delivered her speech with the finest conviction, so that anyone who had not seen her wink would have believed she did intend an atrocity.

Mary now cleverly added to the drama.

'Oh miss!' she exclaimed, giving us a wink. 'I don't want to go to prison. Who knows what will happen to the gentleman if you get carried away?'

'Have no fear, Mary – and you too Darma,' Estelle replied. 'I will take all the blame, no matter how fearful the consequences of my actions.'

Darma now voiced similar pretended concerns, and I too expressed my doubts. Estelle, however, would not be swayed, and we three eventually acted as though we were convinced. David then struggled so much that Darma, Mary and I had to hold him still.

'Now I am going to whip you where it will hurt most,' Estelle told our frantic prisoner. 'I turned to women for love because I was cruelly betrayed by a man, and since then I have sought revenge on the male sex.'

This was of course all nonsense. Estelle had never been betrayed by a man – in fact they were always falling over each other to be polite to her, as, when she wanted to be, she was so charming. It was a fine lie however, as it made David all the more frightened.

Estelle put her fingers to her lips to commend us to silence, then left the room silently. She soon returned carrying a bowl of cold water, to which none of us made any reference. You can imagine David's suspense during this period. He started as much as he was able to in his strap suit, and cried out as much as he could with the big red rubber ball held in his mouth by a strap, when Estelle cracked the cat-o-nine just over his helpless flesh. She repeated the process several times. Darma, Mary and I held David steady. Finally, she cracked the cat in the air inches above his male organ, and at the same time used her other hand to pour the cold water over his penis and testicles.

This was for him a terror! Owing to the coldness of the water and the fact that he was skilfully blindfolded, he naturally perceived the chill of the water as the searing pain of a savage blow from the leather cat. It is an interesting reflection that in all matters, we feel to some extent what we expect to feel. My word, how David did writhe!

We did not want him to have a heart attack. (Well, I did not at any rate. Who knows what Estelle would have found sensually exciting?) So we now removed his blindfold and gag and explained the joke to him. He did not laugh.

'You cunning, cruel bitches, you might have killed me,' he cried. 'Let me go now, I demand it. It would have been better had you truly whipped me, but to be thus deceived is insulting.'

'Oh come now,' Estelle said with her winning smile. 'You have had the most splendid time in restraint, and I am sure an intelligent gentleman like you well knows it, and will be grateful to us.' She paused. 'Mary, perhaps you had better call your master before we release David.'

The servant hurried on her errand. Our prisoner fell silent, apparently reflecting on his ordeal, then suddenly broke into a great laugh, deep and strong.

'By God, but you are clever girls!' he exclaimed. 'I shall never forget what you did to me if I live to be a hundred. It is easily the best experience of captivity I have ever known. Though you should have whipped me harder, Jane.'

Robert entered the bathroom with Mary. He did not so much as raise his eyebrows at the unusual scene that met his eyes.

'You are the luckiest man in the world to have such a wife,' David told him with heartfelt sincerity.

'I know it,' replied my husband.

We all set to undoing the straps that bound David, and soon he was naked and free. We dried ourselves on soft towels. I wondered how David would choose to attain ecstasy after such a long period of extreme stimulation. He did not leave me long in suspense.

'And now it is more than time that I had you, my dear Jane,' he stated. 'Come, let us join the others in the library.'

We went downstairs where most of the servants were waiting. My heart was pounding violently. I was about to be taken by a man who was not my husband, a man moreover, whom I had just been wickedly teasing, even whipping! It was a momentous event indeed – and a sin. I hoped he would at least have the decency to possess me in a private room. But it was not to be. He had determined on his revenge for my cruelty.

'I want you all to form a circle around us,' he said. 'This fine lady has teased me hellishly, and now she shall be made to pay. I will give her a damn good fuck.'

'My dear,' said Robert, 'only go ahead with this if you want to.'

'It should be an interesting experience,' I told him. How could I back out now? Had not the servants already given their bodies to our creditor? Besides, he was not so bad-looking.

The servants, Estelle and my husband arranged themselves about us in silence, staring at us in common fascination. David snatched some cushions from the sofa and chairs and tossed them on the floor. I feared I might faint with the humiliation of being taken in public, but I told myself not to be over-wrought. I guessed that Robert would derive some excitement from seeing me treated thus, and if some-thing pleased a woman's husband, ought she not to be pleased herself?

'Down on your knees and kiss my cock, you cruel witch,' David gasped. He was in a passion of lust after our prolonged teasing.

I knelt down in front of him and took the thick shaft of his huge pulsing cock in my hands while planting a long wet kiss on the gleaming helmet. He trembled and gasped as though I had sunk a stiletto into his belly. Oh, how sinful it was for me to behave thus in front of my husband! And how delightful! I saw his maleness pulse rigidly.

I licked David's organ up and down, and fondled his big balls. After all, it was my duty to save the house, I told myself again. My juices flowed with some urgency. I grazed his shiny helmet with my teeth, then slid my wet lips back and forth across the rim. He made appreciative grunts. David thrust, and I let him slide into my open mouth, turning my head so he could stab against the insides of my soft warm cheeks. He gripped my long golden hair in both hands, using it to hold my head steady, as though I had reins attached to my head for the better pleasure of men availing themselves of my mouth. My tongue worked saliva around his gleaming organ.

'Go down on all fours, my dear,' David gasped,

withdrawing from my mouth by a great effort of will. 'It is time I tried your cunnie.'

I took up the position he demanded and presented him with my raised rear. I was in a fine state of arousal. Indeed, though it may be shameful to admit it, I have to confess that when a lady is in a certain state, there is only one thing that she truly desires, and what that thing is, you may well imagine.

David again took strands of my hair in his hands, pulling it gently so that I put my head back like a high-spirited mare shaking its mane.

David now delighted in making disgusting comments about my body.

'How wet she is!' he exclaimed, putting two fingers inside me. 'And what a gripper! Jane, you have a splendid cunt. And what a marvellous body! How big and round her arse is when seen from this advantageous angle! How it curves out from her tiny waist!'

Suddenly he thrust his organ inside me, and rocked back and forth. Then he pulled my hips down so that I was crouching down on the floor. He squatted on his heels behind me and held my hips, moving them up and down so that his penis slid in and out without his having to move. He kept this up for a time and then stretched me out, unfolding me so to speak. He lay flat on top of me and hammered his triumphant maleness into me with savage strokes. Soon I cried out in rapture, and it was then, with my innards clutching at his staff of life, that he erupted with great force, like the explosion of Krakatoa. He uttered a long, shuddering cry – it was almost a wail. I felt his copious, powerful spasms, and they intensified my own, so that we fed on one another's ecstasy and rose together to undreamed of heights beyond the peak of Everest.

It was a shocking way to spend, impaled face down

on the library floor in front of my husband, best friend and servants.

David withdrew from me, wiped his penis on my backside, and laughed.

'She's well worth a ride, indeed she is. What say you try her now, Robert?'

My husband needed no prompting. His manner of pleasuring me was both impressive and delightful: instead of thrusting into me, he laid down on the carpet beside me, offering his body to me as though to emphasise that my desires were the ones that mattered most and that he was not too proud to be a servant to my lust. He offered himself to me as his equal – an equal far more exciting and powerful than any mere master.

I embraced his rigid penis with my vagina, then bent down and kissed him with all the passion I had known in my entire existence. I was free. I was compelled by nothing save erotic desire. My movements were my own, and I made them with the man of my life. I thrust myself against him, letting his pubic bone dig into my sensitive sexual-flesh, pleasuring my clitoris with my vibrant motions which made his long, thick maleness slide in and out of my well-lubricated parts. I spent quickly for love of him, and nearly fainted, for in that rapture we seemed to have moved to a higher plane, one in which pleasure possessed its own ferociousness.

Recovering, I rolled over onto my side, and Robert rolled with me. We coupled in that most equal and pleasant of positions, on our sides and facing, grinding our bodies hard together as though determined to remain united until death.

Minutes later, Robert rolled us over again, so that he was on top, and he drove his body weightily on to mine, taking me with superb athleticism, holding my shoulders and driving into me as though he meant to bury his whole body in my cunt. He paused, and we kissed one another like a drowning woman and man whose only hope of air lay in the lips of the loved one. I reached the summit of earthly ambition once more, and at the same time Robert released himself within me, spurting jets of soothing balm that eased all the hot desires I had ever known, bringing me unspeakable relief.

My mate gasped and shuddered, groaned and tensed, his face contorted with pleasure that wore the mask of agony. After a long, long time, he collapsed.

'Robert, you have a fine wife,' David said cheerfully. 'And I am glad to tell you that because of her I am more than willing to let your little debt go by in instalments, in return for visiting this house.'

'Splendid!' I cried, and the servants too voiced their great pleasure and relief, embracing one another. How they feared losing their home!

'In fact I had decided to accept your offer from the first, but I pretended to be angry when my instructions were disobeyed earlier – as I had known they must be – in order to add the spice of a little suspense to events.'

'Oh, how could you be so cruel, and so cold-blooded?' I exclaimed, not caring that he was our creditor. 'We have all been on tenterhooks trying to please you, and you pretended to be displeased to make us try harder. It is wicked. I should have whipped you much harder when I had the opportunity, for you deserved it.'

'Well then, the next time I place myself in your power you may have your revenge,' David pointed out with a smile. 'Though to be sure, there are many men far crueller than I, as I fear you may find out one day.'

155

'You are thinking, are you not, of your fellow creditor, Sir Horace Withington-Blathers,' said Robert.

David nodded in confirmation.

'His tastes are rumoured to be on the cruel side,' my husband said thoughtfully. 'We will never satisfy my other two creditors as we have satisfied David. He was the least difficult.'

'Never mind my darling, at least we are trying,' said I, squeezing his hand. In my heart I felt a great determination to succeed, even though the cost might be terrible.

Reader, there is no need for me to describe how David enjoyed himself the rest of the time he spent with us. I have told you that he agreed to forgive Robert's debt in return for erotic pleasures, and there is no need for me to say more about him, for it would merely be a catalogue of carnal delights. You may imagine for yourelves how relieved the servants were to have won over at least one creditor, and how joyfully they joined him in satisfying their every whim. You know of their special predilections, and can envisage how David enjoyed trying them out, putting those men and women through their paces, forming them into every combination that occurred to him, and getting them to give him every manner of erotic delight. Suffice to say that none of us had much sleep that night.

One creditor was satisfied, but we had to have all three agree to the same arrangement David had accepted, as we did not have the money to pay even one. The next morning, Robert, Estelle, David and myself enjoyed a hearty breakfast. We had the healthy appetites and cheerfulness of those who have devoted themselves to the exploration of erotic deviations. The second post brought us a letter from another of the men to whom David owed money, namely Mr Stanley Blanking.

'He says he will give us no grace, that we must leave the house immediately or he will send the bail-iffs in,' my husband informed us, having perused the missive. Robert was not too disturbed by this letter, as now he had my full support.

'I know the fellow slightly,' David told us. 'He is a puritan and a milksop, a deplorable namby-pamby indeed. He will run a mile if you offer him the delights of the flesh in return for cancelling your debt. You cannot succeed with him. I would make a wager in total confidence that I would win, were anyone fool-ish enough to bet with me.'

'Shall we say one hundred guineas?' Estelle said at once. 'I could use a little hat money.'

'This is one bet you shall lose,' David laughed.

'I never lose,' my friend replied complacently. 'I will cheat and lie, I will use every trick – if necessary I will use force. I shall take your hundred guineas, and what is more, you will do something that will help me take it from you.'

'And what shall is that?'

'You will be good enough to pay a flying visit to Mr Blanking – I see from this letter that he is current-ly in London, and you will pass through that jewel of Empire on the way to Paris, will you not?'

'I am at your disposal,' David agreed gallantly.

'You shall lie to him,' stated Estelle, as though there were not the slightest possibility of David refus-ing. 'Lying is always efficacious, and so much more refreshing than the truth. You will tell him that Robert has a remarkable business offer to put to him, that you personally think it a sure way to make a fortune, that you have accepted a share in it – but you will not tell Mr Blanking anything about it, because you promised Robert to let him tell Mr Blanking about it personally. Robert cannot come down to London because Jane is indisposed – how tiresome you are Jane, I am sure it is mere hypochondria.'

'I'll do it,' David promised. 'I shall tell him it is a sure way to make a fortune, and he will come running.'

'Tell him to come tomorrow evening if he can,' said Estelle. 'By then we might have recovered from what you put us through last night.'

'I would be glad to lose my wager with you – you are splendid in your lust,' David said warmly. 'But I will not lose. There is nothing to be done with such a puling milksop as Stanley Blanking.'

'We shall see about that,' my husband stated grimly. There was a kind of menacing resolve in his tone, and I felt he might be contemplating extreme measures.

Chapter Eleven

David departed for his channel tunnel meeting that morning, telling us that the first train would be running under the sea by 1895. We settled down as well as we could to await news from Mr Blanking, though our anxiety kept us from achieving the ease of mind to which we would normally have aspired. The servants were lucky in that they had work to do to distract themselves – I positively envied them as they caught up on the tasks they had not been able to perform the day before. For my part I toyed with a little crochet, though I fear I did not work with that single-mindedness which my mother tried so hard to instil in me. That evening we were greatly relieved when a telegram arrived from Mr Blanking. It informed us he would arrive the next day at about 6 p.m., so we knew that David had played his part well. If we could but get our second creditor in our clutches, there was at least a chance of persuading him to cancel our debts by fair means or foul. Probably foul.

Naturally we discussed what course of action to take with this fellow, and we decided that first we would use subtlety. It would be no use to put on a show of the staff, as we had for David, as it would simply frighten him away.

'Perhaps we'll be lucky, and he'll turn out to be a hypocrite,' said Estelle. 'He might be a secret libertine.'

'No, I fear not,' my husband replied. 'I fear he's as religious and puritanical as any Englishman ever was, which is very.'

As soon as we met Mr Blanking, we all felt that Robert was right, and that this young man did not even possess the saving grace of being a hypocrite and a secret lecher. He was indeed an upright, pure young man of strong convictions in the moral sphere. It was intolerable to meet anybody so righteous.

John collected him from the railway station in the chaise. Mr Blanking was a slightly built man in his mid-twenties, with a solemn face and a measured, portentous way of speaking that made one want to finish his sentences for him to save time. He was already going bald. I felt he was a virgin.

At dinner he astonished us by requesting that an eighteenth-century painting of a classical subject be removed or hidden, as it portrayed women in a state of undress. Banks covered it with a cloth. This did not bode well.

Our guest's main subject of conversation was religion, which he thought of in terms of suffering, punishment, discipline, and the finer points in the organisation of the Church of England. It was clear that there was nothing to be gained from bringing in the servants naked and telling him how they liked to reach orgasm.

We invited him to stay the night rather than hurry back to London, and he agreed, saying that the journey from the modern Sodom to the rustic delights of Norfolk was more than enough travel for one day. Robert told him he would reveal next morning what Mr Blanking was anxious to hear of, namely how he could make a fortune, as David had assured him he could if he listened to Robert.

It would have helped had we been able to get our

guest to drink, but you will not be surprised to learn that he was an abstainer.

It was during the cheese and wine, or in his case cheese and water, that he began to talk of ghosts. I was greatly surprised that a man who thought himself religious could believe in such things, which are surely excluded by the Christian revelation, but there, it often happens that men grasp the externals of religion while missing the heart. He not only believed in them, but was clearly fascinated by them, even obsessed. He asked eagerly if there were any to be found in this house, which in parts was venerable. I thought that if ghosts existed there must be hundreds of them in this house by now, so they would be somewhat cramped for space, and have to haunt a dozen to a room. Imagine my surprise when Robert answered Mr Blanking's foolish enquiry in the affirmative.

'Why yes,' he said. 'There is a legend about a ghost in this house, though I have never seen it myself, and think the story untrue.'

'Do please tell me the story,' Mr Blanking requested with real eagerness.

'It is supposed to be a pretty young girl whose spirit can take on physical substance. She is said only to visit certain men of virtue; God-fearing men. She rewards them for their virtue, and if they are patient and accept her gifts, she tells them, on her third or fourth visit, how they can make a great deal of money. Of course it is all nonsense.'

I thought that it certainly was, and nearly said so, but then it struck me that this story might be some stratagem of my husband's, so I kept silent.

'I feel it is far from being nonsense,' Mr Blanking stated, weighing every word as though he were selling them by the ounce. 'Such a strange and poetic legend is clearly the product of events going back several hundred years, and we, in this inferior modern age, must bow to the superior wisdom of our forefathers. I for one believe in this ghost of yours, and I would very much like to see it.'

'I think it unlikely anyone has ever seen it, except perhaps when drunk,' said Robert.

'Your scepticism,' Mr Blanking insisted disapprovingly, 'prevents you from being aware of the spiritual aspects of existence.'

Robert soon introduced a new topic of conversation, and we heard no more of ghosts. It was a dull evening. Mr Blanking had a way of voicing platitudes as though they were new-minted which was far from being the most engaging form of conversation.

When Robert and I were alone, I asked him what he intended.

'You will have observed, Jane, that when our guest talked of ghosts, he showed his gullibility. Indeed, he even betrayed his obsession with the spirit world – an obsession frequently found in those who are too cowardly to enjoy the actual world. Now then, if a woman came into his room, normally he would protest, shout for help, throw her out, and generally be immune to her charms. However, if a young lady enters his room and he believes her to be a ghost, a ghost of a special kind who can be touched – and a ghost who rewards virtuous men by telling them how to make money – his attitude to her may just be a little different. Something may occur. It is worth trying.'

'It is a splendid idea,' said I. 'Of course a man like that would like nothing better than to be seduced by a ghost.'

'And once a man tastes the pleasures of women, he wants more, and indeed must have more,' my husband asserted. 'We will be able to make a deal with him to settle my debt once we ease him past the barrier of his virginity.'

We discussed who would make the best ghost, and agreed it must be Lisa. Mr Blanking had not seen her, and she was of a calm, motherly nature. She could indeed give him what mothers give their babies. We hoped he would accept her milk, and from there other prospects should develop naturally.

This was of course a fantastic scheme, but it had to be tried. How straightforward it had been with David in comparison with this milksop!

Lisa was summoned, and we explained to her what she must try to do. We assured her nobody would blame her for failure, which helped make her less nervous. We waited until three in the morning, so that Mr Blanking would be awakened by the ghost and be in a more susceptible, dazed state of mind. Lisa entered his room wearing only a white night dress that was open at the front along its complete length, so that her remarkably large, firm breasts were fully accessible. She later told us exactly what happened, so I can give you the full narrative.

First, Lisa opened the curtains so that the light of the three-quarters moon could stream in, bathing her in a silvery glow that had an air of the supernatural. More practically, it let her see what she was doing. She saw that Mr Blanking was still asleep, so first she said his name softly, repeating this until he awoke. Seeing her, he gave a start of surprise.

'Stanley Blanking, you are the first virtuous man to come to this house in many a long year,' murmured Lisa, speaking slowly and softly as we had advised. 'To you I shall give the great reward that I have given to virtuous men throughout the ages. First my spirit must flow into you, so that you will be ready to receive the wisdom of the ages,' said Lisa. 'I am to you as a mother, and you are my son.'

She walked to the head of the bed and bent over him, letting her night dress fall open to expose her left breast. She pushed the nipple at his mouth and he took it between his lips, something I am sure he would not have done had he not felt, in his half-awake state, that she was a ghost, a special ghost that could be touched, Robert had told him, by virtuous men. Mr Blanking hardly knew, I daresay, whether he was awake or dreaming.

'Drink my wisdom,' Lisa told him. 'Be not afraid, for it is good.'

He did indeed suck, and he drank her warm milk. He drank it eagerly, as though he were hungry for the touch of women after years of loneliness. So at least we had got him to enjoy an act of sensuality with a young woman.

'Yes,' he sighed after a time. 'It is indeed wisdom. I can feel it entering my soul.'

'You must divest yourself of earthly trappings,' Lisa told the gullible young man. 'Lay yourself open to me, and be not afraid. I shall help you.'

She assisted him in removing his night gown, and soon had him in that naked state which is most suitable for the erotic act, leaving as it does every part of the body accessible to touch.

'Close your eyes and relax,' Lisa stated. 'Accept what I do and know that it is good, for it is the way to wisdom.'

He did as she said. Lisa let him wait a short time, then began gently to caress and kiss his body, avoiding his penis for the time being. She trailed her fingers up and down his skin and brushed his chest with her teats, she licked his own little nipples and blew on them, she stroked his belly and thighs. His maleness grew erect.

Finally she touched it, at first so lightly he can hardly have known whether she was touching him or not. Very gradually, she increased both the frequency and the pressure of her caresses. Her hair brushed his penis. Lisa naturally began to hope that she had won the day, and perhaps this made her a little too hasty, though the end result would probably have been the same had she been more cautious. She took his male organ in a firm grip, moved her hand up and down, and kissed the helmet. Who would have thought that any man could tell her to stop when he was enjoying such pleasure? How surprised poor Lisa was at what next occurred!

Mr Blanking's puritanism was so deeply ingrained that at this late stage he abruptly gave a strangled cry, clawed at Lisa's head and hand to push her away, at the same time clutching at the bedsheet to cover his nakedness. Lisa told us later that he was like a live eel escaping from the chopping block.

'You are a succubus, an evil succubus sent by Satan to seduce me,' he cried. 'I repudiate thee, demon. Get thee hence from here, and go back to the infernal regions from whence you came.' He still imagined she was a supernatural being, but had now decided she was evil rather than benign.

Lisa was so started she did not know what to do with herself. Seeing her confused gave Mr Blanking more courage. He looked at her closely, then grabbed her arm and felt her hand.

'Your hand is rough with work,' he said. 'You are merely some ordinary creature of the lower orders.'

'Oh sir, do let me go, you're hurting me,' Lisa protested. 'I didn't mean no harm, I'm sure.'

'You are a harlot, a whore. Kneel down with me and repent. God has sent you to me to repent. Let us give ourselves to God.'

Lisa thought she would rather not, so by a sudden effort she pulled herself away from him and ran out of the bedroom into the passage. Robert, Estelle and I met her there. We realised our scheme had failed.

'What can we do now?' I cried, wringing my hands in despair.

'Don't be a wet blanket, Jane,' Estelle admonished. 'Now we shall simply switch to plan B. With the whole alphabet laid out before us like a cheap slut, there is no reason to abandon hope.'

With that she hurried to her room, returning with something wrapped up in a silk scarf. I asked her what it was, but she shook her head and stayed silent, smiling a smug smile as though she was enjoying herself more than somewhat. This was typical of her irresponsibility.

Robert sent for Franklin and John, and told them on their arrival that they would prevent Mr Blanking from leaving. With splendid loyalty they simply agreed.

'Oh, but we cannot imprison him,' I gasped, horrified at the turn events were taking. 'That will be a crime. He will –'

'Calm yourself, Jane,' my husband stated. 'Trust me. Trust and obey like the good wife I know you to be.'

His words and accompanying embrace steadied me. How admirable were his self-control and manly bearing! I resolved to support him even in taking desperate measures.

In a short time Mr Blanking rushed out of his bedroom, having dressed with great rapidity.

'Are you aware what has just transpired in my room?' he demanded. 'A wanton harlot came to me with intentions that were distinctly carnal.'

'Heavens, how I envy you!' Estelle exclaimed. 'I

have to ring the bell several times just to get a hot water bottle.'

Her levity was totally unsuited for this serious occasion, and I would have liked to give her a good slap.

'I know all about it,' Robert told Mr Blanking. 'Lisa was following my instructions in paying you a visit. I intended you to enjoy yourself.'

'You amaze me, sir!' cried Mr Blanking. 'You dare to tell me that you initiated this outrage?' His eyes protruded further than one would have thought possible.

'I dare rather more than that. I tell you now that you will not leave this house until you have enjoyed carnal relations with my servants.'

'You are deranged! I must leave this evil place now before I am polluted by its dark sins.'

So saying, Mr Blanking tried to get past us, but at a signal from my husband he was held by John and Franklin. They had an easy task of it as he was but slightly built.

At that moment, Estelle surprised me by revealing that the object she had fetched from her room was a little bottle of ether. She unwrapped it, poured some onto the scarf, and held it to Mr Blanking's face.

'Oh, you can't do that,' I cried.

'On the contrary, it presents no insuperable difficulties,' Estelle replied as Mr Blanking went limp. 'There we are. Look how convenient he is this way – he is almost bearable when he is unconscious.'

'Why do you carry ether in your luggage?' I enquired.

'Ether has many uses,' Estelle replied cheerfully, though it was not much of a reply. 'You shouldn't ask me a lot of questions, Jane. I might accidentally tell you the truth one day, and then where would you be?'

'It is better that he is unconscious,' Robert told me. 'We would have had to imprison him otherwise, and that would have been very awkward. Tomorrow we can introduce him to the pleasures of the flesh, and once he has tasted these he might become addicted to pleasure, and so forgive my debt.'

'Or he might have us put in prison,' I pointed out.

'Of course I am the only one over whom that threat hangs,' my husband assured us. 'If it comes to a trial I shall take all the blame upon myself and exonerate everyone else.'

'I shall blame you and exonerate myself too,' said Estelle. 'So we'll achieve a happy unanimity at our trial.'

Our unfortunate guest, or rather our prisoner, was taken to his room, undressed, and put to bed. It was arranged that he should have a man watching over him for the rest of the night, with the men taking turns. I went to bed, though it was some time before I could get to sleep, as not only was I anxious at this turn of events, but there was a thunderstorm, as though nature were echoing the stormy conflict within our souls. I could not help but imagine my beloved husband going to prison.

I awoke a little late the next morning, though so did Mr Blanking, due to the effects of the ether. The gardens and countryside were fresh and bright, for the rain had cleaned everything and left a cheerful scene for the sun to play on. Mr Blanking awoke, protested, dressed, and came down to breakfast, watched all the while by McBean and Robert.

'Good morning,' I greeted him. 'The kippers are very good, and will you take some toast? It is so good for the digestion.'

'How can you ask me to think of kippers when I am being held captive?' he groaned theatrically.

168

'Can I etherise him again?' Estelle enquired languidly. 'I much prefer him in an unconscious state.'

'Restrain your anaesthetic enthusiasms for the moment,' Robert advised her before turning to Mr Blanking. 'Now then sir, you see we have means of dealing with you should you become unpleasant. For your own sake you had better be cooperative, had you not? Sample a few of the servants and you will be free to go.'

'Sample a few of the servants!' Mr Blanking exclaimed. 'You are asking nothing less than that I assist you in the process of my own damnation to the eternal fires of hell.'

'That's one way of looking at it,' Estelle murmured, and sipped at the brandy she liked to have with her breakfast.

'We propose to help you to enjoy yourself,' Robert told Mr Blanking gently. 'You will be a better, happier man afterwards.'

'And then you think I will cancel my debt to you, I presume?'

'If in gratitude you choose to reduce it in stages, while making visits to this house in order to enjoy erotic pleasures, that is a business arrangement I shall be glad to enter into.'

'You want to besmirch, befoul and pollute me, and send me to hell,' Mr Blanking cried in a voice tense with horror. His face was even whiter than usual, and the piece of toast he held trembled visibly.

'Of course you're a virgin,' sighed Estelle. 'What rotten luck for us. And worse luck for you.'

'Naturally I have never known the touch of women – at least until last night – how could it be otherwise? I am an unmarried man,' Mr Blanking replied indignantly. 'Only a fool would, for brief pleasure, condemn himself to the eternal fires of hell.'

'Shall I etherise him now?' Estelle enquired. She produced the bottle of ether suddenly, with the air of a stage magician.

'Oh, do put that away,' I admonished. 'You are developing a positive mania for making men unconscious, and it is not altogether seemly.'

We all made as good a breakfast of it as we could under the somewhat tense circumstances. Even Mr Blanking had two kippers – they really were very good. There was obviously no time to be lost in initiating him into the delights of eroticism, for his friends and relatives would enquire after him after a while, so we decided to start at once.

Estelle and I left Mr Blanking with Robert and Banks, and went to the large soft room, after sending Edith, who was waiting on table, to tell all the female servants to join us there. When they came we instructed them on what was to be done with Mr Blanking. They went to disrobe and wash, then returned to the soft room in a state of nudity. It was most affecting to see so many young women eager for erotic excitement. I rang the bell, and when Banks came in response, I told him we were ready to receive Mr Blanking. We girls were all very much determined he should not remain a virgin.

He was half-dragged, half-carried to us by Robert, Banks and John. Estelle took the opportunity of asking Banks to bring us some wine, which was rather shocking, as we had only just had breakfast, but she had the excuse that this was a special occasion, and I had to grant there was some truth in this claim.

Mr Blanking was struck dumb with horror to see so many naked young ladies. He was pushed into the room somewhat in the manner of a virgin sacrifice being pushed into the crater of a volcano on some primitive Pacific island. He had been stripped naked

170

by the men for our greater convenience. It was amusing to see his terror of us. He gave a gurgle of fear, and tried to escape through the door, but the men had closed it instantly, and he scrabbled at it in vain.

Here was an interesting situation: eight ladies, full of erotic skills and desires, holding a virgin male captive with the purpose of persuading him to know the delights of female flesh.

Chapter Twelve

Mr Blanking looked at us in our alluring nakedness, then gave a choking cry and burst through the cordon of female bodies almost completely, nearly reaching the window. I do believe he intended to jump, preferring death to dishonour. Fortunately, Mary brought him down with a determined tackle, as though she were an expert rugby player, and he fell back on to a silk-covered mattress. In an instant we were all over him, and we held him down easily enough, he being so slightly built. He became quite hysterical in his fear of bodily contact, so Estelle gave him a whiff of ether – not enough to make him unconscious, but enough to stop him fighting. We kissed and caressed him, and each other. Paying special attention to his male organ, we soon had it in a fine state of rigidity.

The wine arrived, and we were able to make Mr Blanking drink a good quantity of it with the aim of helping him forget his moral objections to erotic enjoyment. He was too dazed from the ether to know what he was drinking, and after that he was too influenced by the wine to know clearly what he was doing, so the situation was already improved.

We ladies also had a little which made us all merry. I cannot say it made us wanton, for we were already wanton. We caressed and kissed our captive male with increasing abandon and passion, rubbing our naked bodies against his, jiggling and squeezing his private parts, and generally indulging in every manner of lewdness. We lay him down and took turns to press our bosoms and nether lips against his face, which became wet with our vaginal flow. Charlotte and Darma suckled on his maleness like babies feeding from their mother's breast.

We enjoyed competing with one another for what was left of his attention. Estelle was especially vigorous in mounting the servants and in having them mount her right next to Mr Blanking, and her loud vocalisation of her rapture was pleasant to hear, even if she was showing off. I parted my legs at her direction and lay back while she went on all fours above me, her head to my tail and vice versa – mainly vice, as matron used to say. I sucked Estelle and she sucked me, a fair enough arrangement, and one that brought me to the heights of rapture. I spent with great force thanks to the hungry voraciousness of my friend's mouth, which indeed seemed to draw my sensitive parts far out against her open lips and between her teeth. What suction! What a tongue! I felt my clitoris sticking right out, and her busy tongue whipped in warm wet circles around it until I nearly fainted with the burning delight of it. How good it is to live, and to feel all that God in his wisdom has allowed us to feel!

We sent for Franklin, the muscular brooding stable man (I never did find out what he was brooding over), and had him plunge his thick organ into Edith, demonstrating many positions to Mr Blanking. For a time Edith rode her brutish partner, and we had Mr Blanking closely watch their united sexual parts. Edith moved vigorously up and down so we could see her nether lips sliding up and down his penis, all shiny with her juices. Lisa frigged Mr Blanking as he witnessed the moving scene of Edith writhing her hips and gasping with delight, holding her own breasts tightly.

Finally Edith knelt before Franklin. We all licked her splendid globes to make them wet and slippery, and then she held them together while Mary held the stable man's shaft and moved his helmet between Edith's breasts, until he spent with great groans, unleashing a fine flood of cream that burst forth in mighty spasms. Charlotte then licked her fellow servant clean while playing with herself.

We sent Franklin away after he had recovered his wits, so that Mr Blanking would not feel intimidated by the presence of such a strong fellow, and then we set about the pleasant task of giving him his first spending at the hands (and other parts) of ladies. He had sufficient presence of mind to make an occasional protest, but it was so feeble we hardly noticed.

The giddy maid, Edith, insisted on being the first to mount him, and you can imagine how glad she was to impale herself on him and move her hips in vigorous actions – back and forth, up and down, round and round. She brought her thighs together to increase the pressure on his organ, and it was a fine sight indeed to see her arching her back and working her powerful thighs and other muscles as she exerted herself with all her strength. On her fair skin glistened a fresh perspiration. Finally she closed her eyes and held herself taut and still like a knife blade against her partner, for she was lost in the throes of ultimate pleasure.

We persuaded Mr Blanking to take a little more wine. Edith was unwilling to get off him, as she was a greedy girl, but we persuaded her to let someone else have a turn on Mr Blanking, so Mary took her place. Darma and Estelle squeezed her breasts as she sat on him. Next she leaned forward over him and held her body raised on her extended arms. She wriggled her shapely behind vigorously so that we had a fine view of Mr Blanking's maleness churning between her long, full nether lips.

I have to admit that we were not thinking so much of saving the house as we were about our own pleasure, but then, that was only natural. Mary now did a clever thing: she turned around a half-circle so that she was facing her partner's feet, and then she bent right down and suckled on his toes. This meant that Mr Blanking could see nothing of her at all save for her strong buttocks moving slowly up and down, with full lips between them that devoured his penis.

It was a stirring sight for any man, even Mr Blanking. His eyes opened wide, and he gave an inarticulate cry, then struggled wildly in our grasps, making a final effort to escape his pleasurable fate. It was all to no avail, for there was no avoiding the reality of his male organ being inside the warm, clutching, juicy vagina of a young woman. He spent with a series of choking gurgles as though he were dying. We knew that he was throwing the essence of his being into Mary's tightness, and it was oddly delightful to have triumphed absolutely over a man's moral scruples. It served him right for putting on airs about being better than the rest of us.

It was also delightful to have given him pleasure, for there is something dreary and pointless about a male virgin. We cuddled him gently when he was finished, comforting him as women are so good at doing. We told him he could be proud now he was a real man, that he had a big cock, and suchlike pleasantries. We ourselves felt proud, and smiled at one another as comrades in erotic combat, victors against a puritanical virgin. Indeed, I thought a woman could have a pleasant time of it seducing innocents and corrupting virgins. Our victory over Mr Blanking was all the sweeter for being hard-won.

He said nothing, but only wept a little, for he took a somewhat unbalanced view of what had occurred, and considered himself damned. We pressed ourselves warmly against his body so that he could not help but grow more accustomed to the feel of naked femle flesh. I fervently hoped that as he was tasting such pleasures for the first time he would naturally hunger for more, and have to have more, and thus enter into the arrangement which David had already accepted. After all, I told myself, after the first time I had been sucked by my bad friend Estelle, the only idea in my mind was to seek a repetition. Never again did I win the school prize for algebra.

Estelle now told Mr Blanking the details of our erotic preferences – in my case, she said I was a Jill of all trades, but I let it pass, as her idea of friendship is that she can insult her friends even more than she can insult strangers – and she also pointed out that he could have a splendid time in the future, coming here and enjoying the servants. She had each girl in turn stand over him, display her buttocks and private parts, and play with herself. She then pointed out the details of their anatomy, as well as their engorgement and lubrication. As he watched this fine show, Charlotte suckled on his maleness and frigged herself, until, withdrawing her mouth in case she bit, she gave herself to the delights of a prolonged orgasm. This amazed Mr Blanking, as he had not known ladies could masturbate and spend.

It struck me that it must interest Mr Blanking to witness dildos being used on a woman, so I had Sally go on all fours, with her huge fat rear above his face, and then I worked a dildo in and out. Mr Blanking was horrified to find that his organ had grown erect again, and grew a little troublesome once more, but the merest whiff of ether made him calmer, and we had him drink a little wine. Then the girls took turns handling and sucking his manhood, and Mr Blanking, in his relaxed state, sighed with pleasure.

'Now you are a real man,' I told him. 'You need not be shy of us any more, for you have tasted our flesh.'

'Yes, and he has a fine big cock if you'll pardon my way of speaking,' said Mary. 'It did me good and proper.'

'If I had a cock like that I'd use it on girls all the time,' Estelle insisted. 'I'd be proud of it.'

'And Mr Blanking will be proud of his soon, I am sure,' said I.

It now seemed a good idea to get him on top of a woman, and Sally, the enormously fat cook, pleaded for the opportunity, which we granted her. She lay down on a mattress and grinned in anticipation, squeezing her own vast breasts. We lifted Mr Blanking up and arranged him on her. Charlotte slipped his organ into its natural setting. He was too dazed to resist us. We all gathered round and enjoyed ourselves pushing and pulling him, as though he were a toy. The motion of his penis inside Sally so pleased Mr Blanking that his instincts took over, and he began thrusting of his own accord, at which we applauded. Sally enjoyed herself immensely, and spent with piggish grunts.

Suddenly Mr Blanking recollected himself, and withdrew from the cook. I told the servants not to try and stop him, as I thought it better if he did not spend just yet, because we could keep him in a state of lustful erection despite himself, and so persuade him to take an interest in matters erotic.

'Now you will enjoy watching another man,' I told

him. We sent for John. 'Think what fun it would be for you to tell him which girl to pleasure, and to advise the couple, or indeed threesome or foursome, how to arrange themselves in their disports. On your future visits you can enjoy yourself so much, directing the pleasures of a whole group, and taking your pleasures here and there exactly as you choose.'

'You can fuck a girl, have two girls suck you, try a girl's breasts, have a man fuck a girl before fucking her yourself, suck a girl while another sucks you, tie Mary up, go from one cunt to another, spunk over the faces of three girls and then start again,' announced Estelle, with somewhat more detail than was necessary. She worked hard at being wicked, and she enjoyed her work. I thought her self-conscious obscenity deplorable, but then again it might have helped to inflame the imagination of Mr Blanking, so I refrained from criticism.

'You are the devil in female form,' gasped our creditor.

'Oh, you flatter me, you sly creature,' replied Estelle.

John, the black handyman, soon arrived. He was in a condition of nudity, and his large ebony organ was in a fine state of readiness for the combat of Eros.

'Oh sir,' Edith appealed to Mr Blanking. 'You are in charge here, we only want to please you. Won't you tell John to give me a good screwing, for I'm sure I need it badly.'

'No, no, I will not,' our captive protested. 'I will not even watch, for it is evil. You cannot make me watch. I can close my eyes, and nothing you can do shall force me to open them.'

This was an irritating idea, for we did not want to be ignored – what would be the point of displaying ourselves to him if he would not even look? Estelle however was quick-witted enough to think of a counter-attack.

'If you close your eyes, I shall force you to open them by having the girls whipped one by one,' she announced. 'You shall hear their piteous screams even if you close your eyes. I shall also force them to take part in every kind of advanced sexual deviation, every bizarre, forbidden, erotic perversion known to man. Then I'll try the ones only women know about. You can spare them this ultimate obscenity merely by agreeing to watch John. I am sure you know where your duty as a Christian gentleman lies.'

'Oh sir, you must save us,' Mary appealed to Mr Blanking. 'I beg you, agree to watch. I want to be a good girl, but I have been corrupted by this house. Just agree to watch, and save me from a whipping.'

In truth she would rather have liked to be whipped a little, as she was such an ardent masochist, but she was cleverly joining in our attempts to make Mr Blanking watch.

'It is clearly my duty to watch,' Mr Blanking conceded in a whisper.

'You are good and kind, sir,' said Mary.

John's maleness was pulsing with every beat of his heart and we briefly discussed what was the best use to make of it.

'Let Charlotte have it,' Sally said at last. 'Look, she's all juicy, but she's too shy to speak up for herself.'

Charlotte blushed deeply, but voiced no denial of her fellow kitchen worker's claim.

'Let it be her,' I agreed.

The other girls concurred – it was touching to see how generous and unselfish they could be, for all of them would have liked to be pleasured by John, and to pleasure him equally in return. During the ensuing scenes of debauchery Mr Blanking did indeed keep his eyes open, and I suspected that he felt a natural curiosity and was not simply giving way to Estelle's threats, for all he doubtless told himself that he was trying to protect the servants from Estelle's wickedness.

John kissed and caressed Charlotte's slight body with real tenderness. It was a fine thing to see such consideration and mutual pleasure. Their bodies were not only strongly contrasted by virtue of skin colour, but also by build, for John was big and muscular while his partner was so thin and short that it looked as though he must hurt her accidentally with the strength of his embrace, but of course this appearance was misleading, for when it comes to matters erotic we women possess a power fuelled by desire which enables us to give as good as we get in the clash of body against body.

Charlotte lay back on a mattress covered with dark yellow silk, her legs open to uncover her private parts, which looked like a mouth hungry for food. How vulnerable she looked! John licked her cunnie for a time, then sank his organ into her welcoming flesh. It was like a conjuring act to see how a tiny young woman accepted that male flesh inside her body. They engaged in a vigorous coupling, her hands clutching tightly at his back, pulling him against her while he reared and plunged like a bull, jerking his maleness back and forth in its juicy confinement. After a time they moved on to their sides, and Charlotte revealed the surprising strength of her small body, moving her slim hips in a strong, satisfying rhythm that filled me with fresh desires.

I saw an opportunity when John rolled on to his back, holding his lithe partner so that she came over on top, where she rode his strong body with a fine frenzy. This gave me a new way to enjoy myself while at the same time adding to the lust we were striving to kindle in our captive. After Charlotte spent with sobbing moans, I had her lean forward, and then I straddled John's thighs at her back and rubbed the sensitive flesh at the base of my belly against the kitchen girl's pert behind. I kissed her shoulders and caressed her flat, yet sensitive, bosom. It was good. I enjoyed caressing someone involved in the act of copulation with a third party.

'How beautiful you do look, ma'am,' exclaimed Edith.

'Pretty as a picture she is,' Sally agreed.

Usually Charlotte was a shy, retiring girl, but at this moment she was transformed by passion, and so could speak thus:

'Let me turn around, ma'am, so that you can have a good time on me.'

I got off for a moment to let her turn around. She let John's maleness slide from her, then quickly moved so that she lay on him face up. It was Edith who took his organ in her hand and inserted it back into Charlotte's vagina. Meanwhile, Mary and Lisa were caressing Mr Blanking in an almost surreptitious manner which did not arouse him to protest.

John was now on his back, with Charlotte lying face up on top of him, their private parts happily engaged. I went on all fours above the kitchen girl and rubbed my body lightly on hers, feeling delicate thrills of pleasure shiver through my flesh from the grazing contacts, which seemed to migrate to the region of my clitoris, where they prospered and multiplied in the manner of a successful colony. We kissed avidly. Not only her hands but also his caressed me. Delightful, delightful.

181

It is especially pleasant to engage with a copulating couple, as the act is so unusual and supposedly wicked. This gives an extra sweetness. Even Mr Blanking's frozen look of disapproving, disbelieving horror was like a spicy sauce that gives added zest to a meal, and I was at that moment grateful for his puritanism, as it gave me a measure against which I could compare myself and so enjoy the exact degree of my wantonness. Everybody has their uses in this world, even Mr Blanking.

After some minutes of this fine sport, Estelle knelt beside me with a dildo in her hands, and pleasured me with it. This added a touch of coarseness to events in my opinion, but it also had the effect of hastening my orgasm. Charlotte reached the depths of pleasure (pleasure has depths as well as heights) soon after, turning her face away and biting her lip. I got off her and was struck by a curious idea, which shows how completely the spirit of that house had entered into my soul.

'Take my place on Charlotte, Edith,' I said. 'I want to try something.'

The maid was on the kitchen girl in a twinkling, and I did a wicked thing: I had Charlotte lift herself slightly, and I pulled John's wet and rigid organ out of her – and then, when both women had lowered themselves, I transferred it into Edith. Mr Blanking had a clear view of the three sets of private parts, and he literally groaned in horror and disgust at what I had achieved. His own organ was rigid, and it was clear from his expression that he was fascinated by these somewhat unorthodox proceedings.

'Oh, how good it feels!' cried Edith, writhing around so that she, Charlotte and John were all stimulated. She did not put her full weight on her fellow servants, as this might not have been quite comfortable for John, even though Charlotte was so very insubstantial.

'How disgusting!' Estelle commented approvingly. She was making love with Darma in a manner notable for its gentleness.

'I've only just started,' said I, for my imagination was in a state of activity. I took hold of the base of John's penis and moved my fingers up and down while squeezing tightly. Soon I moved him back into Charlotte, moving his cock in and out of her manually while he and Charlotte lay still. I kept moving his organ back and forth between Edith and Charlotte, so giving John the experience of being frigged by me while at the same time enjoying two girls in turn. Was this not rather clever of me?

John gasped with delight as he used his powerful muscles to thrust up at first one woman, then another, while all the time my hands played with not only the base of his shaft but also his big dark balls. He looked happy.

'I wonder which one he'll spend in?' Sally mused. 'Have you decided yet, ma'am?'

'He shall spend in both, and in my hand,' I asserted boldly. This caused a great flurry of interest among the servants, for they all wanted to see if such a fine ambition could be realised.

After a great deal of enjoyment, John finally reached the point of no return. His maleness was then in Edith, but it was obvious from his loud cries and groans that he had begun to ejaculate. I pulled him out and gripped the shaft of his penis tightly. A great gout of cream erupted, spraying and splashing over Edith's shapely buttocks. I stabbed him into Charlotte and he gave a loud cry as he shot once more, then I took him out again and instantly slipped him into Edith's cunnie, feeling his spasm between my clenching fingers. I left him there a few seconds, then slipped him out and squeezed his shaft in both of my hands while his final spasms shot cream over Edith's back in long streaks. It had been a prolonged and powerful orgasm, and it had taken place inside two women and in my hands. It was a memorable occasion. The applause of the servants, was, I believe, heartfelt.

Charlotte and Edith got off John, who was in a dazed state, and proceeded to lick and suck one another, laying on their sides with their heads between one another's legs. Sally went to lie with her favourite, John, cuddling him and calling him a fine man. Mary's hand crept to Mr Blanking's organ and began to manipulate it with knowing skill. Could any man return to celibacy after witnessing such stirring scenes? That was the key question.

He came near to spending as he watched the girls lick one another. Estelle and I conferred in whispers, then had Darma go to the sofa on which he sat. We hoped that her great charms would tempt him into enjoying her of his own free will.

Shuddering with desire and horror, he clutched at Darma's naked body as she straddled him. Mary slipped his penis inside her and she rode him, straddling him as he sat on the sofa. He could not bring himself to push her away, though clearly he thought he should. She proffered him a breast, and he took the nipple between his lips with a sob. The Indian beauty clearly clenched her highly trained vaginal muscles, for he groaned and rolled his head, actually banging it on the back of the sofa like a man being tortured.

It was impossible that he could last long in this feverish state, and soon he was spending with the cries of a wild animal caught in a trap.

'I have possessed an adulterous woman,' he sobbed a minute later. 'I am damned for all eternity.'

'Never mind, sir,' Edith said in her artless way. 'At least you'll be damned as a real man.'

'And if you believe that you're damned,' said Estelle, 'you can now enjoy yourself without fear of further repercussions.'

Darma kissed and comforted him – she was a good-hearted young woman – and after a few minutes he cried himself to sleep like a child, due to the after effects of spending so strongly combining with those of the wine and ether. Darma gracefully moved off him and we watched him in his slumbers.

'I do believe we're making some progress with him,' I said.

'I do hope so ma'am,' John told me fervently. 'For this house is a wonderful place to live, and that's the truth of it.'

We amused ourselves quietly for an hour or so until Mr Blanking woke up, at which time we all went down for luncheon. Mr Blanking insisted on dressing, but the rest of us did not bother, as it was such a hot day. The women servants went to their dining room, and John escorted Mr Blanking until Robert met us and took over this duty. Estelle and I enjoyed erotic activities with the lower classes, but we did not wish to go so far as to actually eat with them, as it would hardly have been proper or desirable.

Robert was delighted that we were making some progress with Mr Blanking. I told my husband this good news privately, because if Mr Blanking heard me say such a thing it would only inspire him to be contrary and stubborn.

'How long do you intend to keep me here, sir?' Mr Blanking demanded. I fear his mind was not on the pleasant cold collation we had laid on the table.

'Not long,' Robert assured him. 'If we held you here a long time, it would only vex you, and so make you even more determined not to agree to our proposals.'

'Are you not ashamed that you encourage your wife to take part in such sinful orgies as I have today – unfortunately – witnessed?'

'On the contrary,' Robert stated, taking me by the hand. 'I am highly proud of my dear Jane. She has shown herself to be the ideal mate for me: a strong, sensuous woman capable of independent eroticism and daring, fearless acts. She is a triumphant female warrior, and I love her more than words can say.'

Reader, these generous words of my husband warmed my soul, and made me more determined than ever that he should not suffer the humiliation of being turned out of his home.

'Mr Blanking,' said Robert, 'I have a proposal which I think will interest you. It is an opportunity for you to regain your freedom this very day.'

'I desire nothing more – but I presume you will attach unreasonable conditions.'

'Not so unreasonable. I hope you will see that you can benefit by accepting. You can leave on the train to Norwich at 7 p.m. All you have to do is give us orders to put on a show for you, a show of an erotic nature featuring copulation, masturbation, and sucking. You will give us all instructions and we will be your puppets. The only point to be borne in mind is that Estelle will only touch other ladies, not men.'

'That is the only point, is it?' Mr Blanking exclaimed in an impolite, sarcastic manner. 'And what is the alternative?'

'The alternative is that we keep you here as long as we can fend off the mounting concerns of your friends and relatives. A week, ten days. We will keep you here, and you will have to witness every sexual act we can think of, which believe me is quite a number. You will witness advanced deviations and bizarre obscenities, and you will be tempted to join in. If you are a truly virtuous Christian, it is clearly your duty to give us instructions this afternoon, for by doing so you will save yourself and the women of this house from a prolonged orgy. If you refuse, you are actually choosing the longer period of debauchery.'

A short silence followed these impressive words. I saw Mr Blanking's face go white as he faced this unique situation. It was Estelle who was first to speak.

'I do hope you refuse,' she announced. 'I'd rather have a long orgy than follow your instructions for an afternoon. You're bound to give us something boring to do.'

'How,' enquired Mr Blanking, 'do I know for sure that you will let me leave this evening if I do tell you what to do this afternoon?'

'You have my word,' Robert replied. 'And please do not doubt my word,' he added quickly, in a dangerous tone. 'I would be considerably annoyed if you did. So, there you have it. You have only to think where you want us to perform this erotic show, and what you want us to do. You will instruct us, we shall obey, and then in the evening you may leave.'

We awaited Mr Blanking's reply with keen interest. I understood that my husband's aim in making this proposal was to get our creditor to direct a group of attractive young ladies and gentlemen in their erotic actions, and in so doing discover such a sense of pleasure and power that he would be eager to repeat the experience, and would have to forgive our debts in order to do so. I thought it a fine, bold plan, for after all it was an exciting idea indeed to tell a man to spend here, or a woman to adopt such and such a position and give to some man her splendid naked body. Heavens, I wanted to do it myself. Very much.

'I envy you such an opportunity,' I told Mr Blanking.

'You shall do it yourself one day, my dear,' Robert assured me with a smile.

Mr Blanking looked at us both as though we were insane, then gave his reply with a sullen reluctance.

'I accept your proposal. I must, as it is the lesser of two evils. To refuse to choose would be a sin of omission. It is my duty to save these poor fallen women from further sins. I only pray that God will forgive me – and that you will keep your word.'

I saw Robert clench his fist, and I sensed he was sorely tempted to give Mr Blanking a sound thrashing in return for the fellow's doubting his honour. I held his wrist for a few seconds, until he was calm.

'Now then Mr Blanking, you only have to chose where you would like to start,' he said. 'We have an excellent bathroom, and the room where you passed time this morning is also a pleasant choice. The garden is also a possible setting. Of course, we may move from one to the other. You might like to start with a small group and work up to a bigger one. Would you like an hour to lay your plans?'

Mr Blanking hesitated. A pleased expression slowly spread over his features. To see Mr Blanking looking pleased was not one of the great joys of my life.

'There is no need to delay,' he said. 'I have an idea. Am I to understand that you will follow my directions whatever they may be.'

'Yes, so long as there is no danger in them,' Robert replied. 'And excepting Estelle, as I explained before. We are yours.'

'Even if what I tell you to do humiliates and dirties you?'

'Yes, even then.'

'Then I know what I want you to do,' said Mr

188

Blanking. There was no doubting the fact that he was excited by his own idea. 'It is my clear duty to make you see the error of your ways, to make you see that the sins of the flesh make you descend into the mire. God has placed this opportunity in my hands.'

'He's thought of something jolly nasty,' Estelle said. She grinned.

'In the corner of your garden wall is a pond,' Mr Blanking stated. 'It looks extremely muddy. I want you all to dress up in your sinful finery – indulge your vanity to the utmost – and then go down into the filth and mud like beasts. I will direct you to act in a way that will shock you with the horror of your own sins, of your own lives. This conjunction of physical dirt and moral corruption will make you see just how be-smirched you truly are. I may by this means be able to bring you to repent – yes, I see my duty clearly. Well, do you accept this challenge, or do you fear that by this humiliation your servants will see the light, and repent of their wickedness?'

'Of course we accept,' my husband said at once. He squeezed my hand. 'Don't worry Jane. The mud will be pleasantly cooling, as it is so very hot today.'

I understood that he wanted Mr Blanking to have his way with us so as to try and lure him further down the path of wantonness. It was a desperate at-tempt, and our chances of success seemed absurdly slim.

Chapter Thirteen

We broke the news to the servants. They were taken aback. Robert said he would understand if any of them did not want to go through with this muddy erotic drama, which Mr Blanking had invented for the purpose of humiliation.

'Excuse me sir,' asked Edith, 'but do the drains from the house go into that pond? I mean, is it clean dirt or dirty dirt?'

My husband was able to reassure everyone on this crucial point: the drains went the other way, into the river, which had no connection with the ornamental pond in our garden. All the servants then evinced their complete willingness to become muddy. It was a touching scene. We told them that Mr Blanking wanted them to dress up in their finest clothes, but suggested they wore their second best instead. They muttered harsh words about that puritanical gentleman, who did not care if he spoiled their clothes, and I could not but agree in my heart.

We separated to dress in our own rooms. I put on a light blue silk dress with French lace trimmings, a dress I no longer liked, while Robert wore one of his finest tweed suits. Estelle was wearing one of her favourite gowns, a very expensive creation in creamy silk that would be ruined by the mud and green slime of the pond. She wore it cheerfully, to defy Mr Blanking's assumption that we would care what happened to our fine clothes.

'He will try to revenge himself on us,' I observed nervously.

'Of course he will,' Estelle responded. She smiled. 'That is what makes this so amusing. He will be trying to humiliate us, telling himself it is his Christian duty, and in so doing he will enjoy himself despite himself. He will be hoist by his own petard, with any luck. And for my part I am determined to enjoy myself.'

We three went downstairs to rendezvous with the servants and Mr Blanking – John and Franklin had been in charge of him. The sun was positively blazing, so the ladies all wore hats. Estelle and I also carried parasols for further protection against its unfortunate skin-darkening properties. We all went outside and walked through the garden towards the pond, like a valiant troop of soldiers going to do battle in the mud. I must confess to experiencing the most ticklish feeling of curiosity as to how this slippery mud would feel on my body, and I keenly wondered what Mr Blanking had in his puritanical mind. Certainly I could not justly complain, as so many ladies do, that my life lacked variety of incident.

We waited at the edge of the lawn where it gave way to the muddy fringe of the pond and awaited Mr Blanking's instructions.

'Mrs Shawnecrosse,' he addressed me, 'I feel it is my duty to single you out for special treatment. You are of the upper orders, and it is one of your prime roles in life to set a good example to those placed by God beneath you, so that they might not wander from the narrow path of righteousness. Instead you have been a leader in licentiousness. The same is true of you, Miss Havisham.'

'Thank you,' said Estelle, as though acknowledging a compliment.

'It is only fitting that your servants should see the two of you punished by having to wallow in filth like the beasts of the field, and so come to realise that the sins of the flesh leave permanent stains on the body and soul. Forbidden pleasure and a descent into the glutinous mire are one and the same thing. Go, you unrighteous pair! Step into the dark pit of filth that is a foretaste of the damnation that awaits you unless you repent.'

'Gosh,' murmured Estelle. Vastly amused by this speech, she winked at me. We folded our parasols and handed them to Robert, then gingerly stepped onto the edge of the mud, which at first was dry and hard, cracked into biscuits by the heat of the summer sun. I felt a strong sense of trepidation, so strong in fact that it made the lower part of my belly tingle as though it were being caressed – my mother had always insisted on the highest standards of cleanliness, and it was curiously thrilling to deliberately get dirty. When one added the consideration that Mr Blanking was going to direct us in some erotic act intended to humiliate us, one had a situation that was not altogether without its interesting aspects.

With every step we took, the mud grew damper, until we reached the water's edge. We paused. Mr Blanking looked excited. At the water's edge the mud was wet, sticky, and dark brown.

'Take one step into the water and filth!' exclaimed Mr Blanking.

We did so. The mud was very soft, and I squealed as my foot sank in. I instinctively stepped back onto firmer ground.

'Don't be a coward,' Estelle admonished me, as she so often had on the hockey field.

'You're right, I must not give Mr Blanking the satisfaction of being afraid of a little mud,' I muttered, and stepped back into the shallow water beside my friend.

I thought that this was a fine way for two refined young ladies to be treated. Here we were in England, the model of civilisation for the entire world, in the progressive late nineteenth century, and we were being sent fully dressed into the mud.

'You have sinned greatly, and must be made to see and feel that immorality and filth are one and the same thing,' our tormentor said with mounting excitement. It was very provoking to follow the directions of this fool who thought he was better than us, but I was comforted by the hope that soon he would come to realise he was no better. 'You shall see yourselves as you truly are under all your finery – dirty beasts, animals smeared in every kind of filth. Vanity, all is vanity. God has sent me here to punish you, and I must do His will. Accept his punishment with due humility, and see yourselves as you truly are beneath your finery. Acknowledge Him! Become beasts of the field. Go on, throw mud at one another. Dig your fine ladies' hands into the mire and throw filth at one another. Throw, I say! Reveal unto us the true noxious filth of your immoral, sinful, corrupt beings.'

I was annoyed by his criticism, which put me in no mood to obey him, and besides, I was not accustomed to standing in a muddy pond and throwing mud at anyone – not even at Estelle, who deserved it more than most.

So I hesitated. As for Estelle, she gleefully seized the opportunity for fun, to which she might be said to take the attitude of a naughty child. She scooped up a handful of brown ooze and flung it at me as though she had been awaiting the opportunity for several years.

'A mud fight!' she exclaimed.

The nasty mess spattered all over my light blue dress, and a few drops even went on my face. I gasped in shock, for I had not expected even Estelle to behave so deplorably. Before I could pull myself together she had thrown a second handful, but she was over-eager, and most of it missed me. Naturally I could not accept that my friend should triumph over me in any conflict, for it is truly said that it is easier to bear the success of one's enemies than that of one's friends. All my scruples against touching mud vanished. I took some in my hand and flung it at her, but, typically, she dodged aside with such cowardly adroitness that she was untouched.

This was most vexing. You can imagine the strength of my feelings when that bad girl dug both hands in to the wrists and flung a great spray of mud and water at me. It went high, and I bent down and angled my head so that most of it spattered noisily all over my broad white hat. However, a considerable quantity dirtied the upper part of my body.

All my ladylike qualms about touching mud deserted me. I became a savage, because I could not bear the thought of my best friend scoring over me. My best friend in all the world, formerly my hockey captain in many a thrilling game, the chess champion whom we girls had applauded so warmly when she led the team that beat our hated rival school in a tournament, my dearest confidante to whom I had whispered all my secrets, the person who had initiated me into the delightful pleasures of the flesh – naturally I was furiously determined to utterly smother her in mud and take the silly smile off her irritating face.

Her next handful was a good one, splashing all over the front of my dress in big patches and streaks of runny browns, with some bright green slime. Estelle laughed. Pulling a nasty face, she stuck her tongue out at me. This was intolerable. I dug both my hands deep into the mire, withdrew them with a large scoop of mud, and took a few steps closer to Estelle to make sure of my target before throwing the whole mess of glutinous ooze all over her expensive white silk dress, ruining it in an instant. This was one of the most satisfying moments of my life. I was delighted to see that she was momentarily nonplussed, looking down at herself as though amazed that anyone should dare to defile such a fine young lady as herself, but I gave her little time for reflection, as I flung a fresh gob of muck over her Parisian creation, making her squeal like an unhappy piglet.

She recovered quickly, and caught me in the face with her next delivery, if I may use a cricketing term. A little went into my left eye, so that I had to bend down and wash it with pond water. As I did so, I heard the repressed giggles of Edith and John, for which disrespect I can hardly blame them, as I must have presented a ludicrous sight.

Estelle, expert in treachery, crept up on me unawares and liberally smothered my back in mud while I was bending down. She then hurried away. I recovered my sight and ran after her, throwing mud. She dodged well, but then justice caught up with her for once in her life, as she tripped over a tree root and fell headlong in the shallow water with a mighty splash. I might have felt sorry for her, had I not been so pleased.

'Serves you right!' I exclaimed.

'What a beast you are, Jane!' cried Estelle. 'And you never were any good at hockey. I should have thrown you off the team and given your place to Nellie.'

'You've always been jealous of me because I'm better looking than you,' I replied.

We both bent down and threw mud and water at each other in earnest. Here I should remind the reader that we were in Norfolk, a county singularly bereft of stones. A mud fight in Yorkshire would be a more risky proposition.

Out of the corner of my eye I noticed Mr Blanking staring at us with absorption. The truth is that he was fascinated by the spectacle of two attractive young ladies becoming filthy, and I hoped he might indeed become trapped in an erotic snare of his own making. Indeed, all through our lives the most dangerous snares for us are the ones we make ourselves.

Estelle and I now partook of a perfect frenzy of mud-slinging, deluging one another with glutinous brown ooze. I was immensely pleased to see my dear friend covered in muck, and my triumph was not spoilt by the knowledge that I no doubt presented the same picture. After a couple of minute we were exhausted by our exertions, and fell into a ceasefire. Panting for breath, we were simultaneously struck by the ludicrousness of the situation, and joined in united laughter.

'Nellie was a rotten hockey player really,' said Estelle. 'She lacked your determination and bad temper.'

'And you need be jealous of no lady in the world,' said I. 'As you know all too well, you mirror-loving creature.'

Overcome with emotion at the renewal of our status as best friends, we embraced.

By the by, to stand there in wet clothes was not unhealthy, for it was such a hot day that any cooling effect was welcome.

'Now you are to strip off your soiled finery and

expose your corrupt nudity to the filth,' Mr Blanking said in a voice vibrant with erotic excitement. He thought he was punishing us, but actually he was arousing himself, as my extremely clever husband had hoped. 'You like to wallow in debauchery in a naked state, so now you can embrace the dirt of the world in that state also, to understand and illustrate the stains that besmirch your very souls. Filthy, filthy ladies!'

It was quite a task for Estelle and I to undress, for not only were our fingers slippery with slime, but the many little clasps and buttons of our garments were clogged and concealed. We largely undressed each other, one squatting in the pond while the other undid and pulled off an item of clothing, then reversing roles so that we kept pace with one another in our slow disrobing. The skin that we revealed was largely clean and white, for our dresses had protected it from the mud, but rivulets soon ran down from our wet faces, hair and hands. Gradually we took off our boots, underclothes, corsets, and stockings, until finally we were naked save for our broad-brimmed hats which we kept on, for, of course, no lady would risk having a sun-darkened skin. At Mr Blanking's insistence however, we unpinned our hair, throwing the pins, as we had our garments, on to the lawn. It was an emotional moment for Estelle to loose her gorgeous long auburn tresses, and for me to let down my no less fine golden hair. We were exposing our crowning glories, laying them down as sacrifices to a man's perversity.

'Now go down in the mud and caress one another with it,' said the nasty little man. 'You have enjoyed these caresses before, under the illusion that you were clean, but now you shall see and feel and smell the filth and corruption that is in every contact of flesh.'

Estelle and I looked at one another. Abruptly she dropped down on all fours and wriggled her shapely bottom at me. It looked very fine, curving out like a violin from her narrow waist.

'Smear me, Jane,' she requested.

You had to admire a young lady so spirited that, naked in the mud, she could offer such cheerful defiance of decency and modesty. I put my hand in the mud, then placed it on her behind, making a splendid brown palm print on her left buttock. She wriggled her behind again and smiled at her audience.

'Estelle, don't tease the men too much,' I protested.

'Who's teasing the men? I'm only teasing the ladies,' she replied. This was rather too nice a distinction to make, but then perhaps the men were not altogether adverse to being teased by an unobtainable woman. If everything were obtainable, the world might lose some of its lustre, and seem dreary.

I noticed that all the men had significant bulges in their trousers, including Mr Blanking. I felt I should strive to create unforgettable images for him to absorb, so that he would not be able to refuse our offer, so I accordingly made a slow and sensuous job of muddying my friend's delightful young body. First I put my hands and wrists deep into the ooze so that I seemed to be wearing shiny brown leather gloves that reached almost to my elbow, and then I delicately dirtied Estelle's curvaceous form, making long streaks on her thighs and back so that she resembled a tigress – well, a muddy tigress – and then I heaped a great quantity of muck over her shoulder-blades. I had her stand up, and the stuff ran down her in streams, rivers of dirt flowing over white female skin. Her hair, still largely clean, hung over and glowed reddish gold in the sunlight. It was piquant.

I worked mud into the front of her body while she

stood hand on hips, superb in her insolent posture. I gave her shapely breasts a good massage, then her belly and thighs. My tender application of the slippery, cooling balm clearly left her not unmoved. Her nipples were rigid, sticking out from her firm high breasts all gleaming with mud. I smeared her private parts with ooze, and she thrust herself against my hand. As she concentrated on her own pleasure, the tip of her tongue stuck out between her lips and looked very pink by contrast with her dirty face.

Now Estelle applied mud to me as I stood still. She used an individual method, first coating her breasts copiously, then rubbing them all over my body, a provocative action that made some men literally gasp with lust. She lifted my hair when she worked on my back, so that golden waves hung about my shining wet body.

'Now smear one another's hair, you harlots,' Mr Blanking cried in a passion of misogyny. 'If you want to embrace one another sinfully, first you must dirty each other's crowning glories. Admit that your lives are filth!'

'We will do it to arouse him, though he knows it not,' whispered Estelle.

We sat down in the water like grubby naiads, gathered mud in our hands, and smeared it on each other's hair, tress by tress. Mr Blanking seemed to find this particularly exciting. (If Mr Sigmund Freud knew Mr Blanking, he would find him a valuable object of study.)

'And now that you are smeared with the filth of sinfulness, choose,' cried Mr Blanking. 'Choose between a joyful cleansing in the clean waters of righteousness, or a perverse coupling of two women in the mire.'

'Thats a difficult decision,' said Estelle, pretending to ponder. Suddenly she laughed, and pounced on to me. She pressed her body against mine, and we sank down into the mud and water, our hands busy with one another's sweet flesh, our mouths together, our legs intertwined as we thrust our thighs against each other's private parts. We spent most joyously.

'You have made the wrong choice,' Mr Blanking said in a voice husky with desire when we had finished and lay sighing in one tight and squelchy embrace. 'Now it is my duty to try once more to make you see the darkness and corruption inherent in your sinful mode of existence. You, Mrs Shawnecrosse, shall use your hands to relieve the terrible lusts of these male servants who have been witnessing this disgraceful exhibition. That will be a lesser sin than your usual acts of adulterous copulation, so I will have saved you from that at least. Now, filthy as you already are, you shall be further besmirched by the vile seminal excretions of your servants. Surely you must see the light that shines in contrast to this darkness! Since there are a lot of men, you may have one of the female servants to help you.'

'Oh, let me do it ma'am, do let me,' Edith cried out. It was just like that giddy girl to be eager to indulge in such an extreme of erotic activity.

'You raving nincompoop, don't you even know that the agent of the Lord is punishing you?' Mr Blanking groaned in disbelief. 'You men, undress the slut, and be quick about it.'

Edith was quickly stripped by Franklin, McBean and John, and then she came white and naked into the pond. She looked very clean. Estelle and I looked at her, then at one another, and then we fell on Edith with one mind, dragging her down into the filth as though we were a pair of evil water sprites. We smeared her curvaceous young body all over with the shiny brown mud. She giggled and squealed.

Mr Blanking then had McBean, Banks and Robert undress. They stripped very quickly, as they were filled with lust. They came naked towards us, displaying huge erections. Here I was, muddy and naked in a pond with a trio of excited men advancing on me with lecherous intent. I could not help but feel proud.

We three girls had to laugh as we muddied the men, bringing them down to our level so to speak. Edith and I smeared them, while Estelle was happy to throw mud at them in liquid spatterings. I rubbed my muddy breasts on Robert. It felt good. It looked as though the men's organs might burst apart, so bloated and stretched did they appear in the ferocity of their lust.

'My dear, you must satisfy me,' stated Robert.

I hastened to wet my hands with fresh mud to caress his yearning phallus, making sure there were no little twigs that would cause him distress. With a feeling of worshipping the one I love, I knelt before my husband and placed both hands on his organ, gently writhing lubricated fingers around his helmet while pumping his shaft. I saw that Edith had similarly taken in hand the gardener, McBean, but she was a little unorthodox in that she had Banks in the other, and was frigging them both at the same time. The men sighed and moaned with delight as the oozing brown lubricant dripped from her strong fingers.

The issue could not be in any doubt, nor long delayed. McBean was the first, venting great quantities of cream in powerful long spurts that spattered over Edith's breasts. With her blue eyes wide open, she gazed up hungrily at the shuddering man as if to share in his ecstasy. It was a curiously beautiful sight. She knelt there in the shallow water, sunlight gleaming on her mud-coated body like a vision of the world's youth with all the falseness and artificiality of our modern age stripped away to leave only the real.

'Would you like to take Banks?' asked Robert. 'Be a kind girl and give him to my wife, Edith.'

The maid grinned and handed the butler's penis over to me, so that for the first time I had a man in each hand. This was a moment when I envied no one. I laughed for sheer love of life, and tried hard to give the men absolute delight with my strong grip and slithery caresses, while Edith knelt behind the lucky fellows and plied her muddy hands around their buttocks and thighs.

By a happy chance, my husband and Banks spent together. It was most interesting to have their leaping sperm shower me from both sides, and I felt most triumphantly wanton as the stuff ran down my body in myriad streams. The groans of the men were moving, and I felt proud of myself. The spectators actually burst into applause, except of course for gloomy Mr Blanking. Coated in mud and male spending, I felt a pleasing sense of achievement.

'You look pleased with yourself!' Mr Blanking exclaimed in horror. 'So you think it's admirable to wallow in filth and corruption, do you?' He shouted so hysterically that he woke up Lisa's baby Arnold, who had been sleeping under the shade of a tree. Lisa went to comfort him.

'Then you might as well all go into the mud,' cried our boorish creditor. 'Embrace your sins in the filth.'

This tiresome man's keen disapproval actually added to our enjoyment, for if a thing is worth doing at all, it is certain that someone will disapprove of it. The remaining servants, save for Lisa, began stripping. We, in the pond, urged them on, and caressed ourselves and each other in order to excite them further. As they became naked one by one, we pulled them into the mud and smeared their flesh.

John had Sally go on all fours, and took her from

behind with a fine show of manly vigour, while Franklin lay back with Darma squatting over his face and Charlotte riding his maleness – the kitchen girl was like a frail deer coupling with a great bear. It was a splendid pleasure to have such servants and to enjoy the huge range of combinations possible amongst so many fine women and men. I thought how tragic it would be to lose them and our home, and, on looking at Mr Blanking, I felt we had made him angry. The reader may wonder why Robert and I did not feign repentance, tell Mr Blanking we had felt the hand of God, and so try to persuade our creditor to forgive our debt in a Christian spirit. In fact we could not have done any such thing, as neither Robert nor I would mock our Creator with such cynical trickery.

I grew all the more determined to enjoy myself, feeling we would certainly lose the house, so accordingly I jumped on Estelle from behind, startling her out of her wits and knocking her sprawling into the mud. This helped console me for the loss of my home. She was not long angry with me, for I let her smear me with fresh mud and then ride my body while I lay back on the soft mattress of ooze. We seemed to be burrowing down into the softness, as though searching for an erotic antipodes.

Robert meanwhile had a playful idea. He took a bucket from the edge of the lawn and filled it with liquid mud behind Mary's back, then emptied the whole load over her shoulders from behind. She cried out with the shock of it. She was riding McBean at the time, and that most excellent of gardeners laughed good-naturedly.

John and Sally meanwhile reached the peaks of ecstasy together. The handyman rode the fat cook with splendid vigour, shooting his vital fluid into her core while she writhed in the mud, rubbing her huge breasts against the invigorating slime. They made loud squelching noises which mingled with their cries.

Charlotte and Darma enjoyed several orgasms before Franklin, and when he finally spent he arched and thrashed about in the mud as though he were being murdered. The ladies ground their nether parts against his face and around his penis. As Franklin jetted inside her, Charlotte laid her hands on her belly, her mouth open in wonder at the force of the man's ejaculation. His cries were somewhat muffled by Darma's backside, yet still they were loud and thrilling. Estelle knelt in front of Darma and caressed her breasts, brown mud shining on darker brown skin.

Everybody was doing rude things in the mud, but I cannot describe them all, for in every narrative there must be a selection of incident. I am confident that the reader may use his or her imagination to good effect here, where so many interesting women and men are gathered together in such an unorthodox setting.

We all paused to draw breath. I saw that Mr Blanking was standing still and staring at us, with an expression of mingled disgust, hatred, and yearning. Lisa approached him diffidently. Her baby, Arnold, had fallen asleep again in his cot under an ancient oak. This young and gentle mother now showed a concern and sympathy for Mr Blanking, which, I assure the reader, had nothing whatsoever to do with the house or the debt – she was all womanly and Christian in her kindness, she simply felt sorry for Mr Blanking at seeing him so aloof from all the fun.

'Sir,' spoke she, 'will you not come into the mud with me? You see the others are having a fine time. I want to try it too. I think the mud must be very cool on such a hot day, and then it does look so slippery.'

'I cannot join them – mine is the path of righteousness.'

'You are lonely, sir, and it will do you good to spend,' Lisa stated, and took him by the hand. Wonder of wonders, he let her hold his hand and looked at her as though she might be able to impart wisdom.

'I have failed,' Mr Blanking sighed as I approached him. 'I thought that going down into the filth would make you repent, but instead you enjoyed yourselves.'

'The mud feels so good!' Edith exclaimed in her giddy way, idly caressing her breasts with the oozing stuff.

'With respect sir,' said Banks, 'it might be that corruption of the soul does not form a perfect analogy with commonplace mud. Might one not say that to play in the mud like this is a childlike activity, which might be taken to show purity of heart. I respectfully suggest that you join us in the spirit of a happy child.'

'Yes, do join us, come on sir,' was the chorus of cries from the staff. In truth we all felt sorry for him, as he seemed so incapable of enjoying himself.

'I am a sinner, so it is not right for me to put myself above my fellow sinners,' Mr Blanking sighed. 'I should join you in the slimy ooze and fetid filth as a way of abasing myself, of chastising my flesh.'

We helped him out of his clothes and put them on the lawn. He was passive. His male organ was standing at attention. Lisa, who had also undressed, went down on her knees and kissed it, then squeezed it between her breasts.

'What would you like, sir?' she asked him. 'Tell us how you would like to take us, and we shall be so glad. We are all friends together now, you and us.'

Mr Blanking was silent for a few seconds, and then he stared at his own pulsing maleness and gave a deep groan, as though its great lust was a wound to his heart.

'Yes, I must go down into the filth, for I too am a sinner,' he sighed. 'I see now that when I told you to go into the mud, I did so because I wanted to see young naked ladies get muddy, which is not quite the same thing as trying to make you repent.'

'Take me sir, take me,' cried Sally, lying down on her back and opening her legs wide to reveal her cavernous vulva.

Mr Blanking stared at this enormous female for a moment, then abruptly fell on her like a puppet whose strings have been cut. Sally helped him get inside her huge body, and then they set to with a fine vigour, with accompanying sounds of squelching, splashing and grunting. It was an inspiring sight to see him acting naturally at last, and I felt a surge of joy and hope. Lisa knelt beside him and smeared herself as well as him with mud, not to humiliate him but to please him with its slippery coolness. Darma, Charlotte and I joined in, stroking and caressing each other and every part of him while he rutted.

Suddenly he surprised us all by seizing Darma and transferring his penis from Sally to her in one swift motion, as though he had been doing such things for years. She lay back and he rode her splendidly before enjoying Lisa from behind. She wriggled under him and moaned with pleasure as he buried his hands in the soft mud to hold her breasts, and then he gave a savage cry of triumph as he voided his seed into her welcoming embrace.

We were all so glad to witness this moving scene that we cheered, and I prayed that he would join us in the future and forgive our debt, not merely for our sakes, but also for his own.

After another hour or so's further amusements in the mud, we washed off as much as we could in the deeper part of the pond and then went indoors. The servants washed in their own bathroom, while we gentlemen and ladies used the luxurious, one might say heathenish (Mr Blanking did in fact say it) bathroom upstairs with which the reader is fully acquainted. We dried and got dressed. Mr Blanking was very quiet all this time, which I thought was a result of his having had such an enjoyable day. We descended to the library.

'Mr Blanking,' said my husband, 'you have now sampled a little of what we have to offer here.' Robert looked, as I felt, confident that this second creditor must now forgive the debt. 'I only hope you can bring yourself to forgive the way in which we – at first – forced you to sample these pleasures. I hope you will agree that the end result is a happy one, for now surely you will have a better life.'

'Yes, the end result may be a better life for me,' Mr Blanking agreed in a tone of melancholic meditation. He stared at Herbert, a splendid example of the feline race indeed, who had just entered the library, but I do not believe he even saw him.

My husband and I exchanged uneasy glances.

'May we take it as settled that you are willing to accept my offer?' asked Robert. 'You will cancel my debt to you in as small instalments as you please, and in return you may come here and enjoy our hospitality, which is of a highly satisfying nature, as you have experienced.'

'Indeed I am grateful to you,' said our creditor, but in the same funereal tone.

I sensed something – perhaps everything – was wrong.

'I am grateful to you,' Mr Blanking repeated, 'because you have made me see my own true nature at last. Until now I have made the mistake – no, committed the sin – of regarding myself as being better than other men. I believed myself to be pure and righteous. Today I have learned that I am as great a sinner as any. I bade you enter the filth of that pond and I was aroused by what I witnessed. I could not resist falling on those pathetic fallen women like a beast of the field. And I know that once having tasted such animal pleasures, I shall be unable to resist their temptation in the future also, so long as I am in the company of women.'

'So you will join us?' I enquired hopefully, though in truth his dark tone had struck fear in me.

'No, Mrs Shawnecrosse, I shall never join you in your sins,' stated the dreadful man.

'We are undone!' I cried in despair. 'I shall swoon. Oh, we shall lose our home – where shall we live? And what of the poor servants?'

'Sir, you are not a gentleman to upset my poor friend so,' Estelle stated coldly. She used sign language to indicate to me that I must cry a great deal, in order to soften his heart, or whatever he used instead of a heart.

'Calm yourself,' Mr Blanking stated. 'I said that I would not join you in your sins, not that I would refuse to forgive your debt. I see more clearly now, and I know that as I am at heart a great sinner, I must strive harder to be more of a true Christian. You have wronged me, but I must forgive you your debt. I must place myself beneath the heel of the world and let it crush me, to prove that I only care about the kingdom of Heaven.'

'My dear fellow!' Robert cried. 'For whatever reason you forgive our debt, you are welcome to visit us any time. We will be glad to see you – we will teach our children that you are a fine Christian gentleman. You need not touch the servants if you don't want to.'

'Thank you for your offer, but I doubt if I will have the freedom to accept it. I plan to enter a monastery, where I shall be freed from temptations.'

Chapter Fourteen

We thanked Mr Blanking for his Christian kindness towards us, urged him not to enter a monastery, and finally waved goodbye to him as his train steamed away from the village station towards Norwich. We went home, and had the following discussion at dinner.

'Excellent,' said Estelle. 'Two creditors down and only one to go. How can we fail?'

'I fear our situation is not as good as it may appear to you,' my husband sighed. 'It is true that we have miraculously reduced the total of creditors by two, but the third, Sir Horace Withington-Blathers, shall certainly be very hard to satisfy – indeed, I do not believe there is any chance of our succeeding with him. He is cruel, grasping, and unprincipled in the extreme. He loves to wield a cane against female flesh, and besides, I fear he is no gentleman.'

'Let us try our best,' said I.

'Mary might like to be caned a little,' stated Estelle. 'And I could watch.'

'Your watching will be very helpful, I'm sure,' I observed sarcastically.

'I fear that if such a man is given a feeling of power over a household of men and women, he will become more unbalanced by the minute,' Robert mused. 'His cruelty will grow as it digests what it feeds on – that is, suffering and distress. Where will we draw the line and say no to his demands? We must prepare ourselves to deny him what he wants if it is too cruel.'

'Certainly,' I agreed.

'Oh no,' protested Estelle, 'let him do what he likes until he has had enough. Encourage the servants to be whipped if it will save their homes. You should order them to submit to any demand Sir Horace makes, no matter how cruel. That is the only way you can secure your house, their future, and Jane's happiness.'

It was ironic that Estelle should say this, ironic that is in the light of what was to occur, as you shall see.

'My dear,' said I to my husband, 'you must know that I would sooner lose this house than encourage the staff to indulge the cruel caprices of any man.'

'I know that Jane,' he replied, taking my hand. 'I know you have a kind and good nature, and I would sooner lose my home than risk losing your esteem.'

'I hope,' said Estelle, 'that, for your sakes, you are not quite as good as you currently believe.'

That evening Robert wrote to Sir Horace, telling him that he had an unusual staff at Dreadnought Manor who would provide varied and pleasing erotic services in return for a gradual reduction of Robert's debt. John took the letter to the village and sent it on its way to Leeds, where Sir Horace was in temporary residence.

On the third morning following, we had a reply to the effect that Sir Horace would visit us on the fifteenth, though he carefully pointed out that this did not imply acceptance of our offer, either at the present or in the future.

'I wish he had refused,' Robert told me. His tone was sombre. 'You cannot imagine him, my dear. He is bad, he is a man to be feared. I see him as a terrible shark that smells blood in the water and hurries to devour its pitiful victims. Sir Horace knows we are in a weak position, virtually helpless indeed, while he is in a position of power. This will excite him. This kind of sadistic character is excited by weakness and helplessness, and our financial position makes us his natural victims.'

On the night before Sir Horace's arrival, I lay naked in bed with Robert. I might as well mention here that we habitually slept naked even when not engaged in erotic pleasures. I hope this fresh breach of decorum does not shock the reader, but the truth is that sleeping naked is more comfortable.

'If he wants to whip some women,' said I, 'there is one point that must be settled. He may want to whip me, and if he does, I shall say yes.'

'My dear! You must not. The very idea is appalling. I will not allow it.'

'I am very curious about this kind of activity, dearest. I have a mind to try it.'

'You mean you have a mind to try and save the house,' Robert insisted bitterly.

'It is a little of both, I think. Our motives are often mixed throughout our lives. I have a mind to try being the victim of a cruel man – so long as you are there to protect me, of course.'

For some time we discussed the matter, with Robert trying to forbid or dissuade me, and I insisting that if I had complete freedom in erotic matters, then I had a right to sample what Sir Horace had to offer, if Sir Horace had that desire. At last Robert conceded the point, admitting that if he was in favour of freedom, he could hardly draw an arbitrary line. If I wanted to try everything once, I could try being chastised. He conceded with reluctance, and I knew he was deeply concerned that Sir Horace would be too cruel.

The next morning, Sir Horace himself arrived, having spent the previous night at a hotel in Norwich. The sky was grey, with a thundery tension in the air, as though nature itself was subdued and apprehensive at what this man might inflict on frail human flesh.

He was of medium build, and some sixty years of age. His expression and manner were sharp and sardonic, arrogant and untrustworthy. My heart sank to behold his nature. His face was reddened by strong spirits, while the remaining hairs at the edge of his bald head were white, making a strong contrast with his red cheeks and nose. He was accompanied by a valet, Jenkins, a man of powerful build and brutal appearance whom I disliked equally on sight.

Sir Horace was in a cheerful mood, but it was a menacing kind of cheerfulness, for it had an air of triumph, as though he had already won a praiseworthy victory against us. I knew at once that we were in for a bad time, and in my heart I quailed.

'Well, well,' said Sir Horace as we arrived at Dreadnought Manor. He rubbed his hands together. 'Just think of it. A household of servants, mine to do with what I choose. An interesting place, hey?' He gave me a penetrating, rude stare, and came at once to what was for me the crucial point. 'And how about your delightful wife? Will she consent to join the fun?'

'I shall, if it seems amusing,' I replied as lightly as I could manage.

'And you Miss Havisham?' he asked Estelle.

'I am a woman who only enjoys other women,' she replied. 'Ask me to do anything with women, and it is probable I shall comply.'

'Nobody here is under any kind of compulsion,' stated my husband. 'Including the servants.'

'Except the compulsion of financial need, which is rather a considerable compulsion, eh?' Sir Horace laughed. He was clearly delighted at the power he sensed he held over us all.

We had lunch together, during which Sir Horace again made it clear that he was committing himself to nothing, and would have to sample what we had to offer before he decided whether to cancel our debt or not. He would sample us for several days, a week or two perhaps, and at the end of that time he would recognise no obligation. These were the only terms he had to offer, so of course we had to accept. David had said much the same, and things had turned out well enough with him, but this reflection gave me little cheer, for I knew that at heart David was a kind man whereas I sensed Sir Horace was thoroughly bad.

He made it clear to us that he expected something special from us, not just a series of straightforward couplings, as he was used to the great brothels of London, Vienna and Paris, wherein one might obtain anything the human mind could conceive.

'We have here a fine group of men and women, with many skills and varying inclinations and preferences,' Robert told our guest after we had completed our midday repast. 'If you like, Estelle would be pleased to describe these as the staff display themselves to you in a state of nudity.'

'That would be a waste of time,' Sir Horace replied rudely. 'I care nothing for nude shows, nor for the skills and inclinations of the servants. I do not care what they are good at or what they want – I am only interested in what I want. They are servants – very well, they shall serve me. Women should merely be the passive recipients of men's lusts – they are vessels designed for men's pleasure. If their passivity is complete and enforced, so much the better. What does a woman need with skills? The only good qualities in a woman are beauty, obedience, and an ability to endure suffering. That is what makes a real woman.'

This I thought was a dreary way of looking at the physical act of love, which should bring with it affection or at least some concern for one's partner or partners in the game. Sir Horace's ideas certainly deprived him of the greater part of the pleasure of eroticism, which is that of giving someone else pleasure, and in this sharing break down the barriers between one person and the next, so reducing the power of loneliness in this sad world. I could not of course argue about this just then with Sir Horace, as unfortunately we had to satisfy his desires, however bleak.

'You will have no objection to my valet taking the girls on my behalf, I am sure,' said that unpleasant aristocrat. 'At my age I cannot give the females what I once could for long periods, so I save my juice for key moments while Jenkins does the hard work over the long stretch. I use him as a kind of proxy, telling him what to do and putting myself in his place.'

'Of course your man is welcome to act for you in this way,' Robert replied, though I think in reality he would have liked to tell them both to go away.

'Why then, we might as well start,' Sir Horace exclaimed, rubbing his hands together with a kind of unholy glee. 'Jenkins is a model of male prowess, as I was until recently – and I am still twice the man of most fellows my age. Jenkins will wear the girls out, he will leave them sore.'

'Let us go to the library, where I shall have the staff assemble for you,' said Robert. 'Then you can decide at your leisure which of them to enjoy, and in what way – if they are willing.'

Before long all the servants were being inspected by the gloating Sir Horace and his valet. Our staff were subdued, as were Robert and I, for we could all sense that this pair were thoroughly bad. Often, even generally, evil is carefully concealed, but here it was as easy to read as a book in large print, for the simple reason that Sir Horace and Jenkins were both too proud of themselves to even consider hiding their true natures.

'You may all strip naked,' our creditor told the staff. 'And you too, if you please,' he added. This last instruction was intended for Estelle, Robert and myself. 'You too, Jenkins. You shall roger these sluts until they beg for mercy, but you shan't give it to 'em, no by God you won't.'

And so we all undressed, with Sir Horace urging us to hurry, and making crude comments on the human flesh that was disclosed, as though we were cattle he might buy. There was nothing he refrained from saying, and most of what he said was in the form of exclamations on the size of John and Franklin's male organs, Lisa's breasts, and Mary's breasts and protruding genital lips. He rubbed his hands in malevolent glee, and his nose grew redder than ever, as his excitement increased his flow of blood. A big nose it was too, which did nothing to add to his appearance. He was charmless.

'A good enough crew,' he gloated when we were all naked. 'Succulent male and female meat for me, a set of girls and fellows to put through their tricks. It could be worse, indeed it could. It might even be rather amusing. You're all ready, I see, to ride these shameless fillies, Jenkins. What a cock you have! Why, it is almost as good as mine when I was young. It might almost be mine – and since you are my man, we might as well say it is mine.'

'Indeed it is yours, Sir Horace,' growled the brutish valet, whose body was covered with an undue amount of unnecessary hair. A monkey might have need of such hair on cold nights, but not a valet.

Sir Horace also singled out Estelle for special attention. I believe this was owing to the fact that she had made herself unobtainable to him – like many men, he wanted what he could not have.

'What a fine lady, so shameless, and what a pity it is that she's a lesbian!' he muttered. 'What a body, what a wicked young face!'

He praised me in strong terms too, but modesty and a distaste for Sir Horace both lead me to omit his fulsome praise of my form and face. I only mention them so that this account may be accurate.

Robert now suggested that we go to a comfortable place for our pleasures. Sir Horace agreed, so we went upstairs to the large soft room, which could accommodate all of us without any sensation of overcrowding. Our guest was very taken with the room, which he praised as a fine setting for erotic delights – he naturally used cruder language than this, but I tire of the man, and will not write down all of his nasty words. They are not worthy of preservation.

He directed us to sit down on the sofas and chairs that lined the walls, and looked us over once more, cogitating on how best to use us for his maximum excitement – pleasure is too warm a word for the sensations he obtained from women. We were quiet and nervous, sensing that we were in danger. The danger was not only in Sir Horace and his nasty valet, it was also in ourselves, for we might be tempted to concede to cruel demands and to behave in ways we might later regret, not only to save the house but also because we were so enamoured of novel erotic experiences. Would we come to crave dangerous and cruel deviations?

'These are remarkable titties,' Sir Horace said at

last, addressing Lisa. 'I think it would be pleasant to bind, torment and chastise a girl with such overblown mammaries.' He looked at the stretch marks on her belly. 'And you have had a baby, I see. Where is it now?'

'He is in the village, being looked after by my friend there, Rose,' Lisa replied shyly, looking down at the floor. 'Usually he is here with me, but I took him to Rose today so that I could give all my time to entertain you, sir.'

'So normally he lives here with you. Have you a husband?'

'No sir.'

'You are fortunate indeed to be able to live here with your bastard offspring, hey? Robert is a liberal fellow indeed. If he was to lose his house, you would have no home, and you would be separated from your baby.'

'Yes sir,' Lisa replied tearfully. 'I don't know where I'd go, sir.'

'So you'd do anything at all to please me, no matter how painful, and so be able to live in this pleasant, relaxed house with your baby?'

'Yes sir,' Lisa agreed in a whisper.

I was horrified by this development. Sir Horace, by an instinct of cruelty, had sensed one of the most sweet-natured and defenceless of us, and was singling her out for cruel treatment. This is the true nature of a sadist, that he prefers to find a gentle and virtuous victim. A great rage welled up in me.

'Sir Horace,' said Robert, 'you cannot –'

He was plainly going to defend Lisa even at the price of losing his ancestral home, and at that instant I loved him more than ever. He never finished the sentence however, for Mary interrupted with a marvellous ferocity.

'For shame, Lisa!' she cried. 'How can you submit to be tied up and chastised, to be restrained and humiliated? I would never agree to such filthy wickedness in a million years.'

'Indeed?' sneered Sir Horace. 'Then you will be tied up without agreeing to it. Robert, this is the one I want first.'

I was thrilled by Mary's insight into his nature, and by the way she had fooled him completely. She herself wanted to be tied, she was obsessive about that kind of activity, being an ardent masochist, but she knew that if she said so, Sir Horace would lose interest in her, for he did not want to please a woman, but rather to frighten and abuse her. By the stratagem of a refusal to submit, Mary had made Sir Horace eager to have his way with her – what an intelligent young lady Mary was to be sure. She was tricking him into giving her what she desired, and at the same time was trying hard to save poor Lisa.

Robert had Mary stand up, then took her by the shoulders and turned her around so that Sir Horace and his valet could not see her face.

'Mary,' he said, 'will you not let yourself be tied up for the first time in your life, to save the house?'

'No sir, I shall not,' Mary replied, but at the same time she gave him a slow and deliberate wink. 'I have never been tied and I never shall be tied – I am a good Christian girl and I will not submit to any wickedness.' She paused and winked again. 'You could only tie me by force, and I know you would not dare use force against a poor innocent girl.'

'Let us tie the girl,' said Robert. 'In fact I will do it myself, for she is a disobedient servant.'

'Fine, that's the way,' cried Sir Horace. 'And as for you,' he said to Lisa, leering at the poor girl, 'we will give you attention later, my dear.'

Mary pretended to be frightened and rebellious as Robert, helped by Banks, tied her face-up on the mattress at the centre of the room, which was covered by a dark red silk sheet. They used black silk cords, attaching them to metal rings which had been fitted at the corners of the mattress. She lay spread-eagled, her statuesque body naked and defenceless. She could not help looking somewhat pleased, but in his excitement Sir Horace did not notice. Robert, of course, had insisted on tying Mary himself not because he was angry with her, but because he wanted her to be tied safely and comfortably.

'Mrs Shawnecrosse,' Sir Horace said to me, 'you will go on all fours over this wench and lick her cunnie while she licks yours.'

I went on to the mattress on all fours, and Mary and I licked one another's most sensitive flesh. It was certainly interesting to do such a deed in front of so many ladies and gentlemen, and I swiftly grew aroused, especially as Mary seemed to suck me so hard as to draw my parts into her mouth, while her tongue circled and whipped at such high speed that it seemed she had two instead of the normal one.

All of the men had strong erections, and I felt proud to display my body to them while licking a bound woman. I may have been guilty of arching my back and thrusting out my buttocks to arouse them further. I enjoyed too the sensation of using my tongue on the exposed, open nether lips of a helpless girl, and I teased her clitoris in the knowledge that she could not defend that little spot of ultra-sensitive nerves. I lashed it with my tongue, while rubbing my parts over her face, using her bound body for my selfish pleasure.

'She is not ashamed to show her cunnie, though she is such a fine lady,' Sir Horace commented to his valet. 'Put your cock in her from behind, Jenkins.'

This was getting to the heart of the matter in no uncertain terms. I could not be fussy, so I steadied myself, and felt the brutish valet kneel behind me, his penis nudging my nether lips. He inserted it into its natural sheath and proceeded to enjoy me. It was not very pleasant to be possessed in this way, yet I tried to make the most of it, and concentrated on the simple physical sensations of his organ sliding deep into my body, and by its motions pleasuring my clitoris.

I thought too of my husband, and how I was not only helping him keep his home, but also giving him excitement by showing myself to him in this manner, on all fours over a bound girl while simultaneously being possessed by the hairy valet of a guest. It is not every man who has the opportunity to see his wife put on such a performance, and I doubt if Robert found the experience boring.

'Lick my valet's balls, woman, and do a good job of it too,' Sir Horace told Mary.

She told me later that she was tempted to bite them in order to be chastised in the manner of her fantasies, but she reflected that we had to please this creditor, so she obeyed him instead of disobeying.

'Try both their mouths,' Sir Horace told his valet, who was now serving as what we might call his surrogate. I did not see any bulge in Sir Horace's trousers, and decided he must be almost impotent. Doubtless only the most cruel and refined of torments could stimulate him to erection and orgasm, which was rather unfortunate for us.

'Take it out of the lady's cunt and stick it in the servant's mouth,' cried the wretched man, striving to arouse himself by his own vile abuse of language. 'Do as you please! They have plenty of holes between them, and all worth trying I'm sure. Use the tied-up bitch's mouth.'

I shall avoid quoting this man's utterances as much as possible. He did not have, I fear, any wholesome way of obtaining erotic gratification.

Jenkins withdrew from me with rude suddenness and enjoyed Mary's busily licking tongue and fervent sucking.

'She uses her mouth like a good 'un, Sir Horace,' grunted the valet. 'She's had a hell of a lot of practice, no doubt of it. Shall I spend here? I could spray her face and the lady's bum.'

'No, spend in Mrs Shawnecrosse,' Sir Horace cried in a voice high-pitched with excitement. 'Go back to her cunt and tell me what it's like. You forgot to tell me that before, and you know I want you to tell me.'

'Oh, it's a fine cunt,' Jenkins exclaimed, as he transferred himself back into me. 'It's as juicy as they come, and marvellously tight. It's a cunt in a million.'

I understood that Sir Horace wanted to fully imagine what his servant was experiencing, and needed his oafish comments to help him in this endeavour. It was humiliating to be referred to in such terms, but there, if humiliation was the order of the day, I would try to get some pleasure even out of that rather tiresome and overrated emotion. There was at least some excitement in being used by this brutish fellow, though I would not have liked it to have become a habit.

'Spend any time you like,' growled Sir Horace. 'Give the fine lady a damn good spunking.'

Indeed I sensed that Jenkins was on the verge of spending, and I compared him unfavourably with my dear Robert, who could delay his eruption for the greater delight of himself and his fortunate partner. Jenkins lacked his skill. With a series of grunts and moans, he delivered himself into me, obviously having a splendid orgasm.

'It was good, eh Jenkins?'

'One of the best ever, Sir Horace,' the valet grunted in reply. Spent, he withdrew from me and collapsed on to a sofa.

'Now Mrs Shawnecrosse, press your cunnie against the bound woman's mouth. Mind that you suck your mistress long and hard, and let me see you swallow.'

This seemed a little hard on Mary, but in reality she was glad to be the centre of attention. In a way, so was I. I squatted over Mary's face, positioning my cunnie over her mouth, and she sucked me with the eagerness of a masochist who takes pride in humiliation, lavishing attention on me also with her agile tongue, so that as she drained my pleasure channel of its viscous male deposits, I experienced a delightfully prolonged series of orgasms.

'This is not such a bad show,' Sir Horace muttered, 'not so bad at all. You may get off the servant, Mrs Shawnecrosse. Now we shall have a good deal of fucking, and see if the ladies are strong enough to endure being taken by man after man.'

The reader will note Sir Horace's foolishness in thinking that a woman might not be strong enough to 'endure' (a foolish word, in this context), a series of men. As though women were not strong! We are the sex with the great strength necessary to carry the extra weight of pregnancy and to go through the prolonged pangs of childbirth – let no one doubt the strength of women.

'Which of you fine fellows shall fuck this bound female?' Sir Horace asked the male servants.

Before any of them could reply, Mary spoke up in bold terms.

'They would not use a girl in such a helpless condition as myself,' she insisted. 'They have more spirit and Christian kindness.'

'You naive girl,' laughed Sir Horace – he had a

sinister laugh like the villain in a badly acted melo-drama. 'Men would do anything for money. And do you think they care about your feelings? Any one of them would fuck you for a sovereign.'

'You might tempt some of them with a sovereign,' said Mary. 'Banks and that McBean might be tempted by a shilling, come to that.' (This was just her joke, as she was a firm friend of both men.) 'But as for the likes of Franklin, he would not commit beastliness at your beck and call, no sir, not for a sovereign, nor even for so much as a fiver.'

'You think Franklin would not, eh?' sneered Sir Horace. 'Which one is he? Stand up, Franklin, and let us have a look at you, as you are a paragon. So you are the one incorruptible man in the world, eh? I doubt it, I doubt it. Will you not roger this girl for a sovereign, Franklin.'

'No sir, for it is a sin and I'd burn in hell,' Franklin muttered, shy at having to speak in front of so many people. 'Such a sin has to be worth a fiver, sir, and I could not do it for less.'

'Very well,' snapped Sir Horace, though he was an-noyed at having to pay so much. 'You drive a hard bargain, but it is worth it to prove this slut wrong. You see, woman, human nature is evil. Give her a good fucking, fellow.'

Mary pretended to protest as Franklin licked her cunnie, but it was all fakery, because, in fact, Franklin was her special friend. The reader will recall that the dour, taciturn stable man loved to make curious and cunning harnesses of leather for the erotic re-straint of men and women, so I need hardly explain that Mary was keenly attracted by him, and shared with him the specialised thrills of restraint and har-nessing. They also had in common a complete lack of interest in conversation, so that I have seen them sat silently beside one another for hours, apparently ignoring each other, yet in reality enjoying the delights of a tender companionship and a deep romantic attachment.

Sir Horace gloated over Mary's apparent suffering as Franklin mounted her splendid body, spread-eagled and naked on the dark red silk sheet of the mattress. The muscular stable man teased her huge nipples with his strong fingers and worked his penis in and out of her succulent cunnie with the most vigorous enjoyment – an enjoyment that was mutual, though Mary pretended that such was not the case. Franklin grunted with pleasure as he enjoyed Mary's splendid young body.

'I wish to see you with the black fellow, Mrs Shawnecrosse,' said Sir Horace, getting more and more excited. 'You can suck his cock and then mount him. Lay back on the mattress there, fellow.'

John obeyed the unpleasant man, and I at once set to work licking and sucking his large dark male organ. It was an interesting experience to hold a black man's penis in my hands and mouth in front of such a large and attentive audience, not the least attentive of whom was my husband.

Then I mounted John's strong, black body, taking the penis I had just been licking into my vagina. I rode him gently at first, then with more powerful movements. I rubbed my breasts against his face, writhed my hips in various erotic rhythms, and squeezed him with my internal muscles, while his hands made free of my naked flesh, caressing me in a manner that showed no small skill as well as respect for the female body. To copulate with John was no hardship.

Franklin and John came at the same time, brought to this simultaneous ecstasy no doubt by the fact that they could hear one another's gasps and moans of mounting delight. Franklin grunted as he emptied himself into the bound Mary, while John gave what I can only describe as shrieks and pleas for mercy as he blasted a great quantity of semen into the centre of my body, stimulating me to a further orgasm by the power of his ejaculation.

Now I had coupled with two men in succession, a thought that gave me simultaneous feelings of pride and chagrin. I looked at Robert, and he gave me a charming smile that illuminated my soul. I was reassured. I liked being a bad girl, but only so long as I had the support of the man I loved.

'You say that you like women,' Sir Horace said to Estelle. 'Then couple with any girl you like.'

Estelle smiled, took Darma by the hand, and led her to the third, unoccupied mattress. Here they lay down on their sides to kiss and hug, while rubbing their shapely young bodies together in a fine display of absolute wantonness. Sir Horace regarded them keenly. Estelle looked remarkably attractive with her splendid body, lovely aristocratic features and long auburn hair. She took the lead with her dark-skinned partner, now on top of her, then on all fours over her to present her parts to be licked. She sucked Darma, caressed her own breasts, and sighed as Darma slid two fingers in and out of her cunnie, which had never been used for its natural purpose of receiving a man's instrument of procreation, but was, as it were, reserved for the pleasure of its owner.

'What a waste!' Sir Horace muttered to himself. 'Such a fine young lady and she will not entertain a cock!' From his staring eyes and the bulge in his trousers, it was obvious he was greatly attracted by Estelle, as men often are by something unobtainable. I feared this would bode ill.

Franklin and John went to sit on a sofa once more. Sir Horace had me pose on all fours with my private parts a few inches above Mary's face. You can imagine that I dripped somewhat, and this gave our creditor pleasure, for he delighted in that most infantile of erotic activities, namely the humiliation of ladies.

'What a marvellous bum your wife has, Robert!' Sir Horace explained. He gave me a hard slap on the posterior, a slap I would not characterise as playful. 'Come Robert, take her from behind, and you fellow, give her your cock to be sucked at the same time. Let us see the lady taken from both ends at once.'

So I found myself with Robert kneeling behind me, while McBean knelt in front of me so that I could use my mouth for the pleasure of his short, thick penis. My husband's organ entered me as I licked the helmet of McBean's maleness, and I felt I was the most wanton woman in existence. I was now participating in the kinds of activities that helped win Messalina and Catherine the Great their immortality, and I was not ashamed to be in such august company. In truth, I felt a fresh wave of arousal sweep through my body at the thought of acting in a way that would have caused my old teachers at school to die of heart attacks. Anything that had the potential to achieve such a laudable aim must possess intrinsic merit.

'They shall both spend over you,' cried Sir Horace. He directed me to lie besides Mary on my back, then urged Robert to let loose his male fluid. My dear husband went on all fours over me and gave his gleaming-wet organ to my mouth while fingering my parts. I gave him my best attention, using tongue, teeth and lips to play a symphony of varied caresses on his glans, while my fingers squeezed and pressed and moved, keeping him at the peak of pleasure for several minutes, until he erupted in a positive Vesuvius of passion, spraying my breasts and belly for a marvellously prolonged period of rapture. His strangled, choking gasps told the tale of his ecstasy with convincing eloquence.

McBean was next. He sat on his haunches and held his organ down to introduce it into its natural setting in my body, then caressed my thighs and lower belly while wriggling his hips. I was determined to enjoy myself and to give Robert a stimulating vision of his life's partner as an erotically fearless female, so I steadfastly ignored the fact that Sir Horace was doubtless trying to make me feel humiliated. In his own mind I was a wicked woman humiliating herself by engaging in erotic acts with one man after another in order to save her home, but I was pleased to think that the joke was on him, for I did not feel humiliated. I was strong.

The fact that I was a lady thrilled him of course, for we upper class ladies are supposed to be the very model for the world of correctness and propriety, not to say boring puritanism. He was more interested in me than he was in Mary, because she was of the lower orders. From my wantonness he gained a special spur to his jaded senses. He was getting ever more excited, and I feared whatever he might next demand.

'May I spend over you, ma'am?' asked McBean, that most reliable and skilled of gardeners, and a paragon of politeness besides.

I replied in the affirmative, and so, a short time after, he withdrew his male organ and held it in his hand as it spurted over me, so that my flesh ran and gleamed with the copious spending of two men. In ecstasy McBean was silent, with not even a murmur escaping his lips. Sir Horace stared hungrily at every drop, no doubt because his own ejaculations were now few and far between, so that he was unhealthily fascinated by the vigorous spurtings of other males and the way they hosed my shapely young female body to run in streams over my firm breasts.

As for ecstatic pleasure experienced by ladies, he clearly took no interest in encouraging it, and would probably have preferred it if we were incapable of rapture.

'You women,' he exclaimed, pulling at the arms of Sally and Edith. 'Rub yourselves against your mistress. Become as besmirched as she is.'

They were only too eager to comply, for they had become heated while watching the lurid disports I have described, and were desperate to spend. They hastened to me, and licked my breasts like cats drinking milk while pressing their bodies to mine, each taking a thigh of mine against which to rub her mound of pleasure. The three of us tried many forms of wanton pleasure, and we also involved Mary, who pretended to protest. In fact we tried so many variants that it would be a mere catalogue of positions were I to try to explain them to the reader. So I shall trust the reader's imagination.

Finally, Sir Horace unleashed his alter ego on us.

'Take them Jenkins!' he cried, like a huntsman urging his dogs to finish the fox. 'Enjoy all four of them in as many ways as you can. Use their mouths and cunts, fuck them senseless.'

The brutish fellow jumped on us in all his hairiness. And here again it would become tiresome were I to attempt to list all that occurred. Suffice to say that his large steely penis made use of four ladies' mouths and cunnies, switching from one to another countless times, and trying every position and variation, such as for instance having two of us handle his balls and shaft while the other two licked him, two of us kiss his helmet while the other two rubbed against his body and caressed him all over – no, it is fruitless to go on, for it would take twenty pages and would become tiresome, even though the activities themselves were of no small interest.

At the end he spent inside Edith's tight-clenching vagina, with howls of pure delight.

'Splendid!' cried Sir Horace. 'And now for a damned good whipping.'

Chapter Fifteen

My heart sank at these words.

'Now then, who will be the victims?' Sir Horace mused, looking us all over so that many of us quailed. 'Ah, so you are afraid of me, are you? And I can tell you that you are right to be afraid, and I am glad you are afraid.' He looked down at Mary, and added: 'You can release this woman for the present, for I feel we should change the venue.'

Mary was untied, and at once she knelt down in front of me.

'Oh ma'am, she begged, 'protect me against this wicked gentleman, who will surely burn in hell for being so evil. Do not let me be whipped – me who has today been tied up for the first time in my life.'

This lie about being tied up for the first time was her way of telling me that in reality she was trying to trick Sir Horace into whipping her instead of somebody who would not like it.

'Ah, so you are the most afraid, are you?' Sir Horace cried. 'And you insult me besides. Then you are my first choice to be whipped.'

'Hold Mary, John,' said I, as Mary pretended to try and flee the room. 'Mary, you must be prepared to be whipped. It is your duty.'

'Who else shall we try?' mused the odious knight.

'I hope you will give me the opportunity to try these pleasures,' said I. The reader may be surprised that I offered myself to this vile man and his unnatural lusts, but the fact is that I was determined to protect the servants by offering myself.

'My dear, no,' Robert exclaimed.

'I am curious to try this sport,' said I. 'You gave me my freedom – I am using what you gave me.'

'Very well,' my husband agreed with the utmost reluctance. 'You may try a mild version of corporal punishment. But Sir Horace, there must be no serious welts or breaking of the skin.'

'All right, all right, no need to get on your high horse and set conditions,' grumbled the rich reprobate.

Reader, I thought I might faint. I was going to be whipped. I hoped Robert would stop his creditor if he went too far – and yet I feared my dear husband might give way to his natural desire to save his ancestral home. Even if he should put his home first for just one minute, the consequences for me could be severe. I was frightened, but at the same time I was indeed curious to know what it was like to be tied and whipped, for all that I would rather have tried it with someone other than Sir Horace.

'I am glad to whip you, Mrs Shawnecrosse,' said our creditor. 'One can whip members of the lower orders any day as a matter of course, but it is refreshing to have a real lady submit to the biting caress of a whip. And now we need one man to be teased and punished by a lady. What about you, black fellow?'

'I'm willing,' John said at once. 'I have often had a mind to try it.'

'And you, Estelle, will you tease and punish this man?' Sir Horace asked with a peculiar intensity and eagerness.

'It is something new,' mused my wicked friend, smiling at John. 'Therefore I shall try it.'

232

'Now let us go to the stables,' said Sir Horace.

'The stables?' I echoed.

'Yes. Stables offer a good many features for the pleasures of captivity and whipping.'

Robert, Mary, John, Estelle and myself now accompanied Sir Horace and his valet Jenkins to the stables. He told the rest of the staff to return to their duties, and to make sure the dinner was a good one, for he was working up a splendid appetite. Poor Sally was hardly in a mood to cook, for she was worried about her favourite John. Indeed all the servants were despondent, not liking the turn of events.

The old stables seemed oddly forbidding as we entered. Poorly lit and gloomy, they were hardly conducive to high spirits.

It was a little cooler in those equine quarters, but the day was so hot and stuffy that none of us were cold, save for the cold shiver of fear that passed occasionally through my flesh. The first thing to be done was to take all the horses outside and tie them to trees in a corner of the lawn, so that they would not be frightened by witnessing a whipping – I found this concern bleakly comical, as it implied the horses were more important than the women who were to submit to the whip. At that moment I rather wished I had been born a horse.

'Now we must bind the three of them,' said Sir Horace, relishing the words. He looked around at the stable and rhapsodised thus: 'Look at the place, see how suitable it is for the restraint and punishment of erring females! The posts and beams offer so many possibilities – the saddles, the harnesses, the whips!'

There was a great deal of dirty old rope in the stables, and a knife was found to cut this into suitable lengths. Sir Horace was clearly pleased that it was dirty. Mary was the first to be tied. She pretended to be frightened, too frightened to resist. I watched with fascination as she was rendered helpless, knowing my turn would come soon. My breath quickened. My heart beat loudly and rapidly as though it were trying to jump out of my breast.

Mary was bound in the following manner: her arms were stretched upward with the wrists tied to an overhead beam, while her legs were parted wide, with each ankle secured to the posts of stalls on opposite sides of the stable. She was thus left standing and immobilised in the centre of an open space with both the front and back of her body completely exposed. I saw in her eyes a thrill of excitement.

It was my turn next, and I was far from sharing Mary's pleasurable sensations. I was bound in exactly the same manner, but using a different horizontal beam, so that I stood some eight feet from Mary, facing her. It was terrible to be bound helpless in the presence of Sir Horace and his valet – no words can convey my anxiety. I could see that Mary was erotically excited, with her huge teats stiffly engorged, while her elongated nether lips grew turgid, and glistened with her running lubricant juices.

John was bound last, to a post at my right and Mary's left, so that we three could all see one another. His organ was fiercely erect.

'Tease the black fellow, Miss Havisham,' said Sir Horace.

'With pleasure,' Estelle agreed. Standing in front of John, she began to masturbate, and speak to him in the most lewd manner, which I refuse to set down. Suffice to say that she talked about how he would love to stick his cock in her but could not, and so on with many variations on this basic theme. She posed and pouted, she handled herself, she turned around and adopted postures to arouse the helplessly bound man. I thought she was being even more unwise than was her habit.

Now, at last, Sir Horace undressed. His valet took each item of clothing from him, neatly folded it, and placed it on a table in the corner used by Franklin for his hobby of making human harnesses.

Sir Horace was even less attractive naked than he was clothed. His maleness was in a semi-erect state. He caressed me, and I shuddered. He was loathsome. He fingered Mary too, and mocked John for being unable to join in the sport. Jenkins too gave us nauseating caresses.

'You have behaved like whores and deserve punishment,' stated Sir Horace at last. His organ gained stiffness from his own words.

Jenkins fetched the leather belt from Sir Horace's trousers and placed it in the hands of his master. Those hands trembled slightly.

Sir Horace held the buckle and cracked the black belt in the air, drinking in our anxiety. He handled his own organ while making circuits of the stable, cracking the belt in the air repeatedly, as well as aiming blows at us that he did not make. He teased us cruelly for several minutes to increase our trepidation. He revelled in his own power.

Next he touched us with the belt, caressing our breasts and private parts with it, making comments on our bodies that were carefully obscene. Then he made many more feints with the belt. Finally, when Mary had ceased to flinch at these feints, he landed his first blow, a vicious thwack across Mary's behind that made her cry out. I winced. I nearly cried out to Robert to release me – but held back for fear that the brutish Jenkins would use violence against my husband so that his master could enjoy his cruel pleasures without fear of interruption. That would indeed be nightmarish.

'You do look lovely all tied up like that, Jane,' sighed Estelle. I wished she had been bound in my place, and I the one wielding a belt.

Sir Horace handled his nasty penis, and rubbed its head against my belly and thighs, gazing into my eyes all the while. he then had his valet stand in front of me, and Jenkins enjoyed himself greatly, kissing me on the mouth, licking and sucking my breasts and private parts, fingering me, pressing himself to me so that his cock was sandwiched between our bodies and the like nastiness. Sir Horace meanwhile went behind me, and while all my attention was focused on his valet, he suddenly laid a mighty blow across my buttocks, so that it felt as though a red hot poker had been laid there to burn my flesh. It was all the worse for being totally unexpected – Robert cried out to warn me, but too late, as Sir Horace struck me so swiftly. I screamed. He promptly added to my woe by landing two more blows in swift succession, then paused to masturbate.

'That is enough!' cried Robert.

'Certainly, certainly, I shall not hit your wife again, dear fellow,' Sir Horace said in oily tones. I knew he was lying. 'Let us turn to the servant instead.'

The vicious knight then gave Mary severe treatment, landing blow after blow, covering every part of her body, though concentrating, you may be sure, on those sensitive parts where the pain would be most lasting and burning. Her body was striped with pink lines.

'Mary, I must stop this,' said Robert very early on.

'Oh sir, I wish you would,' Mary replied. 'For you know I have never before been tied, and never said nothing about wishing to be treated like this.'

By these lies she told Robert she did not want him to stop Sir Horace, so my husband did not intervene.

In truth, Mary was always aiming to be treated in this manner, and she told us later that she had enjoyed Sir Horace's cruelty considerably, as it was the genuine article and so was exciting to try once, for all that she would prefer never to experience it again for the rest of her life.

Sir Horace and Jenkins took a bale of hay and strapped a saddle to it, then untied Mary only to bind her over this saddle face down, so that her curvaceous behind was raised and helplessly exposed. Sir Horace landed more blows on this shapely posterior, pausing now and then to handle his maleness, which did not seem to know whether it was stiff or limp, but seemed generally more inclined to the latter state. At a coarsely worded command from his master, Jenkins took the belt and landed some telling blows on Mary before mounting her, leaning on her shoulders and driving his penis home into her vulnerable femaleness.

He gave Sir Horace a commentary on Mary's helplessness, humiliation and the like, and enjoyed her body greatly, finally injecting his semen into the core of her being with loud shouts of triumphant passion.

'No, it is not enough, we have not even begun to get near doing enough to these wicked sluts,' Sir Horace muttered, holding his penis with an air of dejection.

Reader, it was soft. I understood Sir Horace fully now – by indulging in sadistic cruelty for too many miserable, wasted, loveless years he had damaged his capacity for normal erotic arousal.

The foolish villain now looked around, trying to decide what act of nastiness would suffice to stimulate his jaded being. He then stared at Estelle, who all this time had been teasing John. Indeed, she was so absorbed with her new pleasure that she was ignoring the rest of us, and did not pay any attention to Sir Horace. At that moment she was actually touching, for the first time in her life, a penis. She was stroking John's manhood with the tips of her fingers. He gasped and sweated and strained.

'That is what I need,' announced our creditor. 'A beautiful young lady, and better still a lesbian. To punish her will do me good, and it will serve her right, the teasing slut. Shawnecrosse, she is the one I want. Help me to rape and punish her, man, and you will have a share of the pleasure, and I will cancel your debt all in one step. We will all rape and whip her in bondage. She will not dare complain to the authorities – it would only be her word against ours, and besides, how could she thus humiliate herself in court? I have important friends too, we would be safe.' In his excitement, he was beginning to babble. 'We would be in no danger, Robert my boy. She is asking for it, she is naked here with us. Let us stick our cocks in her, then whip her bum and breasts – we can gag her, she shall not call for help. I am rich, I can do anything I want to, that is the way of the world. You shall be my partner. This is the real world – think of your duty to your servants and your wife, and your children yet to be born. We can fuck this lesbian bitch. Why, if she accuses us afterwards, we can have her confined to a mad-house. My friends will put her there easily enough, and she shall grow old in captivity.'

Estelle was so appalled she could not move or speak. She must have realised what a tempting offer this must be for a man in Robert's financial position. Yes, tempting for 'a man', but not for my dear husband Robert Shawnecrosse, who now gave the following answer, upon which hung our fates not merely in this world, but also, I believe, in the next.

'You are a species of vermin,' my husband stated. 'And a minor species at that, lacking the importance of the rat or the cheerful vigour of the flea. You are also impotent.'

Sir Horace was stunned by this reply, and spluttered incoherently before he was able to speak again.

'You fool! You imbecile!' he exclaimed.

'I rather think,' mused Robert, 'that I am a gentleman, and that you are not.'

'Overpower him, Jenkins,' gasped Sir Horace.

Estelle now shook off her inertia, and ran to seize the knife that had been used earlier to cut the rope to suitable lengths. She cried for help. Robert meanwhile exchanged blows with Jenkins. I was greatly alarmed, but my husband held his own by superior footwork, ducked under the valet's right hook and winded him with a blow to the belly.

At this point, Banks, McBean, Franklin, Edith and Sally all rushed in and flung themselves pell-mell on Jenkins, who was soon brought to the ground, where he was kept mainly by the honest bulk of Sally. The servants then set about freeing Mary, John and I.

'You fool,' Sir Horace shouted at Robert. His fury at having his desire denied was terrible. 'You will die a homeless and penniless wretch. I shall use my great influence to prevent you from getting any position you may seek. I will leave this house at once and start action to send in the bailiffs to evict you. You will regret this action.'

'I think not,' Robert replied coolly. 'And as for leaving this house at once, there is one thing you had better do first.'

'What is that?'

'Get dressed,' my husband stated.

Mary smiled at Sir Horace. It was odd to see her smile, as usually she was so dour.

'Thank you sir,' said she. 'I have enjoyed the pleasures you have given me. I tricked you into doing exactly what I wanted you to do.'

Sir Horace and his valet got dressed, and departed. Estelle, Robert and I walked back into the house.

'I have no way of expressing my gratitude,' said Estelle. It was as distinctly odd to hear her being serious as it was to see Mary smile.

'I merely did my duty, so there is no cause for gratitude,' Robert replied lightly. He turned to me and grimaced. 'My dear, I am going to be homeless and penniless. I have married you and led you to dire poverty. I am a cad.'

'Oh Robert,' said I. 'I am the happiest woman in the world.'

'What? Why?'

'Because you showed your superior qualities in turning down that nasty man's offer,' explained Estelle. 'Honestly, men understand nothing.'

'We shall remain together always,' I said, squeezing Robert's arm. 'We shall have no money or home, yet have great wealth.'

240

Chapter Sixteen

Reader, how shall I ever explain to you our feelings at that crucial period? What had seemed the greatest disaster was now about to occur for certain – we were going to be thrown out of our home, and go penniless into an uncaring world. We had nothing. And yet we had everything, for we had refused to give way to Sir Horace. We had kept our integrity, which is our only sure possession in this mutable world of deception and decay. We respected ourselves and one another, thanks to the grace of God.

'I feel very sorry for my good friend Roger, though that may sound odd to you, my dear,' Robert told me one evening, as the sun gave us the gift of a spectacular golden and red sunset, a beautiful and moving vision of infinitely varied colours and shades occupying the large canvas of the huge Norfolk horizon. 'He will be upset. I lent him money and he has failed to find diamonds in Portuguese Africa after all. And yet you know, if I had to make the same decision again, I would still lend him that money. He is a good man. If Roger has failed to find diamonds in Portuguese Africa, the deficiency is in Portuguese Africa rather than in my best friend Roger – what a difficult fellow he was to bowl out!'

'Dearest, if Roger were here, and I had some money, I would lend it to him,' I replied warmly.

We embraced, and were as one in the golden light.

Robert and I now exerted ourselves to finding positions for our staff – not the erotic positions which may occur to the reader, but rather positions in our friends' houses as servants. We wrote to everybody we knew, explaining our condition frankly and recommending our servants in the warmest terms, as indeed we might do, for they were all excellent at performing their various household and garden duties.

They were worried and sad. Firstly, they would be separated, and secondly they would once more face a life in which their erotic desires and activities would bring them problems rather than simple pleasures. They would have to return to conventional life, and they would suffer, for when once we have known the exceptional and the good, it is more tiresome and wearying than ever to accept the merely commonplace which is all too often the lot of men and women in this world, a world made beautiful by God, and spoilt by man.

The poor servants indulged in a good deal of wantonness among themselves, knowing that this would be their last chance to enjoy one another's bodies and indulge one another's special desires. They would separate all over the country, and on a servant's wages how could they hope to meet again? Even their ordinary work in the house and garden they did with especial care, as a kind of parting gift to Robert and I – why, even Edith, who was a somewhat indifferent housemaid, could be seen dusting and polishing with an attentiveness and industry we had scarcely suspected her capable of, and as for Sally, she had Charlotte spell out to her the recipes in all the cookbooks Robert had bought her, so eager was she to cook special dishes in her last days.

As Doctor Johnson so wisely observed, the word

'last' has a special significance, and a great power to strike deep into the human heart. And if the last issue of the *Rambler* should give rise to emotion, how much more so the last days of a community which, in its remote Norfolk stronghold, had found a rare happiness in this world of toil and sadness? Like Christians in their great strongholds in the Holy Land, we were being overrun.

It hurt me more than I can say to find poor Lisa crying, worrying about what looked like a bleak future for her baby Arnold. Where could a mother and her illegitimate child find a safe haven? Perhaps she would be driven to live in some nightmarish brothel. Reader, I embraced her, and at that moment we were no longer mistress and servant, but two women sharing the common woe of women.

As for the male servants who wept, I shall not name them for fear of embarrassing them, as there exists a common and foolish prejudice against male tears.

We were all penniless. The contents of the house, as well as the house and its grounds, had all been pledged by Robert against loans in the past, so we could not even contact a dealer in Norwich and endeavour to raise some cash by selling jewellery, paintings and furniture.

Robert and I decided to go to Australia. He would work at menial tasks, we would save money, and obtain land to build our own home. But it was England we loved. Her ancient mossy hamlets, gentle and variable climate, well-ordered society, her small fields bordered with hedgerows standing for a thousand years, her richness of bird song, butterflies, small sweet flowers, white clouds and golden sunsets, the gentleness of a land dotted with churches, windmills, villages and centres of industry that fill the entire world with their manufactured products – all this England was in our hearts and souls, and to leave it was to see the sun go down and to enter a land of shadow.

Some two weeks after Sir Horace's precipitous departure, the local magistrate, an elderly man by the name of Arthur Doughty, came to see us, accompanied by Sir Horace's lawyer, Mr Leadbetter. Robert politely introduced them to Estelle, who was still staying with us to show her moral support for us in our time of trouble.

'The fact is,' said Mr Doughty, nervously toying with his luxuriant white moustache, 'I'm here to serve you with an order for you to leave Dreadnought Manor. I'm dashed sorry, old man, but the law's the law, don't you know. I hate to do this to the Shawnecrosse family, believe you me.'

'I know that you are both only doing your duty,' Robert replied with the pleasant, light tone of a true gentleman. 'Won't you come in and share a glass?'

The five of us entered the drawing room and sat down with the wine Banks promptly brought in. (The competent Banks had, I need hardly say, already found himself an excellent position with a very wealthy gentleman, but had insisted on staying with us till the end.)

We made polite conversation until Banks returned to make a surprising statement.

'A Mr Sanders is here, sir. From the African Bank of Investment. He informs me he is acting on behalf of Mr Appleforth.'

'I suppose Roger needs more money to hunt for non-existent diamonds,' Robert sighed. He told Banks to bring in this Mr Sanders, and in a few moments the gentlemen from the African Bank of Investment had joined us. He was remarkably tall, far taller in fact than any banker had any need to be, and his manner towards Robert was distinctly deferential.

'Mr Shawnecrosse, I congratulate you,' said Mr Sanders. He paused as though to heighten the drama of that moment. 'Our branch in Mombassa has telegraphed us with the information that your partner, Mr Appleforth, has succeeded in his diamond prospecting enterprise.'

'He's found diamonds?' Robert said in amazement.

'He is finding a great many diamonds. In a few months he will be able to start selling them in Amsterdam.'

'In a few months!' I exclaimed. 'But we are about to be turned out of our house.'

'Our branch in Mombassa has recommended that we extend an immediate line of credit to you, Mr Shawnecrosse,' Mr Sanders said. 'We will advance any trifling sums you may request against the security of your share of the future profits from the diamond mine.'

'Trifling sums? Is ten thousand pounds a trifling sum?' asked Robert.

'I am delighted to have the honour of advancing you that trifling sum immediately,' Mr Sanders stated.

Reader, I came near to swooning. We were saved.

'Splendid chap, Roger,' my husband said cheerfully, rubbing his hands. 'A hundred and ten not out against Eton – he and I always shared our hampers of tuck and our tips. Once we picked the lock of a bullying prefect's room and poured five gallons of ink over everything the swine owned. Of course a chap like Roger can find diamonds if he damn well wants to.'

'So you are going to be rich, Jane,' Estelle exclaimed in delight. 'How lovely! I shall call you my best friend, get you to buy me the latest and most expensive dresses, and talk about you behind your back. I shall enjoy myself tremendously until the day you see through me.'

'Estelle!' I gasped, embracing her.

'Congratulations, Shawnecrosse,' said Mr Doughty, the magistrate. He smiled and tore up the eviction order he had been about to hand over. 'I knew you'd come through all right in the end. The Shawnecrosse family are made of the right stuff all right. I knew your father well, and he would as soon knock a man down for insolence as drink a pub dry. And your great-uncle fathered a baby at the age of 81. As for your aunt Elizabeth – well, there's no need to talk about your aunt Elizabeth, may she rest in peace.'

Financial matters were settled, after which Mr Doughty, Mr Sanders, and Sir Horace's lawyer, Mr Leadbetter, all departed.

'Good heavens!' I said to my dear husband and my bad friend Estelle. 'Do you realise what this means? We need not have bothered to try and please David, Mr Blanking, and Sir Horace at all. All our efforts were unnecessary.'

'Yes Jane, but there is more to life than what is necessary and unnecessary,' Robert replied.

'You silly goose, Jane,' said Estelle. 'We had such fun.'

I had to agree with her that our erotic strivings had not been without some moments of keen interest.

Reader, it is time for us to take our leave from one another, for I have finished the tale of how Dreadnought Manor was saved. I hope you have enjoyed my account of these events, whatever its deficiencies, as much as I have enjoyed writing it.

As for how we and our loyal staff celebrated the good news, I shall leave it to your imagination, for it is a good thing to imagine cheerful erotic pleasures rather than brooding, as so many people do, on darker matters, and so growing gloomy. If we all can decide to be happy, and be determined to find happiness, there is at least a chance that we may find some happiness in our lives.

NEW BOOKS

Coming up from Nexus and Black Lace

Christina Wished by Gene Craven
April 1996   Price £4.99   ISBN: 0 352 33066 X
Three flatmates – unrestrained, raven-haired Christina, meek but luscious Susan and mysterious, rubber and leather clad Cathy – embark on a voyage of sexual discovery. Each must face tests and undreamt-of pleasures, and push her sexuality to the limits, before she can release the wanton inside her and revel in the power of discipline.

Pleasing Them by William Doughty
April 1996   Price £4.99   ISBN: 0352 33065 1
Into Dreadnought Manor, home to Robert Shawnecross and his beautiful young wife, come the puritanical Mr Blanking and the wicked Sir Horace. They seek satisfaction through control and cruelty, and their hosts, along with the servants – who have been trained to cater to the strangest desires – must stretch their skills to find suitably extreme pleasures.

Dark Desires by Maria del Rey
May 1996   Price £4.99   ISBN: 0 352 32971 8
A subtle taste of the bizarre renders each of Maria del Rey's kinkiest stories strikingly original. Fetishists, submissives and errant tax inspectors mingle with bitch goddesses, bad girls and French maids, in settings as diverse as an austere Victorian punishment room and a modern-day SM dungeon, in this eclectic anthology of forbidden games.

The Finishing School by Stephen Ferris
May 1996   Price £4.99   ISBN: 0 352 33071 6
Young heiress Felicity Marchant is sent, by Selina, the corrupt trustee of her estate, to be disciplined at a sinister finishing school on a remote island. There, she is subjected to all manner of indignities and humiliations, and must outwit a spy planted by Selina if she is to give her tormentors a taste of their own perverse methods of control.

Gothic Blue by Portia da Costa
April 1996   Price £4.99   ISBN: 0 352 33075 9

Set in a remote and mysterious priory in the present day, this dark, Gothic-erotic novel centres on Belinda, a sensual and rest-less heroine who is intrigued by the supernatural unknown. Written by one of Black Lace's most popular authors, it explores the themes of sexual alchemy and experimentation, the paranormal and obsession.

The House of Gabriel by Rafaella
April 1996   Price £4.99   ISBN: 0 352 33063 5

Journalist Jessica Martyn is researching a feature on lost treas-ures of erotic art for a glossy women's magazine. Her quest takes her to the elegant Jacobean mansion of the enigmatic Garbiel Martineux, and she is gradually drawn into a sensual world of strange power games and costumed revelry. She also finds trouble, in the shape of her arch-rival Araminta Harvey.

Pandora's Box Anthology, Ed. Kerri Sharp
May 1996   Price £4.99   ISBN: 0 352 33074 0

This unique collection brings together new material and extracts from the best-selling and most popular titles in the Black Lace series. *Pandora's Box* is a celebration of the revolutionary imprint which puts women's erotic fiction in the media spotlight. The diversity of the material is a testament to the many facets of the female erotic imagination.

The Ninety Days of Genevieve by Lucinda Carrington
May 1996   Price £4.99   ISBN: 0 352 33070 8

Genevieve Loften discovers that a 90-day sex contract is part of a business deal she makes with the arrogant and attractive James Sinclair. Thrown into a world of sexual challenges, Genevieve is forced to balance her high-flying career with the twilight world of fetishism and debauchery.

NEXUS BACKLIST

All books are priced £4.99 unless another price is given. If a date is supplied, the book in question will not be available until that month in 1995.

CONTEMPORARY EROTICA

THE ACADEMY	Arabella Knight	
CONDUCT UNBECOMING	Arabella Knight	Jul
CONTOURS OF DARKNESS	Marco Vassi	
THE DEVIL'S ADVOCATE	Anonymous	
DIFFERENT STROKES	Sarah Veitch	Aug
THE DOMINO TATTOO	Cyrian Amberlake	
THE DOMINO ENIGMA	Cyrian Amberlake	
THE DOMINO QUEEN	Cyrian Amberlake	
ELAINE	Stephen Ferris	
EMMA'S SECRET WORLD	Hilary James	
EMMA ENSLAVED	Hilary James	
EMMA'S SECRET DIARIES	Hilary James	
FALLEN ANGELS	Kendal Grahame	
THE FANTASIES OF JOSEPHINE SCOTT	Josephine Scott	
THE GENTLE DEGENERATES	Marco Vassi	
HEART OF DESIRE	Maria del Rey	
HELEN – A MODERN ODALISQUE	Larry Stern	
HIS MISTRESS'S VOICE	G. C. Scott	
HOUSE OF ANGELS	Yvonne Strickland	May
THE HOUSE OF MALDONA	Yolanda Celbridge	
THE IMAGE	Jean de Berg	Jul
THE INSTITUTE	Maria del Rey	
SISTERHOOD OF THE INSTITUTE	Maria del Rey	

Please send me the books I have ticked above.

Name ....

Address ....

....

....

.... Post code ....

Send to: **Cash Sales, Nexus Books, 332 Ladbroke Grove, London W10 5AH**.

Please enclose a cheque or postal order, made payable to **Nexus Books**, to the value of the books you have ordered plus postage and packing costs as follows:

UK and BFPO – £1.00 for the first book, 50p for each subsequent book.

Overseas (including Republic of Ireland) – £2.00 for the first book, £1.00 for the second book, and 50p for each subsequent book.

If you would prefer to pay by VISA or ACCESS/MASTERCARD, please write your card number and expiry date here:

....

Please allow up to 28 days for delivery.

Signature ....